The Book of Horrors

The book told of tentacles coming through the windows, slots, cracks, even his sink drain. Why the man stayed in his home, the diary did not explain. Nor did it explain why Claro had not at least left at night, did not call the police, did not ask his neighbors for shelter, or assistance.

Or anything.

What could it have been, wondered Legrasse. *Why was it? What did it want? Why did it come? Why?*

Maybe Claro was just too stubborn to admit defeat. Maybe he simply went insane, bought the traps and spread them out, relying on the only thing that had truly worked for him. The last entry he had made in his little book with his bit of pencil, sitting in his corner, disturbed Legrasse the most:

free, free at last!

Cover art by Ben Fogletto
Desktop composition by The Devil Genghis

Published by Bold Venture Press
website: www.boldventurepress.com

ISBN-13: 978-1502967664

Printed in the United States of America

First Bold Venture edition: December 2014

TO BATTLE BEYOND

C.J. HENDERSON

BOLD VENTURE PRESS • FLORIDA

WHO THE HELL ARE THESE GUYS?

INTRODUCTION BY RON FORTIER

IN THE EARLY 1930S, America found itself locked in the grip of what historians call the Great Depression. The once flourishing, robust economy of the industrial age had suddenly gone bust and millions of Americans found themselves homeless and jobless.

Amidst this atmosphere of despair, the publishing world brought forth a new kind of magazine geared to alleviate, in some small way, the daily woes of the American populace. Cheaply produced on the pulp residue left over in the printing process, these small, inexpensive monthlies with the garishly loud covers were identified as the "pulps."

Each and every month hundreds of assorted titles, covering every conceivable genre imaginable, graced the shelves of drugstore racks and sidewalk kiosks.

Among the most popular, and thereby successful, of these pulps were the hero titles. And why shouldn't they be? In a time when most of life seemed cruel and unfair, what reader wouldn't long to find stalwart heroes ready to combat villainy and confirm that in the end, justice, and the good guys, would win. Among this elite group of pulp heroes, the finest were Street & Smiths Shadow and Doc Savage. Even to this day, generations later, those names ring familiar to folks who have absolutely no clue as to "who" these heroes were. That says much to the lasting impact they had on American culture.

Of course, as in all literature, for every king-of-the-hill, there were dozens of also-ran; the B and C heroes that are mostly forgotten today, except for the few hundred diehard pulp fans. These old timers keep their memories alive via the many conventions they host throughout the country. Some even started their own publishing ventures and began reprinting those cherished, classics tales. A few years ago I became acquainted with this fan movement and it opened my eyes to the cornucopia of long lost, truly bizarre and wonderful fictional characters that existed in the heyday of the pulps. Attending several pulp conventions, I saw first hand the enthusiasm of the fans and their genuine love for this brand of purple prose. Which is where I began formulating the idea of writing new stories about these old heroes. You see, most of them had long since become public domain, i.e. their copyrights had expired ages ago.

With the help of several colleagues, both writers and artists, I began producing a series of "new" pulp adventure anthologies and novels. Joe Gentile over at Moonstone Books, had the same idea and put together a truly beautiful anthology featuring The Spider. Joe invited me to contribute a story, along with eighteen other writers. Among of these was my pal, C.J. Henderson. C.J. had made a name for himself with two series; Jack Hagee, tough guy private eye and Teddy London, occult detective. There have been many of others, but these two are the names most often associated with his by-line.

When I learned that C.J. had done several stories for the Spider book, I contacted him about possibly doing something for us. He asked to see the roster of heroes I had lined up for possible projects and after a few days called to say he wanted to do a Black Bat story. But before he did so, he needed to know who the hell this guy was? Anticipating this question from my contributors, I had assembled a pulp heroes' bible listing all our characters of interest.

From the pages of *Black Book Detective*, Tony Quinn was a young, handsome crusading district attorney on a mission to bring down organized crime. During a murder trial, one of the defendants threw acid into his face permanently blinding him and leaving the area about his eyes horribly scarred. After leaving the hospital, the blind Quinn assumed his crime busting days were over and resigned. He opened a private practice relegating his future to a boring life of a corporate law. Enter the beautiful Carol Baldwin whose father, a local town sheriff, was gunned down in the line of duty. Familiar with Quinn's history, Carol told the doctors she wanted to donate her deceased father's eyes to the former district attorney. A radical new procedure had been developed and Quinn, albeit unconvinced it would succeed, agreed to undergo the transplant surgery and received his new eyes.

Lo and behold, the operation was not only a whopping success, returning his sight, but somehow the unorthodox technique provided Quinn with a remarkable new ability. His new eyes could see in the dark! For Tony Quinn, an unlit room at midnight now appeared as of if it was bathed in the sunlight high noon. Realizing what an asset this unexpected gift was, Quinn devised a new scheme to combat crime. He would keep his regained vision a secret and continue to act the part of a blind man. Meanwhile he created a new persona, a black clad, hooded avenger who wears a black cape with steel rods and scalloped edges to give himself the appearance of a giant man-bat creature. With twin .45 automatics blazing, he became the deadly Black Bat. In this role he was aided by three confidantes, the aforementioned Carol Baldwin, who soon became his love interest, a former con-man named Silk Kirby and a rough and tumble ex-boxer, Butch O'Leary.

Once C.J. had this information, he wasted no time in whipping up a great fifteen thousand word Black Bat yarn. I was thrilled, thanked him and figured that was that. The story would go into the files until the rest of the book was filled. What I couldn't have anticipated was C.J.'s infatuation with pulp writing. He'd gotten the bug. Within days of submitting the Black Bat piece, he called me with an idea for a pulp novel that would team up several of the characters on our to-use list. To say I was pleasantly surprised would be an understatement. Who was he thinking of using, I asked, at the same time guessing the Black Bat would most likely be among his picks. My hunch was right as he rattled them off; Black Bat, the Domino Lady and Ravenwood. It was an eclectic grouping, as the three were very much different types. Then, before I could digest all of this, he dropped his final coup-de-gras.

His plot idea revolved around pitting these three against a Lovecraftian outer-dimensional monster which would allow him to also include Inspector John Legrasse in the mix. Legrasse is the monster hunter who first appeared in H.P. Lovecraft's seminal horror classic, "The Call of Cthulhu". C.J. had, over the past few years, literally adopted the irascible Frenchman and made him his own. Somewhere in all this, I mumbled a whispered okay, still stunned by the entire idea of such a book. C.J. in turned asked me to once more provide him with background data on these other pulp avengers.

Ellen Patrick was a beautiful, twenty-year old blonde with brown eyes and heart shaped lips. She lived in Southern California with her widowed father, politician Owen Patrick. After graduating from Berkeley, the bored socialite/debutante was given a trip to the Far East as a graduation gift from her loving father. While in Asia, she received a telegram that her father had been assassinated. She returned home to bury him and learn the truth of his murder. From various sources, she discovered that her father had been about to reveal to the press the names of several corrupt government officials. The police believed that was the motive behind his killing but without concrete clues, their investigation was terminated and the killer never found.

Incensed by this lack of justice, Ellen pledged to devote her life to uncovering corruption wherever it festered and stamping it out. To do so she became the night time vigilante, Domino Lady. Her outfit consisted of a silver or black form-fitting, strapless evening gown, a shoulder cape and a domino mask. That was it. Part of her ploy was to distract her enemies, most of them pea-brain thugs, by brazenly displaying her rather ample physical attributes. Thus while a crook was ogling her bountiful bosom, she would get the drop on him. This was done with the use of her small, silver plated .22 automatic or by injecting them with the syringe she kept affixed to her shapely leg with a garter; it being filled with a fast-acting knock-out drug.

Logic and common sense had no place in her stories. That a scantily clad vixen could effectively get the upper hand on hardened gangsters and at the same time elude the police was stretching credulity to the max. But pulps, especially the Domino Lady stories, were never about realism. On the contrary, they were about make believe and outlandish imagination. The sexy avenger's career was short lived as she only appeared in six stories via *Mystery Adventure Magazine* and *Saucy Romantic Adventures*. Still she did manage to be featured on the cover of each title at least once which is more than can be said for the third and final recruit in this new adventure.

Many of the hero pulps normally contained one short novel starring the central figure and three to four short stories. Some of these back-up tales were themselves series with recurring heroes. One such that appeared regularly in the back of *Secret Agent X* was Ravenwood: Stepson of Mystery. Gifted with psychic abilities, this handsome young man oftentimes could predict the future and aided the police of New York City in unraveling some of their more spectacular cases. His origin was typically pulp exotic. His father was American and his mother British. They raised him in India where he was trained by a mysterious man known only as the "Nameless One" in the strange occult powers of Tibet. When his parents were killed in a plague that swept through their Burmese village, Ravenwood returned to the states accompanied by the Nameless One. The Nameless One never left the solitude of his room in their penthouse apartment, yet via telepathy, he communicated with the occult investigator and continued to teach him in the ways of the mystic arts. Residing with them was Sterling, a tall, stodgy, stereotypical British butler/cook. Sterling was a voracious reader and a walking encyclopedia of the city. He was uncomfortable around the Nameless One and they had an uneasy relationship, held together by their mutual loyalty to Ravenwood.

Of the three, Ravenwood was clearly the hero that would have lots in common with Inspector Legrasse. It was easy for me to understand why C.J. had chosen him. How Ravenwood and Legrasse would interact with the Domino Lady and the Black Bat was something altogether different. Once C.J. had a plot hammered out, he began to pump out chapters and sent them along. Soon it was clearly evident that he was relishing every scene in this book as the characters sprang to life on his pages. As the heroes started to come together, I was impressed by how well he dealt with their individual personalities and allowed those to shine through in guiding these exchanges. Any good writer will tell you, if you write your characters honestly, they will lead the way, revealing new depths to their personalities previously hidden. Thus the writer finds himself on a journey of discovery, as his characters begin to live and breathe in the world he has made for them.

"To Battle Beyond" is no exception. It is a taut, fast paced adventure with some of the most colorful characters you are likely ever to find assembled in one book.

There is suspense, gruesome murder and pulse-pounding action all in the grand tradition of the classic pulps, with a heady dose of horror thrown in for good measure. C.J. is completely in his element throughout. Oh, and if you are curious as to what became of that original Black Bat tale he did for me, well look no further than the back of this very volume. It's been added here as a bonus. You can find more of C.J.'s work on Lovecraft's acerbic detective in *Tales of Inspector Legrasse* from Mythos Books. And finally, the Domino Lady and the Black Bat join forces once more under his inspired guidance in a brand new team-up story appearing soon in Moonstone's all new, *The Domino Lady Chronicles*. The guy just naturally keeps busy.

In the meantime, buckle your safety belts, fire up your disbelief and get ready to be thrilled, amazed and completely entertained. You are entering the realm of the pulps—there's nothing else like it in world!

–Ron Fortier
10/29/2007
Somersworth, NH

TO BATTLE
BEYOND
C.J. HENDERSON

"So free we seem, so fettered fast we are!"

–Robert Browning

"It is better to die on your feet than to live on your knees."

–Dolores Ibarruri

"Even the bravest man cannot do battle beyond his strength."

–Homer

Prologue

THE UNPRECEDENTED STORM HAD HIT IN THE BLACK DEPTHS OF NIGHT, slamming its way up and down the rocky California coast for hours, then days on end. For all intents and purposes, the raging nightmare seemed to descend on the state from out of nowhere. Despite the accuracy and sophistication of the government's weather devices in the modern age of 1941, none of their advanced machines had been able to predict its coming, and for good reason.

This particular storm was different from any other ever witnessed by modern man. Extremely different. It was not preceded by any of the usual changes in barometric pressure. There was no gradual shifting of the temperature, nor in the humidity levels. The surf did not slowly build to the eventual fever pitch that greeted the black-skied dawn. No, one minute all the world was behaving normally, in the manner made famous by postcards sold from Los Angeles to San Francisco. The next minute it was a tumult, one drowning surfers, smashing pleasure craft and turning a sensible world into nightmare.

What also struck those in the know as off was the fact that usually such storms, ones so massive, so all-encompassing, start far out in the ocean, giving plenty of warning as they traveled toward shore over a matter of days. That was not the case with this one, however. None of the ships at sea, those heading into Californian ports, or sailing out from them, radioed any changes in the weather. Not one—and for good reason. One minute, both the skies and seas had been calm and clear, from Honolulu to San Francisco— from the Baja to Portland. The next moment, however, the wrath of some furious god was evident in every force that nature possessed.

The nightmarish storm that ravaged the Pacific coastline sprang monstrously to life in a blood-drenched instant, full-grown and brimming over with horrible, mind-boggling destruction. The incredible winds set frightening records never before imagined. Roofs were sliced away from houses and sent spinning across the skies. Trees were torn from yards and parks and shattered into splinters. The wind raged and all the air was filled with flying debris—fences, bicycles, garbage cans and milk bottles, even animals.

Even people.

The ever-growing waves coming in off the ocean were equally destructive. They were colossal, gigantic things, near tidal walls of overwhelming destruction. One after another, they battered the coastline driving sand and sea weed more than a half a mile inland. Roadways were shattered, homes washed away, entire families drowned. Water exploded against the unsuspecting edge of America with a power indescribable, destroying buildings, crushing power plants, over-flowing rivers and dams.

The resulting floods flashed up and down the unprotected rim of the continent, swamping hundreds of communities. Nearly every population center on the beleaguered western coast of the United States crawled to their windows in the morning to find water-clogged streets, most with more than one body floating face down in the stinking, brackish spew.

Fish of every kind were found far inland as well, many of them strange creatures never seen before by the eyes of man. Chalk white-skinned and eyeless, their dead, decaying bodies drifted half-above and half-below the surface of a thousand new lakes, the roiling summer heat summoning flies and other vermin to their quickly rotting bodies.

Of course, not all that boiled and lapped and spewed across the land that dark morning had been sent there from the ocean alone. The skies had bled billions of gallons of freezing cold water, as well as massive quantities of a most destructive hail. The majority of the violent bombardment had fallen in the standard sized pellets common to the phenomenon, but far too much of it had not, coming down instead in stone-hard, brick-sized lumps. The withering attack smashed windows, caved in car roofs, and shattered the skulls of those unlucky enough to be caught it the path of the unexplainable occurrence.

Indeed, so violent were the pounding onslaughts of hail and rain that eventually great quantities of the California coast began to lose its cohesion. Those who built there had thought such structures to be safe for a century or more—at least. They had not counted on the coming of such a nightmare falling upon their work, however. By the end of the second day of rain, many mountainsides were breaking apart and sliding downward back to the ocean, taking whatever might be on them down beneath the waves.

Over seven hundred Californian homes were lost simply from being washed down to the sea, if not out to the sea. At least one entire community suffered extinction from having been built too close to the ocean in an age still not prepared to hold nature back with two hands. The loss of life left the entire nation in a stunned silence.

Even before it had ceased, the storm was declared a disaster beyond all proportion. The Pacific coastline of North America had never seen such a devastating lashing. Well, of course, that was the wisdom of the radio pundits as well as the sages who sold the nation's newspapers. And, in their tiny, blindered way, they were correct. Within recent memory, the minuscule sliver of time which began when mankind had begun to chart such events and formalize its records of them, it was, indeed, by far the worst storm humanity had ever recorded.

But, before the ink of man was ever set to paper, there were those whose records extended back far beyond those of the modern news and wire services. Filled with ancient and abominable secrets, the sources of these priests and magicians spoke of elder times when such opulent displays of power were tritely commonplace. Their secret books and scrolls told of times long past when storms of a like magnitude were thought of as simply average weather—as just the way of things. These were times, however, long before mankind held much sway over the doings on the Earth. Times when fierce and terrible creatures held sway instead.

Vast millennia in the galaxy's distant past, the Earth had been a strategic battlefield, a much sought after location prized by various star-faring races, as well as by the mind-boggling God-Things they defied. Over several score millions of years, these beasts and creatures and all-powerful entities struggled one against the other, mindlessly ravaging each other, the planet, and even the rest of the solar system. During their endless combat, more than a dozen entire species saw the end of their existence in the muck and blood-drenched ooze of the tiny world that would eventually be the home of humankind.

One by one, however, as these various races and entities expired, the Earth began to know a rough peace of sorts. As interstellar combat faded within the far-from-central reaches of the end of the galaxy housing the Earth, mammals finally crawled forth timeously from the shadows, picking up the pieces left over from the struggles gone before. In time, man would step forth and claim the crown of master of the world, his ape face smiling idiotically, resplendent in his ignorance of all that had gone before him.

To the human race, the handful of millennia during which it had held sway over the Earth was an endless measure. In truth, humanity had been master of the planet for less time than several of the longer wars that preceded its coming. Thus, blithely complacent in its sweeping arrogance, the race of men could only see the nightmarish storm pummeling California as something new—a test created exclusively for them. Through their utter lack of any perspective, they could only frame the devastating gale as a freak, an aberration. As a thing they could hope would never strike again.

Their hopes were, all too horribly, in vain.

And, their complete and utter lack of understanding as to the true nature of the storm—its ancient design as well as its actual intent—was the key ingredient in a plan put into effect several times before the race of men became conscious.

Foretold it was, that the storm that hit California was only the first of four. The first of four storms meant to end the reign of man, and to usher in the return of the Gods.

Chapter 1

OF ALL THE STRANGE THINGS THE INSPECTOR HAD COME ACROSS IN HIS long and varied career, this was the strangest he had ever seen. The first thing he noticed, as had those few others who had peered into the old house out near the swamp, was the bizarre display of traps all about the doorway. Immediately, there in the front foyer, appearing to be set to surround the mail slot cut into the door, spread in a semi-circle, he had come across two lines of traps.

Mouse traps.

Rat traps.

"In here, el Grande…"

All manner of snares.

"Here is something for you to see…"

All agreed that their positioning had to mean that they had been set for something their owner must have felt was actually going to be able to enter his home through the mail slot. Of this there was no question amongst those gathered at the crime site. A quick inspection of the opening showed the passage way to be only one inch by three, covered by a springed hinge that had to be moved with a bit of effort.

"Come in and meet the former Hector Claro, and"—the

officer's voice shifted to a supercilious tone—"let me tell you right now, Inspector…"

Good and great Mother in Heaven, wondered former Inspector-of-Police John Raymond Legrasse, just what could this man have been expecting to come through such a tiny and hard to open aperture other than his mail?

"You're not going to believe this."

Legrasse hated to admit it, but his one-time lieutenant was correct. Even after all of the unnatural things he had witnessed in his time, he did not believe what he found in the next room. It was too odd. Too despairing.

"This isn't one of your pranks, is it?"

Too perplexed by the oddity of the inside of Hector Claro's home to make one of his usual wisecracks, Lieutenant Joseph D. Galvez shook his head gravely, admitting;

"No… I say this truly, I could but wish my sense of humor were this *magnifico*."

Legrasse nodded, understanding the smaller man without need for further explanation. The scene in the humble home's main room was one snatched from nightmare. Without prompting, the one-time inspector of police unconsciously fell into old habits at once. In less than a minute his virgin notepad was bleeding its first page and a half—

Deceased, identified as Hector Claro, found dead, sitting in an upright position, situated in a corner diagonally as far removed from the front door as possible.

Deceased appears not to have been arranged in corner, but to have died of natural causes. Deceased most likely was facing front door at time of death.

Found in foyer upon arrival: various sizes and strengths of standard rodent spring traps set within the doorway.

Theory: Traps set to catch something deceased suspected would come through front door mail slot.

Immediate placement: three large traps—set out but not baited—spread in triangle formation directly below the mail slot in the door.

Further on, spread outward in semi-circle, two additional lines of traps. These all standard mouse traps, rat traps. This is scene just in the foyer.

Inside the house: traps everywhere—scores? Hundreds? Set out...

Patterns?

"Can you believe this guy," asked Galvez. The man's voice was indecisive, unable to either pick a tone, or to slide one way or the other into humor or concern. "He surrounds himself with traps. Okay—he's scared. I understand that. But, I mean, of what? What? I dunno."

"You're already wanting to know why he did it?" asked Legrasse, half in humor, half seriously. "I'm still working on how he did it."

Galvez snorted, then sprang one of the traps with the cane in his hand, a handsome thing covered with graceful carvings which he had acquired from the umbrella stand in the foyer. The officer did so to clear the path before him so that he might be able to walk forward without setting off any traps with his foot, and also not to disturb the patterns on the floor until Legrasse had finished studying the bizarrely complex and twisting designs in which they had been laid out.

"Crazy," the Spaniard muttered, "set all these traps, but don't bait them. How you supposed to catch anything with out any bait?"

It had been decided that, although they would, of course, need to leave as much of the insane landscape intact as possible to see if there was any clue as to what had happened in the old Backtown house out near the swampfronts, some of the complicated geometry of the trap layout would have to be sacrificed for both basic mobility as well as general safety.

"Smells wonderful," snapped the lieutenant, rubbing another wipe of preventive gel under his nose. "Don't he?"

When Legrasse merely flashed his eyes in response, Galvez went silent. Though his one-time commander was now merely consulting, only a citizen, still he was Legrasse, who had lived through it all, and won against the devil himself. They had been through much together, and Galvez knew his former boss well. Already he could see the old instincts taking over, could sense his boss was closing in on possibilities of what have happened in the old house within his mind. The Spaniard watched Legrasse's hand moving across the pages of his notebook, knowing that somehow he would unravel the bizarre scenario before them.

> *Deceased seems to have bolted all other doors behind him.*
> *All other rooms are cut off from the front room. Cracks*
> *around doors are stuffed with rags, old news-paper, slivers of*
> *cardboard cut to fit. Boards then appear to have been nailed*
> *over all of this wherever*
> *possible.*
> *Deceased seems to have been afraid of something approach-*
> *ing him, something small enough to fit under a door, or*
> *through a mail slot—possibly through any small crack what-*
> *soever.*
> *Deceased does not seem to have been restrained in any*
> *manner. If this is the case, then the only conclusion one can*
> *have is that he remained in his corner,*
> *surrounded by his traps, until he starved to death,*
> *by choice. Dying of thirst and hunger—choosing to*
> *do so. This was preferable to him rather than…*
> *Than what?*

And then, Legrasse's eye caught a detail he had thus far previously missed. Indeed, one that everyone that had entered the old house had missed so far. Staring at the desiccated corpse in the corner, he asked Galvez;

"Do you see that bulge in Mr. Claro's breast pocket?"

The lieutenant indicated that he did. Legrasse asked him to fetch its cause. Galvez stepped into the opening already made near the corpse and slid his hand gently inside the pungent cloth. His fingers returned with a prize, a thin, leather-bound volume with a stub of pencil attached to it by a short length of string. The lieutenant paged through it quickly, then announced;

"It's a diary."

Legrasse accepted the small black book and opened it to its first page. There, in a simple style made up of competent, but uncomplicated sentences of mostly one and two syllable words, Hector Claro introduced himself and his dilemma to the inspector.

The dead man told his tale from the beginning. The first date showed that it had been a handful of days back, immediately after a particularly violent storm which had rained lightning down on the swamps for an entire night and half the next day. Legrasse remembered the storm vividly. Indeed, the radio had made much of the fact that it had rolled across the nation at a leisurely pace, building to its devastating finale in the Gulf of Mexico, spreading floods everywhere across the Louisiana basin as it went. That was not what brought the horrendous weather pattern to the inspector's memory, however.

No, he remembered the storm with an exacting clarity for its unusualness. For one thing, he could attest to the downpour's abrupt beginnings for he had been caught out of doors when it had hit the city. The skies had been clear one minute—the sun bright in a cloudless sea of blue. He could see it in his mind's eye, one moment dazzling sunlight, the next, a horrible ebony darkness which crackled open with a riot of lightning and thunder. He had been completely drenched in moments.

For another, the noise and electrical power of the storm had sent much of their city of New Orleans into a mindless panic. The smell of ozone had been everywhere. Normally calm, well-mannered horses had gone wild in the streets, crashing carriages and trampling citizens. It had been one of those times Legrasse was glad he was no longer a public servant, and the memory of the violent night connected him to Claro in a personal way.

The man's mono-syllabic notes went on to tell of finding scores of dead fish and other swamp creatures the next day, floating on their sides in the muddy, boiled water behind his home. A score of great trees had fallen during the night, and the swamp had gone through such convulsions that Claro even noted a fresh spring bubbling up through the crayfish encrusted mud.

At first he had been pleased by the events. The shocked fish had provided him with a much needed windfall of which his notes said he had taken immediate advantage. Working furiously that first day after the storm, the old swamp dweller had quickly set to gathering and preserving as many of the still living, but insensate bounty as he considered safe for the salting. The new spring proved to be fresh, and looked as if it would be a constant rather than a fluke.

All in all, the storm seemed to have been a blessing for Claro, unlike the disaster it had proved to be for the rest of New Orleans. But then, the following night came, and the decease's opinion of things took a different turn.

The next episode in Claro's diary told of a noise in the night, that of a rat trap being sprung. Due to his proximity to the swamp, the man had many such devices set about in the corners of his home and was not overly concerned by hearing one go off in the middle of the night. But, instead of the squeals such a sound usually brought, if they brought any noise at all, he heard instead a series of strange, unfathomable sounds the curiousness of which forced him to leave his bed. Lighting his table lamp, he went out to examine his small home's main room where he found the most curious scene.

Claro described finding the trap he had heard dragged across the room from where it had been set all the way to the front door. He could tell that this was what had happened easily enough because of the wet, sticky trail left from the trap's original position to where Claro discovered it, smashed and ruined beneath his mail slot. He could only think that he had snared quite a large rodent, one of sufficient size and strength to move the trap, although wounded unto the point where it was bleeding profusely. This line of thinking was diminished, however, when he realized that the smearing crossing his floor was not made up of blood.

Looking up from his reading, Legrasse absently noted a faded line of coloration on the door, one leading from deep inside the large room into the foyer, indeed, directly up to the mail slot, clearly supporting the details of Claro's story. The dead man's words described the trail as a bluish-green, one with neither the coppery smell nor taste of blood. He was confused by this, but with the simplicity of most swamp dwellers, soon forgot the incident, tired as he had been from the ordeal of collecting and salting down his windfall.

The next night, however, he was again visited after dark, and the night after that, and the one after that as well. He lay in his bed on all three occasions, the covers pulled up and over his head despite both the summer heat and the all but unbearable humidity—a result of the previous storm. He unashamedly stated in his memoir that he did so for he was frightened to the point where he found himself questioning even the need to breathe. Every day he set out more traps, but each morning he found fewer of them sprung. On all three nights he listened intently as something, or some things, crawled and slithered throughout his simple home. Whether they were searching for something, or simply madly dancing, he had no idea, nor much inclination to find out.

Legrasse read on, page after page, fascinated. Galvez waited, balancing himself in various poses, using the cane from the umbrella stand to keep from toppling into the myriad traps. On the one hand he was impatient to find the answer to the riddle of the dead man and to close out the case. On the other, he was more than willing to wait to see what his former commander could determine. Together, the two had seen some horrific and terrible things in the bayou land outside their city. Indeed, in Galvez's mind, the mystery of Hector Claro could scarce compare to some of their previous exploits.

"Yes, but better safe than sorry, though," the lieutenant cautioned himself, thinking grimly on times past when such odd portents had been ignored with disastrous results for all in the path of what followed. Content to wait, he continued to play with the odd cane, twirling it in one hand, studying its unusual carvings, amusing himself in any way he could think of while he waited for Legrasse's verdict.

The inspector had almost forgotten Galvez, however, his full attention falling to each successive page of Claro's diary. Legrasse had become completely engrossed with the man's description of the fourth night of his home's repeated invasions and reread it simply to hear its words again within his head. The reason was simple to understand. It was on that night that whatever it was that had been searching about in the other rooms of his home, even under his own bed, finally found its way to what was on top of his bed.

Claro wrote of a weight passing over the blanket he had held still and tight across his face over the preceding three nights. Anything with eyes would have seen his form beneath the covers, he reckoned, but whatever this was, this probing, single length, it merely poked and prodded and rolled, intent in its search, but making no discoveries.

Not at first.

Claro's words dropped icicles down the back of Legrasse's shirt collar, making each vertebrae ache in turn as they uncomfortably wormed their way down his spine.

It were a horrible feeling, truly, not being able to see, not being able to breathe, just scared and waiting for the damn thing to go away. Just holding my breath and waiting and praying and none of it doing no good. No good at all.

It just kept digging and scratching and tugging, like a big finger, but a stupid one. Like something that had never seen a bed or a blanket. I think that how dumb it acted were more frightening to me than anything else about it.

You know, even a bear, or fox, or anything else, really, anything that ever crawled up out of the swamp should have known what it had found. But this thing couldn't tell it had found a man under a blanket. So it just kept poking and digging at me.

And then, it found me. The crawling bastard thing finally found its way under the blanket and it slid under my leg and up over the other in a motion so fast that at first I couldn't react.

But, as it started to circle under my leg, like to grab a hold of it, or squeeze it, my fear left me, or it filled me, whatever, I don't know. I only know that that was all I could stands.

It was a madness that took me then. I rolled out of my bed screaming. In the darkness, I grabbed at the thing coiling around my legs and I pulled it from me and smashed at it, beating it with my fists, thrashing it against the floor.

With a lightning speed it jerked free of my hold and retreated out of the room. I followed it, fast as I could, my hands grabbing for something to use as a weapon. They found a chair. I wasn't thinking, didn't care. I grabbed up the chair and ran to follow the thing, whatever it was, to break it, to kill it. Then, I got to the next room... and I had to stop.

Legrasse read the next few lines, and then was forced to stop himself as his blood went cold, and a terrible fear gripped his soul.

Chapter 2

THE WOMAN REALLY DID LOOK COMPLETELY OUT OF PLACE. THERE WAS, of course, no disputing that she was an amazingly stunning beauty. But, the backdrop against which she was standing was one of terrible devastation—a nightmare setting of twisted, shattered trees, displaced boulders, and the debris of what had once been the opulent homes of the rich and infamous. Everywhere was strewn the litter of the lives of a score of San Francisco's most notorious families. It was a truly horrible scene.

What could be done to cover up the most disturbing images had already been done, but it was far too little. Ever since the still unexplainable storm, the sky had remained filled with unrelenting layers of the darkest clouds, a sinister purple-hued canopy hinting that the deluge might return at any moment. And yet, during the daytime hours, even when the sun was not making one of its all-too-rare appearances, from almost any vantage point one could see human bodies, and parts of bodies, up and down the disaster line.

Normally, of course, such a horrific situation would have been attended to immediately. All mortal remains would have been carefully gathered and removed from the sight of decent folks. And, in the case of the wealthy, such things were usually attended to even more quickly. Not to imply that the well-to-do were more sensitive than others, but rather that they could afford to give in to such sensitivities.

But, the normal flow of emotional commerce had to be restricted in this situation. The storm that had devastated the Pacific coastline some days earlier had literally loosened a massive section of the town of Traversville, a notorious San Franciscan suburb, and sent it sliding violently down into the ocean. Indeed, to many it almost seemed as if the God of the Old Testament had arranged the matter.

All those slain were either gangsters, or of the families of gangsters. All of them were men and women who through money, threats, bribes and blackmail had elevated themselves and their children to positions beyond the law. In the end it had done them little good, however, for after the storm their bodies lie broken and shattered in the mud, picked over by birds, ravaged by coyotes, and devoured by flies as the world watched helplessly.

The reason nothing could be done was that even almost a week later, the ground which had broken away from the mountainside, sending more than half of Traversville down to the ocean was still dangerously unstable. Scores of attempts had been made to reach some of the closer bodies to at least cover them, but these noble efforts had all met with disaster. After three firemen and two policemen met with terrible falls, one from each force receiving near-fatal injuries, a state of emergency was wisely declared by San Francisco's mayor.

It was quickly decided by the authorities that no one would be allowed into the area until geologists from a local university who were studying the unusual landslide, trying to determine if this first terrible disaster might be a warning for future generations, declared the area safe for foot traffic once more. Until then, the police were maintaining a light cordon around the grizzly section, chasing off those ghoulish news photographers, or indecently-minded spectators that might approach the scene.

The woman staring out over the gruesome spectacle was none of the three. She represented neither the police nor the press, and her motive for being at the scene of such a disaster was not prurient. And, unlike some of the women's church groups who showed up on a regular basis to pray for the departed, she was not there out of a goodness of spirit, either. She was there out of anger, because the dark hatred which consumed her heart and soul had been thwarted.

Her name was Ellen Patrick, and although she knew none of the deceased personally, she hated them all on general principles. Her late father had been the district attorney of San Francisco, one of the amoral town's only decent politicians. Certainly its only honest one. For those grievous character flaws, the city's criminal element had declared him a menace and issued an extravagant reward for his demise. Like all such bounties, it was not long before it was collected.

Ellen had been in Europe at the time, enjoying part of a worldwide excursion her father had gifted her with upon the completion of her studies at Berkeley. The senior Patrick had definitely had good reason to be proud. Although officially only a liberal arts student, Ellen had carried a tremendous class load, burdening herself with many more credits per semester than any of her contemporaries.

Cursed with both wealth and extraordinary beauty, while still a teenager Ellen Patrick had determined to become a force with which to be reckoned. Her father, a long-time widower, had always encouraged his only daughter as he might a son. When still a toddler, he had challenged her to climb trees and then to leap from them into his arms. She learned to do so with a wild abandon which thrilled the both of them. The senior Patrick had dubbed her his "adventure baby," and his joy at her each and every accomplishment had pushed her to excel far more than any stern chat about her future might have accomplished.

When he had gone riding, there had been a horse for her. When he left for the mountains to camp, to fish or hunt, she had her own sleeping bag, pole and choice of artillery. Those of his friends that wished to accompany him to his cabin were strong-armed to a man into teaching the young Ellen all that they knew which he had not already taught her.

By the time she was thirteen, Ellen could whittle, hit a bird on the wing, bring down a racing deer, drive a car at top speed on almost any kind of course imaginable, box a full-grown man, gut a fish, fence a one-time Olympic champion to a stand-still, swim in icy mountain water at near championship speeds, dress a fresh kill, play guitar, start a fire from scratch, and knock back a boilermaker with the best of them. Young and tawny, the blonde-haired, brown-eyed beauty was the pride of her father and her dozen doting "uncles."

In fact, so boisterously proud of their tomboy were they, whether at private family functions or out mixing with the city's glittering elite, the group of them finally forced Ellen's maternal grandmother and aunt into desperate and rapid action. Swooping in, they badgered her father until he agreed that Ellen might have learned enough about being a young man, and that it was time she started learning something about becoming a young woman. From then on it was far less of sweat and leather for the blossoming beauty, and far more of face powder and lace.

The thing which surprised Ellen the most, however, and her father the least, was that she took to being a woman with an equal enthusiasm to which she had taken to being a tomboy. In her six-teenth year, she was the unchallenged queen of the debutante ball—and the unrivaled future queen of Californian high society. Boys, young men, and men old enough to know better pursued her from that point on, which was in a large part what drove her to excel in college. She knew it was deemed proper for one in her social set to take only the liberal arts, but shrewdly, she threw her-self into all of them at the same time, determined to be a woman of whom her father could be proud.

Of course, like all extraordinary children, she could not fathom that her father was already as proud as any parent could be. He did not reserve his pride for her temporary moments of fleeting accomplishment, for he already took a staggeringly robust glory in the person whom his Ellen was, and knew with all his heart she would always be someone of whom he would be utterly and unabashedly proud.

Thus when she graduated with honors, he was not only not sur-prised, but armed with a carefully planned world cruise as a reward. He had watched his daughter grind herself relentlessly—advanced mathematics, her abilities approached the theoretical; foreign languages, she had master five, become familiar with an additional eight; world history, comparative literature, music, dance, the arts, et cetera, she had wrung the sponge of Berkeley dry, taking the top honors of three sports teams as well, and thus played directly into her father's hands.

Exhausted from her relentless four years, ready for a break, and perhaps even a bit of fun, especially that which could be had while broadening her cultural horizons further, Ellen was easy to cajole into a year long world cruise. Yes, her father certainly did want to reward his over-achieving daughter, but he had an ulterior motive as well.

While Ellen had been conquering her academics, he had been building his cases against the worst of San Francisco's mobsters. With careful calculation, he brought forth the first of his evidence and demands for trials once his daughter was safely out of the country. In a town as tightly controlled by the wrong elements as his, it was a powerful testament that he actually managed to get five of his three score targets incarcerated before those within his righteous path decided enough was enough and had him brutally exterminated.

Ellen returned home immediately, of course, but there was nothing she could do. Or, more correctly, there was nothing she could do as Ellen Patrick. Not that she was in any way going to let that stop her. On her long sea voyage back to the United States, the unchallenged queen of the debutante ball coldly and carefully designed a plan with which to extract her revenge which not one other person in a million could have come up with, let alone executed. Upon her return, she played the heart-broken daughter, wearing black and visiting her father's grave. But, long before a proper mourning period had passed, she traded in her ebony veils and dark shawls for skin-tight evening gowns of glittering silver and gold.

In but weeks she was all but forgotten by the city's criminal element. To them, she was simply a dizzy rich dame too much in love with good times and parties to worry about doing anything to retaliate against them. Of course, they had been watching for her to give them signs they could understand—going to the police, crying to the newspapers or radio pundits, badgering judges and politicians, hiring detectives.

When she did none of these things, when she acted as they might have, with disregard for suffering and an eye cast toward pleasure, they wrote her off as potential trouble. They had been prepared to send her to her grave, certainly. But, clever if not intelligent, they knew two murders in one family, especially the murder of a beautiful woman, was not the kind of thing that was good for business. So, seeing that she posed no threat, they were content as well as relieved to simply go back to business as usual. They were, after all, for the most part not men of great imagination.

Still it must be granted that never, not if they were given the lifetimes of oaks along with the wisdom of Solomon, could any of them have conceived of what Ellen Patrick had in store for those responsible for her father's death, along with all of their ilk.

Coldly, without fear or hatred, but simply working with a burning, blade-sharp precision, she set out to eliminate those who had murdered her father. And, since there were no clues as to whom had actually ordered his death or performed the deed, she decided to simply kill each and every criminal in San Francisco. To her, it was her leaving town which had caused her father's death. Thus she vowed never to leave again, never to do something for her own personal pleasure, until she had gagged the throats of the mobsters who had stolen the last of her parents from her with their own foul blood.

To do so, she created the identity of the Domino Lady. In this role she wore nothing but black and white, two colors she then carefully avoided during her daily life. Known to be handy with rifles and shotguns, her masked persona carried only a dainty, silver-plated .22 automatic. For anyone but a deadly shot such as Ellen Patrick, such a minor weapon would have been an invitation to disaster. In her hands, however, coupled with her massive intellect, her well-honed fighting skills, and her ability to use her undeniable sex appeal as a weapon, she had devastated the local criminal population ever since her return.

Thus, as she stood at the edge of the roadway which was the last piece of land deemed safe in the remains of the town of Traversville, she found herself shaking, her body unable to decide whether or not to laugh or cry. She did not feel joy over the bodies of the dead she saw before her. She did not feel sorrow for the wives or children of the gangsters who died alongside their thug husbands and gangster fathers. All she felt as she studied the carnage in the waning sunlight was cheated.

"Miss…"

"Excuse me…"

"You'll pardon me," the voice from off to Ellen's side said in a tone trying not to sound too brusk. "Try not to be alarmed. I'm a police officer. John Conyers—" His introduction would have been a standard way to calm a citizen. Ellen could tell from its tone, however, that her charms had worked in her favor once more. Already the policeman's manner was far more friendly, his mouth breaking into an awkward smile as he added;

"Really, no one is supposed to be out here."

Ellen turned to find a young patrolman walking toward her. From his easily interpreted body language, she could tell he believed her some family member come to mourn. Although intellectually she realized this was the most sensible thing for him to assume, still a small part of her soul burned to have such a notion believed of her. Using it to her advantage, however, she opened her large brown eyes wide as she turned toward the officer, focusing her attentions upon him as she said;

"I know, but... I couldn't stay away. It... it's safe where I'm standing here... isn't it? They said we had to stay away, but I just, I mean, I just..."

As Ellen stopped speaking the policeman came closer, believing from her sudden silence that she was about to become emotional. He threw her typical words of comfort, but was surprised when she responded, her baby doll voice of a moment early replaced by a tone one expected more from a head librarian, or a drill sergeant. Her ploy of only a moment earlier forgotten, Ellen snapped;

"Turn around, look out there, straight out, about sixty, seventy yards, right along that ridge leading to those three upturned trees. Do you see where I mean?" When the officer assured her that he did, she added;

"Correct me if I'm wrong, but wasn't there a body there a minute ago?"

The patrolman was about to make light of her statement until a small voice from the back of his mind that had been nagging him all night made him actually look and think back. As he stared out across the unstable, muddy wasteland, he muttered;

"I think you're right, miss. In fact..." the young man removed his hat to scratch his head for a moment, then admitted, "I'm sure you're right."

"You're certain?"

"Yes, I am," he answered, his gaze running up and down the recently created hillside. "When you said what you did, you made me realize, I mean, it just dawned on me, something's been gnawing at me ever since I came on duty, and that's it. Several of the bodies... er, I mean—"

"Don't start worrying about my sensibilities," Ellen said, her eyes still scanning the disaster area before them both, "this is more important. I know I was looking at a body a moment ago, when I looked back in that direction, it was gone. I don't see any sign of a cave in; I didn't hear anything like one. Did you?"

As they both stood on the edge of the broken road, staring and squinting through the rapidly fading sunlight, the officer agreed that he had not heard anything, not shifting earth or even the noise of any sort of scavenger which might account for the disappearance of an entire human corpse. Cursing the fact that just the day before the city had reduced the enforcement team responsible for keeping the five-mile cordoned area clear to only two officers at night, he said;

"Listen, I need you to stay here. I'm going to go out just a little ways into the slide area and see if I can get a better look. Come the morning someone else is sure to notice this, and City Hall will be up in arms if we can't report at least having tried to find out what's going on."

Ellen nodded. All her senses were screaming at her that something was terribly wrong. Indeed, she felt a strangeness come over the universe suddenly which was beyond anything she had ever felt before. Unconsciously grabbing hold of a nearby railing still firmly grounded to the roadside, she watched intently as officer John Conyers unlimbered the over-sized, heavy-duty flashlight distributed to him for this particular duty.

After that, he gave her a wide smile, then stepped out onto the mudfield, gingerly, carefully making his way outward toward his doom.

Chapter 3

THE BLACK BAT'S FIST SLAMMED INTO THE MID-SECTION OF ANOTHER thug. It drove deep—hard and crunching—some three inches beneath the surface, snapping three ribs and rupturing the man's kidney. Most fighters' next move would have been to finish their opponent off, to follow that blow with another which would lay their opposite number out, but the Bat had no time for any such by-the-book niceties.

Even as he pulled his left fist back out of the gasping thug's innards, he made a rapid turn in a half circle, sending his right fist shooting forward at the same time on a collision course with the face of the man behind his initial foe. That blow shattered skin and jawbone, cracking four teeth and sending two others skittering off into the darkness.

"Get him, for Chr—"

This man spun around into another, a hoped-for bonus of which the Black Bat took immediate advantage. With three more men coming up behind him, most would expect the Bat to whirl around to face the newcomers. Indeed, so prepared for this response were the newly arrived trio, that they had pulled their guns and were ready to eliminate the number one menace of the

New York City underworld. Their problem was the fact that like most people, they could only think a mere one to two moves in advance.

Knowing this would be their reaction, having subconsciously heard the subtle sounds of metal being scraped across leather behind him, the Black Bat unexpectedly threw himself forward into the two men he had just incapacitated. Catching the shoulders of the one still standing, he pulled the man toward him even as he leapt upward, hurling himself up and over the bleeding thug. At the same time, three weapons barked, flinging lead at the space where a split second earlier it would have found the spine of the hated Black Bat.

Thwarted in bringing down this target, two of the bullets buried themselves in the man the Bat had used as a vaulting horse—one in the thigh, one in the chest—the other taking off his left ear, then hitting the first bruiser he had sent to the ground. Both men bellowed in searing agony, the sound of their screams freezing the triggermen. It was a natural reaction. They had not only missed the Black Bat, but taken out two of their own, and made enough noise in doing so to possibly summon the police.

For the gang members, this was enough to drive even men with their limited imaginations to at least a second's worth of caution. As they reacted slowly to what they had just done, however, momentarily frozen in time as the gang of them debated within their heads what to do, the Black Bat continued to act as the well-honed fighting machine he was.

While still in the air, he twisted his body completely around while pulling his twin .45s. Flipping over so as to be facing the new trio upon landing, he began firing a full three seconds before his feet hit the floor. By the time he did so, of course, the trio of gunmen were stretched out in the hallway ahead, two with bullets in their brains, one shot through the heart. Not taking time to congratulate himself, he instead snapped off one more shot from each automatic, sending a bullet each through the brains of the first pair of thugs.

It was a staggering display of self-defense, a fantastic feat of physical combat of which any human being could have been smugly proud. The Black Bat had no time for indulging his ego, though, for the five men he had taken by surprise were only the first squad

33

of several standing between him and their criminal boss. Taking a deep breath to clear his head, he holstered one of his weapons long enough to extract the small tool from his belt which he used to place a small bat symbol on the foreheads of several of the thugs he had just slain.

This was not an act of ego, either. When others found the bodies, that small symbol would tell them whom they were up against. Those few ultra-hard, steel-nerved criminals who were not impressed by anyone's legend but their own might not be impressed. But, the standard type of guard dog did not respond well to such news. After all, this was not some simple policeman or detective—nor was it something slightly more dangerous, such as a rival gang member. No, seeing that symbol would let them know that the fearsome Black Bat was somewhere nearby. That information was something that could frighten most any criminal in New York, which is, of course, the reaction upon which the masked avenger counted.

As the sound of many rapid footsteps came to him over not only the still ringing sound of the previous gunfire, but the thunder of the approaching storm outside, the Black Bat reached behind his back and pulled forth the special pistol he had brought with him that night. Aiming at a nearby window, he pulled the trigger and released the device's single payload, a flare meant to light up the night sky despite the incoming inclement weather.

"Well," said the man behind the driver's seat of a car parked in the darkness outside the mansion from which the signal had flashed, one of two waiting for the fiery signal, "there we go, Butch, old boy."

"I tell ya," responded the first speaker's partner, "there's never a dull night in the employee of Tony Quinn, eh Silk?"

The first man, a balding middle-aged chap with no special look about him, save a predatory glint of intelligence in his dark eyes, turned to his companion, a much larger fellow, and snickered;

"You may have just earned the Understatement of the Year Award, my friend. I'd stop to alert the papers, but then the whole flare thing... Tony's signal... best we do our part, don't you think?"

Butch O'Leary, the towering right-hand man of the Black Bat grinned sheepishly, even as he left the confines of the passenger's side of the front seat while his companion, Norton Kirby, vacated the driver's seat. Without pause, they charged the mansion they had been watching, both with machine guns in hand, a second slung over their shoulders. As they cleared the front gate, one went left while the other went right.

The Black Bat's plan had been simple enough. If he ran into trouble, his waiting crew were to start an assault on the outside of the building which could reasonably convince those inside that the police were conducting a raid. The pair did so even more easily than had been expected, alternating between shouting through hand-held megaphones and then releasing bursts from their machine guns, following these with canisters of tear gas hurled through the windows. Each man had only been able to carry a maximum of five tear gas grenades, considering the machine guns and extra clips, but the reaction inside was all the Black Bat could hope for—and more than he needed.

Everywhere, panicking mobsters were racing for safes or other caches of possible incriminating evidence, hurrying to remove such objects before the police could reach them. Indeed, so frightened were the criminals of "being caught with the goods," as it were, they were barely aware that the dreaded Black Bat was free and roaming through their midst.

Time and again, either the fists of the Bat, or his deadly automatics cleared the path of this or that hallway. It was ironic that in his everyday life as Tony Quinn, the Bat had once been the City of New York's district attorney. He knew the value of the papers and files being carried by those he sent to the ground, or smashed into walls, or whose lives he ended with his deadly automatics, but he did not stop to gather any of it as he usually might have done.

His mission there in Queens that rainy night was far too important. As lightning split the sky repeatedly, and thunder mixed with the sounds of gunfire from within and without, the Black Bat made his way down the last long hallway to where he was certain his prey waited. Reaching what he realized had to be the master bedroom, he kicked in the door with a single strike, wisely jumping to the opposite side at the same time. Over seventy bullets tore through the door and framing walls in deadly response. After a long moment of silence, a voice asked over the echoing reverberations of the gunfire;

"Enough—did you get him?"

"Don't know, Boss."

"Then go find out, ya lamebrains." The gang member nearest the now ruined doorway was just about to peek his head out for a look, when a deep and threatening voice offered;

"No need to send your trained monkeys out to die, Boot. You didn't get me."

The words were accompanied by a trio of grenades sent flying in one after another. The first was a smoke bomb, not only used to disorient, but also to make certain none inside could find either of the next two grenades. These were gas bombs, one a canister of the same stinging tear gas being used by his confederates, a foul, terrible mixture which caused those who came in contact with it to weep uncontrollably while gasping for air. The second was a deadly poison. It was in fact designed to dissipate quickly, but with the deep lungfuls of air the first bomb made those inside so desperate for, it was only a matter of seconds before all within the room were dead.

Taking no chances, the Black Bat entered the room with his own specialized gas mask in place. Swiftly he moved from body to body, searching to see which of the mobsters his attack had taken down. The fourth corpse he came to told him the evening had been a success. Rolling over the fat body, he exposed the face of Vincent "the Boot" Nelfadamo. Vincent had made his way upward through the city's rackets by handling the one game with which no one else wished to become associated.

Drugs.

At one time left to the Negro gangs to deal out of their Harlem strongholds, Nelfadamo had convinced the families that by ignoring this marketplace they were only allowing their dark-skinned rivals to grow stronger. The minor capo offered to make certain the Negro ganglords' influence stopped at 110th street, and never came below.

For the last few years, that understanding had worked fine for everyone, as long as the mobster had been content to only work the clients already looking for drugs—the actors, the musicians, the poets and intellectuals who craved such debilitating distractions. But Nelfadamo had bigger ideas, ambitions he was willing to back in blood. The first step of his plan was easy to predict, he waged a murderous war against all the Negro gangs and driven them completely out of white Manhattan. Then, without taking a breath, the capo had turned his attention to Chinatown at the southern end of the island and made war on the Oriental gangs there, splicing himself into their trade in opiates as well.

His plan had been hinged on the belief the police would not interfere in gangsters slaughtering each other, especially if it were white gangsters driving out their ethnic inferiors. Sadly, his estimation of the police force's shameless self-interest had been correct, and in less than a year, he had found himself in complete control of the flow of all narcotics of any kind throughout the entire city save for a few uptown pockets of Manhattan and the Bronx.

To be fair, his dealings had not come to the Black Bat's attention in any great way at first, either. The Bat kept tabs on all gang-related activity as best he could, of course. But as long as the criminals were murdering one another, like the police he had better things of which to take care. Two weeks previous, he had found one of those things.

In the basement of an abandoned building, one of his many contacts throughout New York had brought him to a scene too horrible to describe. There, the bodies of over a score of the city's indigent population had been found, dead from experiments conducted by Nelfadamo's people. A simple bit of leg work led him to one of the mobster's men who quickly spilled the beans from his boss's stove after the Bat made it known what kind of persuasion he was willing to use.

Nelfadamo's plan was a thing insidious. The dead had been used as guinea pigs, given all the free drugs they wanted merely so the gangsters could determine the proper doses for the new and sinister types of dope into which they were branching out. Having secured the operational territory for their personal racket, they now planned on expanding their customer base as well.

The stoolie, enjoying the ability to breath and wishing to continue to enjoy it, told everything he knew to the Black Bat—how plans were already in effect to move their product on college campuses, and among various working classes, promoting their foul junk as not only a party favor, the "in" thing for any event, but also as a handy tool for staying awake. Like medicine, really. Study longer, work that extra shift, then go out and celebrate. Jump on the bandwagon with those in the know. Don't be a sap, was their rationale, enjoy the wonder drug!

Attorney Tony Quinn stared out through his mask, remembering all the suffering and misery he had seen during his days in the DA's office due to drugs. Thinking of them promoted far and wide, circulated through colleges, maybe even down into high schools, his vision went scarlet. Forgetting his feared bat insignia for once, the avenger decided on leaving behind a different calling card. Pulling the bloated corpse of the Boot up off the floor, he slammed the lifeless form against the wall, shattering its skull, screaming at it;

"Not in my city, you don't! All of you, figure it out, understand—this kind of filth stays in the gutter where it belongs as long as I'm alive—so help me, God!"

Throwing the dead weight of flesh back to the ground, he placed both his .45s to Nelfadamo's face and pulled the triggers— twice each. Let that be a warning to the rest, he thought. Sell drugs in my town to decent people and when they bury your miserable remains, your own mother won't recognize you.

By that time, the few remaining thugs at the mansion that night had already run off. The pseudo-police raid had worked as perfectly as Quinn had expected. The notion gripped the lawyer's soul and squeezed at it, making the handsome features beneath his mask contort hideously. If it had been a real police raid, if they had come in with unbeatable evidence that proved Nelfadamo had murdered a thousand babies and their mothers with them, all the officers of the law could have done would have been to take him into custody to stand trial.

How long he would have stayed in custody, however, was anyone's guess. He had witnessed it all too often when in the DA's office; thugs and butchers and worse going free because of technicalities and bought-off judges. He remembered instances of the police and other city officials cynically running pools on how long it would take for mobsters to buy their way back out onto the street after being arrested.

Well, he thought, not in my town. Not while the Black Bat has anything to say about it.

Turning his back on the twisted, pain-etched scene in the bedroom, Tony Quinn headed quickly for the outside. His offensive planned to destroy the Nelfadamo mob had worked with textbook precision. Outside, Kirby and O'Leary would already be back in his roadster waiting for him several blocks away. He expected the police to arrive soon in reaction to the bullets fired, but he was not overly concerned.

The Black Bat knew that even if the police were to arrive on the scene before he could exit the building, there was no chance they could spot him. They would be looking for gangsters—men who used doors, or possibly windows. They would not be looking for someone prepared to leap from rooftops. Especially not in the rain. That was one thing Quinn knew about New Yorkers—they never looked up when it was raining.

And indeed, the police were entering the mansion through its front door even as the Black Bat leapt into its back yard from the second story balcony. Making his way quickly to the eight foot stone wall that surrounded the Nelfadamo estate, the Bat made his way up and over the obstacle in a matter of seconds. Landing in the shadow of a large, city-planted tree, he was just straightening up when a voice asked him;

"Ah, there you are, Mr. Quinn. Tell me, could you spare a few moments for a chat?"

Chapter 4

LEGRASSE BLINKED, THEN RE-READ THE LAST FEW LINES OF CLARO'S ragged diary quietly to himself.

Although not as violently, the same terrible fear came over him once again, chilling his blood and gripping his soul as few things had throughout his lifetime. Without further hesitation, the former inspector continued on in the spellbinding tome, half-trembling, half-fascinated.

Claro had halted his forward progress through his home that evening for he had found the room before him filled with vast lengths of roping flesh. The things he saw were something like the tentacles of an octopus, or squid, but longer, thinner, and possessed of individual skills no cephalopod imaginable had ever displayed. Claro wrote of having stood frozen, terror gripping his every muscle as he watched the roaming tendrils poke and pull, slithering hither and yon in the moonlight. Then, the one he had just eluded found him again, and Claro beat at it with his chair until the seat had become splinters.

Racing about madly, the man had smashed at the tentacles, beaten them with his fists, even biting into several of them. And, although the tendrils retreated completely within seconds in the face of his mindless, howling attack, still the old swamp dweller was left drenched in sweat from his encounter.

The man spent the next day completely closing down the side of his home facing the swamp. He was thorough and methodical, but it did him no good. The next night the lengths returned, and again he was forced to do battle with the sucking, grasping coils. They came over the next two nights as well, and Claro began to take note of certain things. Each night the tentacles came earlier and stayed longer. They were beginning to be able to predict where he would be, what he would do. They were beginning to not fear him. Which is when he had decided to start setting the traps.

Legrasse gave the book over to Galvez at that point, suggesting to him that he familiarize himself with at least some of it while the inspector threw some brain power at all the facts they had gathered so far. The Spaniard nodded, handing over to the inspector the cane he had been toying with so that he could hold the book in two hands. While Galvez started, Legrasse thought on what he had read.

The book told of tentacles coming through the windows, slots, cracks, even his sink drain. Why the man stayed in his home, the diary did not explain. Nor did it explain why Claro had not at least left at night, did not call the police, did not ask his neighbors for shelter, or assistance.

Or anything.

What could it have been, wondered Legrasse. Why was it? What did it want? Why did it come? Why?

Maybe Claro was just too stubborn to admit defeat. Maybe he simply went insane, bought the traps and spread them out, relying on the only thing that had truly worked for him. The last entry he had made in his little book with his bit of pencil, sitting in his corner, disturbed Legrasse the most.

free, free at last

The inspector studied the cane in his hand in an absent fashion as he tried to piece the bits they understood of the sad occurrence into some kind of even semi-logical whole. Certainly the storm had unleashed whatever had found Claro. He could not call the notion a fact, but to assume any other premise given what he knew from former cases involving such things would have been insanity. Perhaps, he mused, it was some long lost horror, sealed away within the fresh spring so recently uncovered.

Legrasse stared at the corpse in the corner and wondered, did the dead man somehow possess a bit of arcane knowledge that some outre thing wanted for itself, something it did not want anyone else to know? Or was Claro just the poor unfortunate bastard who happened to be the only creature nearby when the storm somehow opened a random portal that some bug just happened to accidentally poke its way through?

The inspector quietly checked Galvez's progress. He could see the man was nearly halfway through the notebook. Looking about, he scanned the room once more for anything they might have previously missed—any scrap or innocuous bit of flotsam that might possibly unlock the mystery before them.

Well now, he thought, there's something.

Staring once more at the corpse, Legrasse took note of a section of the dead man's leg. Just above the top of his sock, in between there and the spot where Claro's pants were up far enough to reveal flesh above the sock line, he spotted round red welts like sucker wounds which appeared to circle the deceased's leg.

Legrasse wondered at it all, at what the searchers could have been after. What was the point, he mused, of coming night after night, but never taking anything, never actually doing anything—anything. Why?

Absently smacking his hand with the butt-end of the cane, the inspector took a closer note of the intricate carvings etched into its length. There was nothing truly remarkable about them, although he did notice they seemed somewhat fresh. Still, distinct as they were, they still did not seem of any great importance. Indeed, his mind left them instantly as he noticed Galvez coming to the end of the notebook. Tossing the cane back to the Spaniard, Legrasse turned around slowly within his small clear space in the traps, studying.

Wondering.

"Hey, John," called Galvez, "anything you want me to do while you stare off into space at the tax payer's expense?"

"It's your investigation," replied Legrasse absently. "Be creative."

The lieutenant nodded, looking for a direction in which he

might possibly be able to head. Legrasse looked down at the traps, wondering about them once more.

He had been puzzled about them in so many ways since he had first arrived he could not list them all. So far the few bits of information he had gathered about them had only added to his growing puzzlement. He still could not believe Claro had set out all the traps. Their placement was so finely meshed, so intricate. And the patterns he had noticed, swirls and star-shapes, intersecting each other over and over throughout the main room, the madness of it all—

Why, wondered Legrasse. Why would he do it?

The traps had not been working, the inspector remembered. Yet Claro had gotten more and more of them, ultimately painting himself into the corner, so to speak, with them.

Across the room, Galvez picked the next spot where he would knock a new hole in the traps so that he could move toward the back rooms. Sealed off as they were, none of them had been investigated yet. To the lieutenant's way of thinking, it was high time they were opened.

Ignoring Galvez's actions, Legrasse concentrated on the traps. There was something he was not seeing, something that was passing him by. He stared down at the floor again, trying to look at everything once more from the beginning, struggling to gain a new perspective.

The infernal traps were everywhere. In tight, sophisticated patterns. Why? How could Claro have managed it, with only two hands? It did not seem possible. And, even if it were, why would he have done so?

Galvez spotted the point where he could place his next footfall without disturbing too many of the traps.

Of course, Legrasse thought, the traps aren't so tight everywhere. Fairly sparse back by the door when you first come in. And where the patterns run up against one another. Indeed, that was where Galvez had been making his strikes, in the freer areas between the patterns.

Convenient, whispered a voice from the back of Legrasse's mind. He caught the tone, realizing instantly his subconscious was trying to tell him something.

Indeed, the footfalls had been conveniently made, slivers of space left between each of the patterns, just right for a human of average height, spaced just so, placed directly where the average human eye would see them—where any typical human mind would pride itself on being able to take advantage of them.

Galvez's arm stretched out, positioning the cane for its next strike. And, as it did so, the inspector's memory superimposed another image on the scene. He thought back to voodoo rituals he had witnessed, to the foul priest he and his men had stopped only months earlier, all of them, scratching patterns in the sand or the mud, making their magic gestures with their totem sticks—

"I'm going to take a look in the back rooms."

The lieutenant pulled his hand back, even as Legrasse's mind raced. What if Claro had not set the traps, or even if he had, if after his death, something else had moved them? Changed their positions, moved them into patterns...

Galvez's hand began to descend—

And, what if the same patterns it then carved into Claro's cane, the cane left at the front door, where the traps were not so thickly spread, so that one could enter, look around, be amazed, wonder what they could do, and...

Pick up the cane!

"No!"

Legrasse screamed at Galvez, even as he threw himself at the lieutenant. The lieutenant shouted as well, raising his free hand in response, trying to bring up the one wielding the cane, but it was too late. Both men went down painfully, rolling over and over in the flesh-tearing maze.

Chapter 5

"LISTEN, I NEED YOU TO STAY HERE. I'M GOING TO GO OUT JUST A little ways into the slide area and see if I can get a better look. Come the morning someone else is sure to notice this, and City Hall will be up in arms if we can't report at least having tried to find out what's going on."

Ellen heard the officer's parting words in her head over and over as she watched him making his way forward. One part of her hated the fact there was nothing she could do. She had come to the area merely as a civilian to witness the mass destruction of her enemies for herself. To risk appearing as the Domino Lady, or even as competent as her alter ego, when she had no real objective would have been foolish. Indeed, even dropping her "helpless female" role in front of the patrolman had been risky. But now, she wished she had done so. She wished she were out there making her way across the field of carnage along with officer Conyers.

Of course, a familiar voice from within her mind whispered, looking at his progress, perhaps a thigh-slit evening dress and ultra high heels were not the most appropriate garb for such maneuvering.

Despite the almost numbing fear that had been clawing at her a moment earlier, Ellen giggled at the notion of herself trying to make it across the unstable mud flats to where the missing body had been in any of her Domino costumes. Even as her other senses continued screaming at her that something was terribly wrong, she had to admit that Conyers looked more than a bit the comic figure as he slipped and slopped his way across the still wet mud. Several uncomfortable sounds he emitted let her know his landings were not the softest. And then, as Ellen covered her mouth so the young man would not hear her laughing at his expense, it happened.

As officer John Conyers tried to make his way even more carefully across the expanse, he suddenly found a sinkhole which swallowed his left leg up to the hip. He cried out as his one leg unexpectedly sank into the ground, nearly losing his flashlight as he fell. Ellen gasped as well, thinking something far worse had happened to the brave officer.

"Don't worry," he called out. Turning so she could see his face in the last rays of the waning sunset, he grinned sheepishly, telling her, "just a hole."

Ellen was grateful for his thoughtful gesture. Of course she knew he was paying her more attention than he would the average citizen. All men did. Blind men did. She could turn more heads than any woman in the history of San Francisco had ever managed, and on a bad hair day if necessary. As Conyers laughed at his predicament, working to extricate himself, Ellen smiled, the back of her mind snickering that the young, handsome officer most likely could turn a few heads himself.

"In a nice suit," she whispered to herself with appreciation, "anyway."

Her miss-nothing-eyes summed him up in a moment, rating his large, ranging shoulders, his tapered waist, strong-looking hands, clean-shaven, squared-off chin, soft eyes—charming eyes, really—allowing Ellen to shove the moment of horror she had felt away from her mind as she began to map out several possible ways the evening could work out once large, strong-looking, soft-eyed officer Conyers returned to her side.

Indeed, her mind was getting quite playful with the idea. Unfortunately, officer Conyers was destined to not return to her side. Officer Conyers was destine to never be seen again.

Suddenly, even as Ellen's momentary fantasy caused her to close her eyes, a scream from across the mudfield forced them instantly open. As the sun disappeared completely, in that last split second of light she watched helplessly as the policeman was dragged beneath the surface!

"John!"

Without hesitation, without regard for her own safety, Ellen threw herself over what was left of the restraining rail and sprinted to the spot of Conyers' disappearance. Her razor-sharp mind had imprinted upon her subconscious the safe foot-falls while watching the officer make his way carefully across the mud. Thus what took him a laborious, several minutes took her but a few, quick seconds.

Still, she was too late.

Staring into the ebony black hole which was the last place she had seen Conyers, Ellen desperately searched for the slightest trace of the missing officer. For a moment she wondered if she might have reached the wrong spot, for down the dark crack in the earth she could not see even the slightest trace of his flashlight's beam. The quite panicked young woman called the patrolman's name out repeatedly, but received no answer. At least, not until after several minutes when a voice behind her called out;

"What in tarnation are you doin' out theres, miss?"

Turning, Ellen saw a second police officer, this one an older man, making his way across the mudfield. Slipping and sliding, he told her;

"Of all the ridiculous... don't you know nobody's allowed out here. It's off limits because of the sli—"

"No," she shouted with authority, hoping to focus the approaching policeman's attention. "You don't understand. Another officer came out here to investigate something we saw, and he disappeared!"

"Disappeared," responded the slowly advancing lawman skeptically. "What, you mean in a cloud of smoke, like ol' Mandrake the Magician?"

"No, officer," snapped Ellen coldly. Her eyes narrowing, she dropped her voice to a growl and added, "I mean down this hole, like a man falling to his death!"

Ellen's cold retort galvanized the older policeman. No longer worried about getting his pants dirty he reached her side in seconds.

Snatching his own special issue flashlight, the officer played his beam into what proved to be a terribly deep opening. For a moment, if was all either the observers could do to simply try and see down to the bottom of the endless pit. Scratching his head while keeping his light playing down the hole, the policeman offered;

"You know, I don't right see how anyone could have fallen down this here... I mean, the sides aren't that wide. Why... he'd hav'ta been a midget not to catch on to the sides..."

The officer's mind went from confused to suspicious in only a handful of seconds. Like most simple beat cops, the easiest answer was the one he fastened onto first. If his partner on the cordon duty was missing, and this girl was the only other person around, she probably had something to do with him going missing.

On the surface, such a thought made little sense, especially considering how he had discovered Ellen, kneeling over the hole frantically calling Conyer's name. But, following procedure, the patrolman began to wonder just what the young woman in the obviously expensive clothing was doing kneeling in the mud beside him. What was she doing in the restricted area in the first place? What could her motive for doing all these things be—in crossing the "Restricted" barrier, in doing a policeman harm?

Turning away from the hole for the moment, the older patrolman pulled his flashlight from the crack in the ground and played it over Ellen. His common sense told him she had no more to do with his partner's disappearance than he did, but still, old habits forced him to ask;

"Lady, just what are you doing out here, anyway?"

"I saw officer Conyers pulled down this hole. He screamed in pain—or at least shock. I was trying to help..." And then, as realization of what the patrolman was thinking dawned on Ellen, she pulled back from him, shouting;

"Oh my goodness, you think I had something to do with this? Are you an idiot? Of all the—"

The suggestion she was about to make froze in Ellen Patrick's lovely throat. All thoughts of continuing her tirade ceased, such ideas evaporating completely as her ears caught the tiniest sound of something sliding slowly through the mud. And then, as the officer began to say something in return now that Ellen had gone silent, she suddenly grabbed his hand holding the flashlight and jerked him toward herself with all her might—

Only a split-second too late.

The officer jerked harshly to a halt despite Ellen's desperate tug, his body restrained in three spots by gray, ropey lengths which had grabbed onto him. Ellen screamed in defiance, digging her heels into the mud, straining to keep the patrolman from suffering the same fate as his partner. His flashlight, dropped when he was first snared, fell at a perfect angle to show Ellen all that was happening.

A trio of pulsating, slime-covered vine-like tentacles had sprung up out of the ground and grabbed hold of the policeman— one wrapped tightly about his neck, one his left arm, the last his right thigh. From the indentations they were making in the man's flesh, Ellen could tell the lengths were exerting a massive pressure upon him. Indeed, so great was the strength of the horrid things she could feel herself being pulled through the mud, her shoes slipping from her feet, her desperate grip beginning to weaken.

The officer managed to pull his sidearm and aim it down the hole. Without hesitation he pulled the trigger again and again, emptying his service revolver without bothering to question the nightmarish implications of what had attacked him. Amazingly, his frantic defense worked. The lengths released their hold upon him, dropping him to the ground.

The backward force suddenly gone, the officer and Ellen fell one against the other, both going down awkwardly in the mud and the darkness. Both struggled desperately with a kind of nervous terror to push themselves up and out of the mud, their mouths jabbering questions faster than their brains could even attempt to answer them. Finally, getting his hands back on his flashlight, the officer gasped;

"Thank you..."

"Are you all right?"

"Who cares," answered the frightened officer. Grabbing Ellen's arm, he added, "com'on, lady, why the hell are we s-s-standin' around here? Let's get the..."

The patrolman stopped speaking so abruptly, at first Ellen thought that perhaps he had simply changed his mind about leaving. Then, almost as if she were seeing events in slow motion, the flashlight dropped from the officer's hand, spinning as it fell toward the Earth. As it rolled off the tips of his fingers, his chest was torn open as from behind, six of the terrible lengths smashing their way through his body like spears.

Ellen screamed as quarts of blood exploded outward from the policeman's body, spattering her from head to foot. Yes, she was tough, hardened in fact beyond the point of which no more than a handful of women had ever known.

But, what she had just experienced, no one living had ever seen and survived. And now, as her desperate mind surged and pleaded with her to regain control of her faculties, the half-dozen writhing lengths which had just slain a man before her very eyes, turned their attention toward finding her!

Chapter 6

"WHAT WAS THAT YOU CALLED ME?"

Standing up out of his crouch, the Black Bat continued to face away from whomever it was that had managed to take him unawares—who was now standing behind him. He could understand not knowing anyone was there; yes, he told himself, he had been in a hurry, it was dark, raining, the street was lined with trees... but, whoever it was that had called out to him, they knew his name—his *real* name.

He called me Quinn.

As the Bat started to walk off into the rain, the troublesome thought ringing in his head, the voice called out to him;

"*Huuummmmmm,* you know—really, one would think a guy like the fearsome Black Bat would prove to be a touch more quick-witted. But, you've had a full evening of casual murder, so I'll repeat myself.

"I had just said, '*Ah, there you are, Mr. Quinn. Tell me, could you spare a few moments for a chat?*'"

"Oh, I see, now..." responded the Bat, his voice not betraying the tiniest strain of the growing nervousness he was surprised to discover he was feeling, "of course, you're one of those members of the police department in this town who still think I'm that blind chap, Tony Quinn—correct?"

There was something in the voice behind him that made the Bat hesitate treating its owner as he might normally anyone else who approached him in such a manner. The man did not seem smug about his knowledge to him—neither triumphant, nor greedy. He did not seem overly-pleased with himself, either. As a lawyer, not to mention his years as DA for the City of New York, Quinn had learned just about everything one could know about the reading of people. This man's voice screamed out that although he was some sort of rough character, he was a noble one as well, a man possessed of integrity. He knew the man wanted something of him, but as the back of his mind whispered to him;

"You know, you meet the Pope, he wants your immortal soul to go to Heaven. Wanting something of someone doesn't necessarily make that someone a bad guy."

Slowly, the Black Bat turned to face whomever it was that had spotted him coming over the wall. Looking out through the heavy rain, his eyes came to focus on a large man, staring at him with tired eyes. He was thick-shouldered and barrel-chested, casually leaning against a street lamp in the steadily increasing downpour as if he had nothing better to do that wait for the Black Bat to decide what he would do next. A derby sat pushed forward on his shaved head, its brim slightly discolored from the constant cloud of cigar smoke he used to screen himself from the world.

Tony Quinn had once been blind. During those days his senses other than sight had become heightened to an astounding degree. When through an amazing opportunity his ability to see was returned to him, he found his other senses somehow remained heightened. More over, the sight he was then newly gifted with was far greater than that with which he had been born. Indeed, it was greater than that of any feline. He could not only see as a cat does—their eyes capable of reflecting even the tiniest speck of light to be able to see clearly even in near total darkness—Tony Quinn outshone the cat world for he could see clearly in complete and utter darkness as if it were a normal day.

Thus the man before him was not disguised to him in any manner, neither by the rain nor the darkness. The Black Bat could easily see that the man was armed from the large bulge under his coat, but also that he seemed in no hurry to use his weapon even for defense. He could tell the man knew much about self-defense, and most likely offense as well. But that did not seem to matter at the moment.

No, the Bat was certain, the man leaning so casually against a street lamp there in the rain simply wanted to talk.

And, all of Quinn's senses told him, whatever it is he wants to discuss, it's of major importance to him.

The large man was about to speak again, when suddenly the long-awaited sound of police sirens cut through the night. Patrol cars were coming toward the Nelfadamo mansion from every possible direction. Breaking off what he had been about to say, the man in the bowler hat growled;

"Fade, get outta sight—I'll get these guys outta our hair."

Dropping back against the wall surrounding the Nelfadamo estate, the Black Bat found himself forced to make an instantaneous decision—use the distraction as an opportunity to escape back over the wall, or play along with the armed man who knew his identity simply because he seemed trustworthy.

Grinning to himself, enjoying the moment to take a chance, he decided to find out what the bald man wanted, and stepped into the shadows created by an overgrowth of ivy. Hidden from view, he watched and listened as two patrol cars screeched to a halt, one from each direction, to confront the mysterious man in the derby to whom he had just been talking.

"So, lookie-here—we get a report on a thousand gun shots goin' off in'da night, and who do we find loungin' outside said shot-to-hell real estate in question, but the great and wonderful detective Mark Thorner. Oh, tell me, you deep and mystical pain in my backside, oh Lord, why is there no notes of wondrous surprise leapin' inta my throat?"

"That's lieutenant Thorner to you, Sergeant O'Donnell. And, would you really like me to detail why I suspect I happen to be on the spot at a major crime scene long before you and the rest of the Keystone clean-up brigade? Or should I just talk about the good time I had with your sister last night?"

The officer behind the wheel put his hand on the sergeant's shoulder, not so much to stop him from getting out of the car, but to keep him from rushing out foolishly. His eyes bulging, teeth grinding together, O'Donnell slammed his fist against the car door, shouting about what he would do to Thorner for talking ill about his baby sister. Putting a hand up in mock-apology, the lieutenant offered;

"Relax, ya knob. All we did was go to the picture show. Yeah, we went to see that one where the big monkey falls off the Empire State Building." Thorner gave the scene a moment, allowing O'Donnell to calm down slightly, then added;

"After all, how could I possibly miss your mother's debut on the silver screen? You know—I gotta admit, she climbs almost as good as you drink."

With that the sergeant roared, trying mightily to exit the patrol car, but the driver as well as those in the back seat grabbed hold of him, restraining him from what they knew could only be a futile display of violence destined not to end well for their superior. Shaking off those with his best interest at heart, slapping their hands away, a slightly calmer O'Donnell shook his fist once more at Thorner, shouting;

"You miserable bastard, you're just lucky I've got no time for the likes of you right now, or there'd be wigs on the green for sure, I'm telling you that."

"Whatever you say," answered Thorner agreeably. Then, as if an afterthought, he grabbed the brim of his hat and exposed his shaved pate, adding, "Of course, we know whose wig that would be, right, O'Donnell?"

Thorner laughed as the patrolman behind the wheel gunned their squad car and sent it racing forward to the front gate of the mansion. When a more friendly officer from the other stopped vehicle asked the lieutenant his opinion of the crime scene, Thorner pulled at his jaw absently, then suggested;

"It's just a hunch, but I'm thinkin' this just possibly could be the work of the Black Bat. I'd look in that direction if I was you guys."

The other officers gave Thorner the thumbs up and headed off for the front gate after the other squad cars. Stepping out of the shadows, the Black Bat asked;

"Is everybody in this town so sure you always know what you're talking about?"

"Those with any common sense." Giving the Bat a wink, the

lieutenant added, "the tip I gave them... I mean, you did want the credit for that, didn't you?"

"What I do," the Black Bat growled lowly, "I don't do for the credit."

Thorner sighed. It was a weary sound, one Quinn thought might actually be more aimed at its emitter than himself. Thorner stood with his head hung low, his large hands in his pockets. After a moment, he finally pulled his over-sized mitts out of his pockets, using them to help him say;

"Yeah, all right—sometimes maybe I don't take guys like you seriously enough." While the Bat wondered over exactly what the detective might mean by 'guys like him,' Thorner tilted his head back up, adding;

"Look, you got no reason to trust me outsida whatever your gut is tellin' you. I figure you gotta have pretty good instincts, or you wouldn't have lasted a year the way you have. So, what'dya think, you willin' to hear me out or not?"

"Where?"

"Well, I figure you got that ox of yours, O'Leary, and your reformed con artist, Silk, stashed somewhere nearby. Good as you are, you can't fire weapons inside and outside a building at the same time. So, we can either pile into your car to get out of the rain, or we can use mine and you can fill them in later."

Tony Quinn congratulated himself on having designed a mask that covered most of his face. He was certain that Thorner's utter confidence in his information must have left him looking at least a little surprised. Still, the man was a police officer—a cop who seemed to know a great deal about his operation as the Black Bat who had not tried to either capture him, or turn him in, indeed, who had just now sent fellow officers off in another direction when he could have taken him in, or at least attempted to take him in, right then and there.

Every instinct the man in the mask possessed, those honed during his years as lawyer Tony Quinn, and those sharpened by his time as the Black Bat, all of it now assured him that Thorner was an honorable man—one whom he could trust. Not wishing to force his confederates to make that same leap of faith just yet, however, he asked;

"How close is your car?" Sweeping his hand over a black Ford roadster with numerous dents in it, and what appeared to be a half-dozen bullet holes, the detective answered;

"You're lookin' at it."

"Warm, dry, right here... let's use yours."

As the two men got into the car, the sky was shattered by a callosal thunderclap, one followed by an immediate swelling in the level of the driving deluge pelting the city. The increase of the rain came down so violently that neither man could see a thing through the windows of the Ford once they had clambered inside, the detective in the front seat, the Black Bat into the back. Pulling what appeared to be an old shirt from the floor, Thorner took off his hat, wiped down his head and face, then threw the shirt back to its place around the gear box. Replacing his soggy derby upon his head, he asked;

"So, like the weather tonight?"

"I'm sure the ducks will enjoy it."

"They're gonna be the only ones."

"What do you mean?"

The lieutenant stopped for a moment. Pursing his lips, he looked downward for a long second, releasing a breath through his nose. His pause lasted but a moment, however, after which he finally asked;

"Do you follow the news at all, the weather across the country? If you do, you mighta taken note about a story around a week back, California gettin' hit by a storm right outta Hell. Sound familiar? Yes, no?" When the Black Bat confirmed he was aware of that storm, Thorner said;

"Good man. How about the one in between that one and this one, the hurricane that cleaned up around the Gulf of Mexico?"

"Yes, took note of that one, too."

"Well, take a good look outside, because now it's our turn. And if what some guys who know a crapload more about this stuff than I do think turns out to be right, that soak workin' on breakin' through my windshield is not just a nasty howler, its the goddamned calling card of Armageddon."

Both men paused as suddenly the enveloping blackness all about them was shattered by a trio of lightning bolts that blazed the night sky, accompanied by another stunning roll of thunder that frightened children in their sleep and silenced men in their hearts. Pulling a cigar from a cheap cardboard box on his dashboard, the lieutenant fumbled in his pockets for his lighter as he said;

"Hey, woud'ja look at that—just like in the movies, least little mention of the end of the world, and there's your thunder and lightning, right on cue."

The sky was split by an even fiercer display as Thorner lit his cigar, almost as if to prove him right.

Chapter 7

"WHAT IN ALL THE GODDAMNED HELLS DID YOU DO *THAT* FOR?"

Galvez had not been able to stop cursing since he and Legrasse had been rolled across the floor through the scores of set traps by the inspector's rash action. Amazingly, though both had been bloodied, neither man had sustained a severe injury. Each had been stung by plenty of the mouse and rat traps, but these had been released more by contact with their clothing that bodies. The larger snares, those with teeth or bone-crushing power had been, for the most part, luckily avoided.

Pulling a rather distressing rat trap from his elbow, Legrasse explained to his former deputy what he had noted that had made him act so desperately. He showed Galvez the odd relationship between the swirling formations of the traps as they had been laid out, and the freshly carved patterns to be found on the cane. After that, the inspector did his best to explain what he had learned about the interconnected manner of most magicks, and how, quite possibly the lieutenant had been maneuvered into striking each of the patterns he had in turn with what, oddly enough, in most occult circles would be thought of as a wand.

On his own, Galvez made the connection that considering the

detail in which Claro had written in his journal, the fact he did not mention either patterning the traps or taking the time to carve a cane in the middle of his nightmares certainly seemed to both an odd omission.

Together, all the facts gave the pair of police officers a moment's pause. What could the patterns in which the traps had been laid out have meant? How could the tentacles, working blind, have positioned, or re-positioned them so perfectly? Or carved the cane in such intricate detail? And, certainly far more important, to what end would such things be done? Indeed, if they could manage all of that without Claro, why not simply set the traps off themselves as well?

Why was an intermediary needed to do so?

As the two lawmen finally staggered to their feet, Galvez hurled the last trap he had to remove from his jacket toward the corner, growling in disgust. A shorter man, as well as a quite passionate one of Latin descent, his dignity meant overly much to him. Brushing wrinkles from his jacket, his ego still as sore as his flesh, he glared at Legrasse as he muttered;

"You know, you could have just told me not to hit the traps again."

Legrasse sighed. What could he say, he wondered. His hands and legs and arms and face had been snapped and gouged in just as many places as had Galvez's. He had lost as much blood, had pulled one of the crushing things off his nose and one from an ear. He did not answer his one-time aide, however. Remembering the man's sensitivity about some things, there was no point.

At least, not on that matter.

"So, el Grande, what do we do now?"

Legrasse stood staring at the walls all about him, at the floor and its layers and circlets of traps. He knew if he studied the house, if he returned to his library, contacted those others he knew with deeper magical knowledge than his own, that he might be able to determine more, to learn the significance of what he was now staring at so blankly.

But, he thought, he was no scholar. Not yet, anyway, no matter how determined Fate seemed intent on creating one from the naught but rough material he had to offer it. He had been from birth a man of action, and thus all his thoughts on the subject were those of one used to acting first and worrying about the consequences later.

Still, the back of his mind whispered to him, what if someone else gets pulled into releasing the traps? Even if the house is left under a heavy guard, who would be left behind to guard the guards? And, who's to say things haven't already been set into motion by the amount of traps already sprung?

Indeed, another voice within his brain nagged, what if your mad little lunge to stop Galvez was actually the last stroke being awaited?

What if, the first voice laughed, you've set off the end of the world yourself with your foolish blundering?

"Burn it."

Galvez was certain he had heard his one-time superior correctly, but standard protocol demanded he ask;

"What did you—"

"You heard me," snapped Legrasse. "Burn it. Consign the whole damn place, traps and all, to the pyre. You smell the stink of evil in the boards of this moldering old calamity as well as I do, don't deny it." When his former lieutenant remained silent, the inspector repeated;

"Burn it down—before it's too late."

It had taken Galvez less than a minute to consider all aspects of the his one-time commander's suggestion. He would have a bit of explaining to do when he made out his report. Taking it upon himself to destroy a citizen's home, cremating a city resident without approval of his next-of-kin, these were not acts one performed lightly.

On the other hand, however, Claro was not known to have anything much in the way of family, nor was his home worth any amount to raise the concern of most—not really. And, of course, if nothing else it could all be put down as an "unfortunate" accident. With a touch of creative writing, his report could read that Claro had burned his home down in the middle of the night. After all, once the place was cinders, what or who would be left to dispute him?

In Galvez's mind, signing off on a forged tragedy made more sense that risking not following the advice he had been given. When it came to the supernatural, the lieutenant was not one to argue with his former commander. Indeed, as long as he allowed Legrasse to investigate these types of things, and kept his own mind clear of them, he was certain his sleep would continue to come to him much more peacefully than the inspector would ever know again.

In minutes the officers that had been patiently waiting outside were ordered to gather kindling. Claro's own firewood pile as well as his furniture, found stacked on the back porch so he might lay out his ocean of snares, was all added to that which could be gathered from a nearby hardwood grove.

With one patrolman's volunteered newspaper crumpled sheet by sheet in the center of the floor as the tinder base of their fire, it took no more than a single match to start what would be in minutes a conflagration unnaturally hot. As officers of the law in a city as volatile as New Orleans, all those present had witnessed more than one raging house fire in their time. Even so, they all quietly agreed that Claro's rotten old shack burned with an intensity that none of them had ever before witnessed.

As the group of police officers continued to stand on the edge of the swamp, watching the old house burn, Legrasse did not see what they had accomplished. When the madly roaring blaze was finally finished, the officers waiting nearby would dynamite the spring Claro had written of, the one they had found with so many sinister gouges roping up through the mud surrounding it. Afterward the entire area would be salted, then forgotten.

Officially, anyway.

Holding the cane for a moment longer, Legrasse wondered if what he had seen in his mind were even possible. Could the blind lengths have carved the patterns, planted the wand, arranged the room to be discovered just so, waiting for some unsuspecting wretches to trigger the ritual?

And to what end?

"Just to take advantage of the fact that a storm somehow opened a random portal that some bug just happened to accidentally poke its way through?" Legrasse watched a swirl of flame detach from the others, then whiff out of existence. As the old shack disappeared into the night sky, atom by atom, the inspector told himself;

Seems like an awful lot of coincidence to me.

At that point though, Legrasse did not care if he were right or not. Better sore ribs and a swollen ear than some foul horror flopping about loose. One poor dead bastard was enough.

But, maybe Claro was not the only one that had gotten too near the edge. The inspector wondered if, perhaps, he too might not have seen more than he could bear at this point. Maybe he was growing overly paranoid over the unspeakables he had encountered. Perhaps he was weakening, assigning them too much credit, too much ability.

Really now, old man, the voice in the back of his mind that delighted in laughing at him snickered, exactly how can one ascribe such beings with too much ability?

He might've been wrong, he snorted, but that didn't mean it wasn't possible.

Muttering a curse in Hector Claro's honor, Legrasse studied the cane in his hands one last time. He had memorized much of what had been carved in the simple piece of wood. But he wondered, with what he was contemplating, perhaps he should keep the cane for a while.

It might come in handy, he thought.

Then again, another part of his mind whispered, reminding him about the old notion of Greeks bearing gifts, the cane had been left purposely for them to find.

"Galvez," the inspector asked of a sudden, "what was it Gracián said, about right-minded men, and gifts?"

"'To a right-minded man,'" quoted the Spaniard, "'nothing costs more dear that what is given him.'"

Tight-lipped, Legrasse nodded at the wisdom in the statement and threw the cane as hard as he could into the blazing cremation before him. Without waiting to see what else might happen, he then turned and walked back toward the police wagon parked well back from the swamp and the burning house. Like the snorting horses waiting there, he had grown tired of the smell of the swamp.

He wondered if New York City would smell any better when he arrived there this time.

Chapter 8

"NO, NO—I, I DON'T BELIEVE IT," ELLEN PATRICK SCREAMED, HER VOICE out of control, practically ranting. "I don't... I can't..."

Her words trailed off into a kind of humming silence, then Ellen screamed again, unable to hold back her emotions any longer. Only minutes earlier she had simply been gazing across a field of the mangled dead, cursing the fact she had been cheated of the chance to exact her vengeance upon them. Now she was covered with the blood of one man and in some ways responsible for the certain death of another.

Her normally unflappable confidence rattled by the horrendous, yet utterly fantastic display she had just witnessed, the beautiful young woman sat staring, unable to move. Frozen for the moment, overwhelmed by the insanity of it all, she watched helplessly as the half-dozen writhing lengths which had just slain the men in question groped about aimlessly.

"Oh God, oh heavens..."

And then, as she spoke, her mind began to focus as she saw the tentacles responding to her words, as if they had somehow heard the small handful of syllables and had now turned their attention toward finding her!

"No-o-oooo," she muttered, terror throwing her voice several octaves higher. "No, no—s-s-stay b-back."

Her hands shaking, lips trembling, a desperate tiny scrap of her instinct for self-preservation slapped at the blind fear smothering her, screaming within her brain;

Helpless!? Is that what you're feeling? Is that who we are— someone that feels helpless!?

With a supreme effort, the shivering girl who had turned the most deadly gangs and mobsters of San Francisco into frightened hysterics forced herself to take a backward step. It was a small thing, a movement of only inches, but as the terrified young woman forced her stockinged foot through the mud, the minute voice from the back of her mind encouraged;

That's it. Keep moving. Keep moving—go, girl—go. Go. GO! For God's sake—GO!

And suddenly, Ellen Patrick somehow found herself sprinting across the mudfield at her top speed. The record-breaking college athlete within her grabbed hold of her heart and soul and threw her toward the broken edge of the road from where she had started. Behind her, she could hear the flopping, slashing sound of the tentacles, stretching themselves insanely onward as they swept the open field, twisting and spinning as they hunted for her desperately.

Reaching the edge of the roadway once more, Ellen threw herself with near-hysteric abandon up onto the still-solid half of the street. As she wobbled on the edge, catching her balance, she suddenly noticed she was holding a flashlight. It had to be one of the police officers' light, she thought. Somehow she must have caught it when one of them dropped theirs, or picked it up unconsciously.

"How," she whispered, feeling the lush, soft warmth of insanity calling. "How did I get this?"

What does it matter, howled the back of her mind. You somehow end up with this thing in your hands and you don't even know how? Who cares how you got it? Goddamnit, Ellen, pull yourself together. For God's sake, start acting like who you really are or you're going to end up dead in that damn mudfield yourself!

And then, she heard the horrid slapping noise of the terrible lengths coming once more from behind her. Whirling around, her hand automatically extended the flashlight within it. As the beam wandered jaggedly across the landscape, a part of Ellen Patrick's mind cursed her shaking hand. The rest, however, was remembering what had just happened to her. Endlessly, it replayed the fearful monstrousness of it in her mind.

Her ears heard the breeze around her, her skin could feel it. But, what her ears strained to hear was the sounds of police officers dying—the sounds of men screaming, and her screaming right behind them. Her skin felt the air as it was then, recalled the feel of flying blood as it splashed across her face, her shoulders —fingers, breasts, knees, thighs—dripping, sticking, still sticking—sticky...

Wipe it off, get it off me, it's so horrible

Her taste buds, reminding her of the copper taste of a man's blood in her mouth, her nose remembering the smell of it in all its disgusting horror, the smell of the older patrolman's fear—the smell of her own.

So horrible...

All of it, all the sensations replayed in her mind, accenting the visual memory of every bit of it. She saw and felt and heard it all again. The feel of the mud against her feet—soaking through her stockings, clinging to them—the feeling of defeat as she was pulled toward it, her shoes torn from her feet, all her senses combining into that elusive sixth sense which whispered unto her that she was facing something from beyond the ken of mankind, that she was up against that which she could not comprehend, that she was about to lose—

About to die...

"No!"

Ellen Patrick used her free hand to grab the wrist of her other hand. Steadying the flashlight beam, she snarled aloud in a voice even her beloved father would never have recognized;

"No—goddamnit! No!"

With a supreme effort of will, Ellen Patrick forced the debilitating memories away from the front of her mind. She could not get shed of them entirely. Indeed, she did not wish to do so. There was no doubt within either the beautiful blonde's brain or her soul that she could ever afford to do so. There would be no forgetting any of it ever, but she was done torturing herself with it—done leaving herself open to destruction. Her hands and eyes working together, using the flashlight beam to spot the various squirming lengths coming forth from out of the ground, her mind tackled what she had witnessed as it would any other problem she placed before it.

It's not anything I've ever seen before, she noted. Not anything I've read about, or been told about. Not even in myth, or fairy tales.

She felt certain that the lengths were not aware of the flashlight beam as it pinpointed their advancement for her. She did not know what to make of the fact that the things did not retreat, or even recognize the light, since they did not come out until the sun went down for the evening.

This is something new. Something unprecedented—

Ellen Patrick knew she was right. Even though she had spend but the briefest time near the horrid lengths, what the sight of them did to her mind, the unnerving manner in which just seeing the horrible manifestation had completely overridden her confidence and faith, her ability to cope, her rational outlook, she would never forget. The handful of seconds were without a doubt the single most terrifying experience of her life.

When Ellen Patrick had learned of her father's death, still she had gotten through that terrible moment for the knowledge did not so completely step outside her world view as to incapacitate her. Part of her knew people died, that her own father had to die sometime, that as DA his life had often been threatened... people died, she knew that.

But tentacles with seemingly no limit in length rising from the ground, pulling people under, stealing corpses, vines or roots or whatever they were, possessing great strength, being able to attack and murder, the way the hideous things made her feel, she knew this was not merely something out of the ordinary. She knew these terrors could only be—

Something from beyond.

She watched the lunatic sight of the silent coils for a few minutes longer, sliding over and across the landscape, searching for her.

Or are they?

Were the slithering tentacles actually searching for her— for Ellen Patrick, for a woman even, for a threat, or merely looking for anything they might snag and drag back to... and then, her analytical mind asked;

Yes, that's the question... all this time, and I haven't even wondered yet. For God's sake, what are those things? Where do they lead? Are they alive, are they part of a machine? Are they animals? Maybe just one animal? Or then, perhaps they're merely a part of one animal, like a cat's whiskers.

As she realized the grasping lengths had finally gone into full retreat, she told herself;

"As if I were inconsequential, not worth their notice."

Well, the snide part of her mind whispered to her, weren't you?

Inside Ellen, the part of her that was the Domino Lady curled her fingers until they became fists. Knowing there was nothing more to be done on the unstable hillside that evening, the young woman turned and began to make her way through the near complete darkness back to her car. Walking a touch slowly, because of both the darkness and the loss of her shoes, Ellen worked on her plan of action.

Like most people, she was not a woman who enjoyed looking foolish. Even though no one had been there to witness it, she had fallen apart, just another hysteric, when the universe had finally revealed its ultimate insanity. She had just seen the unseeable, and her only reaction had been blind, gibbering panic. Yes, she told herself, it was unexpected, no amount of training prepares anyone for such a thing. More over, her fearful episode had only lasted a handful of seconds.

Still, the fact that she had panicked at all, let alone so utterly, filled her with a deep, unshakable shame. It also filled her with a burning resolve, however, and even as she made her way to her car she began piecing together what exactly she should be doing next. True, there was little to be gained by opposing the thing in the mud. It helped not her crusade to destroy the San Francisco mob.

But, the back of her mind whispered, what if this thing is bigger than any of us knows? What then?

Well, she told herself, maybe it'll be good to let the crusade go for a minute. Fighting devils from Hell, or whatever's set up camp out there, might be a refreshing change.

Besides, she thought while a wicked grin spread across her face, if nothing else, this gives me an excuse to make a trip to New York.

As Ellen Patrick turned the ignition key in her car, across the continent a young man only several years older than her, but one whose eyes held the knowledge of the pharaohs, and the age of the Himalayas, closed in relief.

His mental message had been received.

All the pieces were falling into place.

Chapter 9

"CALLING INSPECTOR JOHN RAYMOND LEGRASSE," CAME THE VOICE once more, "this is a transportation pick-up for Inspector John Raymond Legrasse..."

For a moment, Legrasse felt a twinge of suspicion. But, he wondered, was it justified? After the occurrence at Hector Claro's sad residence, he had told no one of his plans to travel to New York City. The purchasing of his train ticket had been accomplished on board so as to avoid anyone knowing that he was even leaving town until the moment he actually left. There had been no tangible reasons for him to take such precautions, but trifling about in the mystical world always worried the inspector, and he found comfort in the knowledge that there were as few eyes watching his movements as possible.

"Calling John Raymond Legrasse, Inspector John Raymond Legrasse... this is a transportation pick-up for Inspector John Raymond Legrasse..."

Then the notion struck him that if the party he had come to confer with was already aware of the menace which had struck New Orleans, perhaps he had somehow 'felt' Legrasse approaching the city. The inspector realized it was possible for these occult types to know all manner of things before hand. And, they did know each other—had a connection, as it were. For any one of these supernatural fellows, such would not be out of place.

Still, he wondered, why would his New York contact send a man to collect him whom he did not know?

"Inspector John Raymond Legrasse... this is a transportation pick-up for Inspector John Raymond Legrasse..."

From his position in the middle of the rapidly-moving crowd still disembarking from the various noon arrival trains there in Manhattan's opulent Grand Central Station, Legrasse gave the man calling out his name a second careful once over. He was a tall character, but not someone one would think of as immediately threatening. Instead, he seemed somewhat stodgy, almost what one could describe as a stereotypical British butler. The man's manner of dress was very proper ... a full suit with vest, gloves and hat despite the sweltering humid afternoon heat of a New York City summer.

"Legrasse... this is a transportation pick-up for Inspector John Raymond Legrasse..."

Indeed, the inspector had to admit, if the man droning his name over and over had been sent to do Legrasse some sort of harm, he was the absolute perfect choice for the job, for never did a man strike the inspector more as just an amiable chap, one whose idea of high excitement was most likely a night at the cinema, or perhaps an extended journey to the library.

"Transportation pick-up for..."

"Here, good fellow, I'm John Legrasse."

"Ahhh, very good, sir," said the butler type without the slightest bit of surprise or concern. As if he had greeted the detective at the station a hundred other times, he merely asked, "Do you have any other bags we need to recover?"

After the inspector assured the fellow that the one bag which he had in hand was all he had brought with him to the city, and that he preferred to carry it himself, the stodgy character replied;

"That's fine, sir. My name is Sterling, and I will transport you to your destination. This way, sir."

The pair made their way out of the somewhat confusing platform area and into the magnificence which was the central hall of Grand Central Station. Despite the fact he had been in the cavernous

Arrivals/Departures/Ticket Purchasing center more than once in his life, still did Legrasse look around himself once again at the incredible structure like any other tourist might. The vaulted cathedral dome of the building, the dozens of stairways leading off to different levels, the banking concerns, subterranean restaurants, shoe shine shops, bakeries, as well as the constantly moving mass of humanity all about him, the whole of it combined to spark a sensation within him he had trouble putting into words.

The truth was that the southerner greatly enjoyed his visits to New York City; for all its many faults he still found the place, especially the central island of Manhattan, fantastically alive, filled with an energy on a daily basis which his home of New Orleans seemed to need a year to build up to, at which point it released it all into its annual Mardi Gras, an event he found at its best childishly distasteful.

As the pair made their way through the city streets in the well-appointed roadster the man Sterling had somehow been able to park directly outside the nearest exit, Legrasse sank back in its extremely comfortable stretched leather seat. Setting his hat on the cushion next to him, he cradled his hands behind his head and then simply enjoyed watching the handsome art deco buildings roll by one after another. Their splendor always awed the inspector, and he greatly enjoyed rediscovering their beauty all over again.

Within a few minutes, however, Legrasse found something nagging at him, a wrongness the back of his mind could not pinpoint, but of which it could not let go, either. It was true he did not know his way around Manhattan Island to any great extent, but on the other hand, he knew where the sun should be at different parts of the day, and if it were in the West where it certainly belonged at that time, then he was being taken uptown, and not downtown where he had been expecting to go.

Quietly, Legrasse's hand gently released the snaps on his valise. Opening the lid just as softly, the inspector wrapped his fingers around the handle of the heavy automatic inside, as he asked casually;

"So Sterling, where is it we're headed, by the by?"

"Mr. Ravenwood's penthouse in the Sussex Towers, sir. It really is the most fashionable penthouse in the city. You should find it most comfortable."

"Yes, ummmm, that very well could be, sir, but why exactly would I want to go there?"

"Why, to confer with master Ravenwood about this bizarre supernatural business that's approaching."

Legrasse blinked. He had certainly come to New York City for no reason other than to confer about things from beyond the ken of mortal man. But, he had not come to do it with anyone named Ravenwood. Indeed, he had never before met anyone with the name Ravenwood.

No, he had come to meet with someone of a far different name, a master sorcerer with whom he had worked with previously to great success. He had no idea who this Ravenwood character might be, had never heard mention of his name, and certainly did not mean to change horses in mid-stream. Sensing his agitation, however, Sterling offered;

"I believe the master did say something about you coming to see someone downtown, in… the China Alley area, was it, sir? They who reside there are apparently away from their residence at the moment. Mr. Ravenwood will be working with you on this little venture—if that suits your purposes, sir."

Legrasse scratched his head with his free hand. As odd as the situation was, nothing actually seemed out of place to him. Sterling appeared a decent enough sort, and he had to admit that the more he dealt with those who emersed themselves in the worlds of the occult and the beyond, the more he did not understand their ways in the slightest. As his mind clung to its last remaining shreds of distrust, the driver, slowing for a red traffic signal, added in a quiet voice;

"I have been instructed to take you to China Alley if you desire, so you might check for yourself. I believe the young master does wish you ready to face what is coming with a certain confidence." Shifting the roadster back into gear with the changing of the light, the chauffer said;

"Considering the seeming magnitude of whatever it is that's coming, sir, I don't mind suggesting that shedding yourself of all doubts might not be a bad idea." Feeling enough at ease to play the cards Fate had just dealt him, Legrasse released his grip on his automatic, saying;

"So, your Mr. Ravenwood's penthouse, in this Sussex Towers,

it's really something, eh? Well, who am I to miss lunch in the most fashionable penthouse in the city. Oh, unless I'm overstepping myself…"

"Oh, no sir," answered Sterling. "Luncheon will be served shortly after we arrive. I oversaw the menu myself."

"Well then," said Legrasse in return, "leave us off to the Sussex Towers."

And so saying, the inspector sat back in his seat once more, returning to simply watching the city speed by his window. A cautious man by nature, however, he did not refasten the snaps on his valise.

Chapter 10

"AHHH, THE FAMOUS INSPECTOR LEGRASSE, DO COME IN, SIR. DO COME in. This is assuredly quite an honor. Please, come this way, the others are already here."

The speaker was a strikingly handsome young man—one graced with unusually gray eyes and wavy brown hair which he kept arranged in one of the more modest styles of the day. Legrasse noted that although the fellow was of but average height, he nonetheless possessed a deceptively superb physique. The inspector was quite certain the younger man would have no trouble handling himself in the meanest of backroom brawls—even one where the odds were slightly off-kilter.

And if he can't, thought the inspector, there's always that somewhat conspicuous bulge under his left arm.

The man stood before him sporting an ensemble Legrasse could only describe as dapper. He was certainly well dressed, but in the way one of the radio press might label as "the debonair playboy type." But, while his wardrobe was indeed both fancy and of high quality, he did not seems to be out to give anyone the impression he was a banker. He also carried a walking stick, one the inspector was certain was an affectation—until he noted the intricate carvings which encircled it from top to bottom. Its engravings were in no way reminiscent of the stick he had consigned to the pyre made of Hector Claro's home, but it did give him reason enough to say;

"Thank you; nice stick you have there. Oriental?"

"Yes—keen eye you have. Carved for me by some monks in Tibet. How was your journey up from New Orleans?"

"It was your average no-frills train ride," answered Legrasse curtly, "and while we're on the subject, it was one of which none were supposed to be aware. So, Mr. Ravenwood, is it, would you like to tell me now how you knew I was coming to this city, and why you had me shanghaied? Or do we start hurling lead at one another right now?"

"Oh, do let's discuss your rerouting over lunch, shall we? We can always square off with pistols in between the nuts and sherry."

Legrasse smiled. If this Ravenwood character was working on some side differing from that of the angels, he was certainly an expert at making it seem otherwise. Poised, charming, and friendly in a refreshingly honest way he had never expected to find in the bowels of New York City, the inspector found himself taking to the young man as he had none other in quite some time.

Of course, the back of his mind whispered, don't be too quick to balance those scales. After all, casting influence over mortal minds... that's one of the first things these magicians learn, isn't it?

Grinding his teeth over the levels of double and triple dealings one had to expect when faced with the supernatural, Legrasse shifted gears, going back to his original idea of trying to uncover as much information as he could. That thought in mind, he answered Ravenwood, saying;

"Well, then, lead the way, sir. Oh, and by the by, who are these 'others' you assure me are already here?" There was a flash of mystery in his host's blue eyes as Ravenwood answered the inspector, telling him;

"They're right in here. So, as you say, why don't we join them? To be perfectly honest, I've held off telling them much of anything, hoping we could get all our introductions over with at once. Right through here."

As Ravenwood threw open the doors to his library, the inspector was greeted by the sight of two amazingly robust individuals. The first to capture his attention was a stunning blonde, a woman nearly as tall as Legrasse, himself. Her hair was cut to below shoulder-length. It hung in bunches, thick but silken, and all of it obeyed each small turn of its owner's head like a well-trained animal. The woman had chosen a chic blue dress just the right shade for her skin, a barely-sleeved affair that dared reveal not only her elbows but upper arms as well. It also let the world know a great deal about the length and shape of her legs, two things of which even an older gentleman like the inspector found himself taking note.

The other waiting for them in the library was another younger man, this one in burstingly excellent physical condition. Ravenwood had struck Legrasse as fit, but this fellow seemed ready for the Olympics. At least, he would if he were not blind. Then again, despite his dark glasses and cane, the handicap they implied was something the inspector thought might possibly be false.

If that man's actually blind, thought Legrasse, *then I'm a registered Republican.*

The younger man certainly held himself as if he could not see, but despite his glasses and cane, he still did not seem very handicapped to Legrasse. His look was too well-groomed, his creases too pressed, his manner too polished for a blind man—at least, those were the inspector's feelings about it. But, on the other hand, considering what he himself had survived in his time, he probably did not look much like a battler of demons and monsters from beyond to any of them.

One step at a time, old dog, Legrasse told himself. *Let's see what stories are being passed out before we decide what we believe and what we don't.*

As the pair entered, Ravenwood hurried his three guests together into the center of the room, and then began a round of introductions. He introduced the group one to another by their given names only, offering no professions or titles, and then turned to Ellen to whom he said;

"Since I try to maintain my standing as a gentleman at all times, the old maxim, 'ladies first' brings me back to you. Would you like to do the honors, or shall I?"

"What do you mean," she asked back, fairly certain she knew exactly what he meant.

"Secrets are always hard to let go of," he told her. "I understand. But if we are all to work together, then we are all going to have to know something of each other's business. I'll give you an example."

So saying, the clean cut young man cleared his throat and then turn so that he could face all those who had been assembled. So doing, he revealed;

"The three of you know me simply as Ravenwood. Miss Patrick here came to New York to see me because of my reputation as an author of books on Eastern Mysticism. I also travel the lecture circuit speaking on the world of the supernatural, especially as it exists in the Orient, which I believe is how she came to know of me in the first place.

"But," he said with more than a bit of drama, "that is not all there is to my story. You see, I've only been in this country since I was twenty-five. But, in the few years I've been here, the New York City press has been kind enough to dub me the 'Stepson of Mystery.' I'm not quite certain what that appellation means, actually, but there's little doubt it is meant to refer to the fact that I am a psychic, or more precisely, a clairvoyant, and it's also been good for business on several levels, so I've allowed it to stay around."

"Several levels..." asked the man in the dark glasses.

"Yes, to those who understand little or nothing of the mystic arts, it makes me sound all-knowing. To those who understand much, it makes me sound like some harmless fakir. Having both attitudes out there is very helpful to me considering my actual goals."

The young man's green eyes flashed as he indicated with several suggestive movements of his hands that perhaps they should all take seats. Ellen guided the man in the dark glasses to one, and while all settled themselves in the various overstuffed chairs there in the well-appointed drawing room, Ravenwood continued, telling them;

"To be blunt, I often get impressions of coming events—I know things long before they actually happen. I'll explain as best I can. You see, my father was American, my mother British. Before I came here, I lived the whole of my life in India. My parents were taken from me when I was still quite young during a time of great plague."

"How did you manage on your own," asked Ellen, female

curiosity and maternal concern forcing her to interrupt. Ravenwood stopped for a moment, his gray eyes taking on a faraway look. Blinking finally, he said;

"It's a scene I still see clearly in my head after all these years—we were in the mountainous crags of Brumah, near the Border of forbidden Tibet, in my father's hunting camp. Everyone was on alert because prowling tigers were near. There was a sound on the trail, guns were brought to the ready, and then all was fascinated bewilderment. We were bewildered because there was no settlement within miles of our location, yet out of the brush came this hoary being, walking with slow majesty, empty-handed—a man who seemed old as the mountains rearing behind him, white-bearded, with the all-understanding of a great sage."

"That's a lot for a youngster to notice," commented the man in the dark glasses. "Might some of these details be later life embellishment?"

"Not really. For this is the moment that changed my life forever. As all stared at the wizened figure, there was a tawny flash at the trail's side—a tiger leaping for the snowy-bearded man. While others froze, my father fired with lightning swiftness. The extended claws of the tiger fell within an inch of the venerable pilgrim—claws which would have torn him to shreds fell limp. In all the excitement, however, the ancient one had not moved, save for a lifting of his luminous eyes. In his native tongue he said, 'Always the Nameless One will guard you and your flesh.' He then vanished from the trail as mysteriously as he had appeared…"

Sterling reappeared in the background and stood off to the side. Like any good servant, he knew when to make an announcement, and when to wait. To those gathered the butler appeared quite aware his master had taken note of his arrival, which seemed more than good enough for him. In the meantime, the young occultist continued, telling the others;

"After the death of my parents, the mysterious sage appeared again, this time to fulfill his promise. He raised me from that day forward, and schooled me in all the mystic arts."

"Sounds straight out of a pulp novel, I dare say," said Legrasse almost as if he had only meant to think the comment rather than voice it aloud. Without embarrassment, though, he added, "Still, I supposed I'd be one to talk, eh?"

"I don't know about the rest of you," the gentleman in the dark glasses threw out, "but I've found that the truth is most often far more unbelievable than that which the penny-a-word hacks can dish up."

"Yes, I think we could all agree to that one," answered Ravenwood, nodding his head. "I know I certainly can. I will tell you now, that when alone, the Nameless One will speak to me telepathically. He has guided me through the calling upon of forces quite inconceivable to the knowledge of the rest of humanity. I will admit that I understands very little of my actual abilities even now, which is why, I believe, the Nameless One still helps me to this day when I need to call upon these strange forces."

"So, might I guess that that's where the telepathy comes in," asked Legrasse, who had some small understanding of the faculty himself. "He advises you, as it were, through the ether all the way from India?"

"No, sir," answered Ravenwood, almost sheepishly. "The Nameless One lives here, in this penthouse with Sterling and myself. If we're lucky, he may grace us with one of his rare appearances outside his quarters."

"Might I suggest, sir," said Sterling, knowing how to pick his moments, "that we announce the serving of our luncheon. Perhaps that might bring him to us."

"Whether it does or not," said Ellen, rising from her chair immediately, "the smell coming from the kitchen's been driving me wild. Why don't you point us toward the food, Sterling, and earn my undying gratitude?"

"Master Ravenwood...?"

"Far be it from me," answered the young occultist with a trace of humor in his voice, "to interfere with your gathering of undying gratitude. At your age I don't suppose you get all that many chances any more."

"In your employ, no sir," responded the butler with a less than amused tone. "But the master is too kind to allow me to gather what rosebuds that I may." The butler's cheeky answer surprised all of those assembled, getting grins from both Legrasse and Ravenwood. Giving no sign he had noticed, the older man simply turned on his heel, suggesting;

"If you would follow me, everyone."

As Legrasse, and Ellen, guiding the gentleman in the black glasses fell in line behind the butler, Ravenwood lingered for a moment, looking to a door off to the side. It was one thinner than the others in the penthouse, and the wood of it had not been cut from any tree that ever knew Earthly soil. The young occultist's green eyes stared at the aperture for a long moment, hoping to see even the slightest bit of movement from that direction.

Yes, he knew his guests were a group used to the most fantastic things the modern world could throw against them. But, he was about to attempt to enlist their aide in a battle beyond the puny devices and threats of the modern world. He was about to ask them to most likely throw their lives away in a struggle against a deep and abiding evil, a long forgotten menace so overwhelmingly powerful that in ancient times, the sight of it alone had often been sufficient to drive men mad.

The tall, thin door did not move, however. Using all the visions he had at his command, Ravenwood could see that no help would come to him via that particular passageway on that afternoon. Musing absently, he closed his eyes for a moment, thinking;

Why did you have to die, Father? Mother? Why did this cup have to be set at my place at the table?

Of course, as whenever any ask such a question, Ravenwood received no answer. Taking that as answer enough, though, the young man struggled to arrange his face in a manner that would not frighten his guests as he turned and headed off to join them in the dining room.

After all, he thought, what he had to tell them would do that all on its own.

Chapter 11

"OHHHHHH, THIS IS JUST SIMPLY TOO MARVELOUS FOR WORDS."

Ellen had just tried one of the lobster tail thirds wrapped in bacon and the drippingly warm taste of it had rolled her eyes backward up into her head. She was not the only one to voice their appreciation, arguing over what it was their taste buds detected besides butter, garlic and onion. On the other hand, the food was not the only source of conversation at the table.

"So, you dabble in my line of work as well, eh?"

"To a small degree, inspector," Ravenwood said modestly. "The truth is, among the 'smart set,' I'm known around town as something of an amateur detective with a flair for occult cases. You know, it's funny you mentioned earlier how much our lives can seem like they're out of pulp novels. I realize it makes my life sound more like parody than anything else, but I've got a nitwit of a policeman, this Inspector Stagg... the man's thinks of me as some meddling do-gooder, and that my occult abilities are all a sham."

"Sounds familiar," said the man in the black glasses noncommittally.

"Sorry to hear that, for your sake, I mean," answered Ravenwood sympathetically. "Stagg, for a while I tolerated him, found him amusing, I suppose. But now, really he's becoming something of a pest."

"And, you're thinking if he keeps it up, he's going to get either you or himself killed... yes?"

"The thought had crossed my mind," admitted Ravenwood. Raising his index finger, he waggled it intently, adding, "Of course, there's always a third possibility..."

"What—that he'll get you both killed?"

The gentleman in the dark glasses and Ellen laughed as both of them filled in the exact same punch line. Ravenwood stared at them for a moment, wondering if the pair might be serendipitously aligned, or if perhaps the response was actually that obvious.

"You know," interjected Legrasse in a long, pulled-out drawl, sitting off to the side, observing, "back outside we were all supposed to give one to the other our histories. Shining the light on that part of our personal tale of which most others aren't aware. I think you did an admirable job of revealing yourself, Mr. Ravenwood. But so far, the three of us," he indicated himself, Ellen and the man in the dark glasses with his fork, "don't know a thing about each other." Cutting into the slice of poached salmon on his plate as if he cared about it, he watched the others carefully as he added;

"Shouldn't we continue that?"

"Sounds good to me," said Ellen. "So who goes next? Ladies first? Age before beauty?"

"My name's Tony Quinn," said the man in the dark glasses that everyone else had been wondering about. "Unlike you two," he used his fork to indicate Ellen and Legrasse, "I didn't have to come that far. I live here in New York City. And, as you might now be guessing, I'm not blind."

"Pointing us out with your crawfish spear did make one wonder, I must admit," answered the one-time inspector of police, not bothering to add in any of his earlier suspicions. "But not being blind, while a sizeable admission, doesn't explain your interest here. Pardon my bluntness—a bad habit of mine, I'm told, but tell me, what brings you here today?"

"It's my job to protect this city."

"You elected to that position," asked Ellen with a smile, "or is it salaried?"

"Self-employed, so to speak," he answered with a bit of a smile. "I must admit it's quite the sinecure. During the day I work toward that end as myself, 'blind' Tony Quinn. I used to be the District Attorney here in Manhattan. Now I work the other side of the row, trying to make certain innocent people don't get railroaded." Taking a spoonful of rice from under the lobster-bacon rolls, thick with its buttery sauce still both warm and salty, Ellen pulled the spoon clean with her lips, then removed it from her mouth slowly, asking suggestively;

"And during the night...?"

Quinn had been quite the playboy earlier in his life. Of course, that was before he had met a platinum blonde named Carol Baldwin who had turned that earlier life around, intertwining it with her own. She was his fiancé now, and he would never dream of looking at any other woman in anything like a serious manner. Still, the skills he gained during his years of dealing with the opposite sex, as removed as they might have become, had not deserted him completely. Aiming a playful glance in Ellen's direction, he answered;

"When I'm not entertaining my fiancé, I hunt for criminals throughout our wide and ranging streets in the guise of a crimefighter I dubbed the Black Bat. I try to find those undeserving of any mercy—the truly despicable. Sometimes I come across one or two who are only 'spicable.' I don't go quite so hard on them."

"Ohhh, why not?" asked Legrasse, completely missing the tone of Ellen and Quinn's banter. Taken somewhat aback by the question, the young lawyer actually sputtered for a moment, then answered;

"All right, to be serious for the moment..."

"Ohhhh, fudge. And just when things were going so well," interrupted Ellen playfully.

"Something tells me, as much fun as this is, my love, we don't have the time for it." With a rakish tilt of his head, Quinn leaned across the table slightly, then continued.

"Why don't I throw in the white towel and surrender to your charms here and now," asked the young lawyer. "If I freely admit you have femininity a'plenty, enough to drive the entire world of men completely bananas, can we go ahead and get back to what we came here for?"

Within her head, Ellen Patrick gave Tony Quinn a great number of points. She had heard of the Black Bat—everyone in the country had heard of the man who single-handedly had turned the tide in the war on crime in New York City. But, it was one thing to call oneself a hero, and another to be one. She could tell from the cut of Quinn's suit and the easy way he wore it that he was a member of higher society. Such men often spoke one language but believed another. Flirting with him, even for as short a time as she had, told her volumes about him.

He claimed to be engaged, and then acted like such words meant something to him. Also, when he had still wanted others in the room to believe he was blind, he had never stolen a glance at her. That might have been training, staying in character. But, after he had admitted he was not blind, he had not once stared at her, even after their flirting had begun, and she had purposely given him some provocative poses.

For most women, thinking of themselves as so completely irresistible would be bordering on the vulgar, but such was not the case with Ellen. She had come to terms years earlier with the fact that she had something—a quality, for lack of a better word—that made her stand out. In a line up of fifty other girls, all equally radiant, all with the same measurements, standing exactly as tall, et cetera, she would be noticed over all of the rest—it was simply fact. Indeed, any woman in her position who did not come to recognize this fact would have been preyed upon by men at large unmercifully.

Luckily, when she did begin to blossom, and her grandmother and aunt had swept in to her feminine rescue, her father had understood. Thinking back on her childhood, Ellen had even decided years after that her father had subconsciously seen this attraction of hers coming a long way off, and had thus made a son of her to help protect her until she was old enough to handle things on her own.

A female professor once told her that her justification of her father's motives might be justified, but it was equally possible he was just another "typically greedy male" who wanted her all for herself. The benefit, her professor said, was that while kept a tomboy, she had learned how to talk to men on their own level, to not fear to compete with them. Ellen was willing to give the woman's ideas some credit. On the other hand, her continual insistence that the two of them get to know each other better outside of class made her think that perhaps it was not only the males in this world who were sexually greedy.

Still, the point was made. Tony Quinn was a right fellow by any of her standards. Blushing slightly as she turned her head in his direction, she said surrender was out of the question, and that she thought a truce much more advantageous. Her answer made everyone present smile, even Sterling.

As the luncheon continued, Quinn explained to the others what it was that drove him to protect New York, to fight crime, to risk his life when he could simply sit back and enjoy all the pleasures money can buy. Ellen did the same. The group nodded their heads quietly, feeling for her loss of her father, but proud to see someone with her gumption at the same table with them. It was one thing for Quinn to fight against evil as a way to thank Heaven and its Fates for returning his sight to him. That which happened to him was practically an act of God. After all, the world was filled with blind people, but not that many formerly-blind people.

Ellen, however, received very high approval from the group for she was in a particularly unique situation. Criminal organizations slaughtered the innocent every day. Good people were put to the sword by evil on an hourly basis. For her, a woman, one with no special abilities, to turn away from a life that could have been strife free, to shun the comfort of the truly pampered to instead match wits and brawn and luck with that possessed by the lowest elements the universe had to offer was something the men gathered had to look upon as exceptional.

They were, all of them, heroes. The fact that the idea made any of the trio of men at the table uneasy to the point of laughter merely made the label all the more appropriate. The fact that Ellen was cut from exactly the same cloth they were made her all the more extraordinary. After all, in their individual situations, it was amazing enough for a man to do as they did. But a woman—it was practically unheard of outside of ancient myths.

"But what about our fourth bridge partner here," said Quinn, referring to Legrasse. "We're all sputtering over ourselves as if we were important, and here we have a man so modest he says nothing at all. Come, tell it, sir. What brought you here?"

"Cornered at last, eh," said Legrasse, rubbing his lips with his napkin, "Very well, Mr. Quinn, I will explain my comparative silence as merely my great delight with our Mr. Sterling's wizardry in the kitchen. As to why I'm here with you, our host had me kidnapped, so to speak. I came to New York to speak with another, and yet here I am."

"And what did you come to talk about," asked Ellen.

"Well, miss, knowing how these things work to some degree, I'm willing to bet I came here to talk about the same thing you did—the possibility that if something isn't done and done soon, the world is going to end in flame and misery."

Chapter 12

"DESSERT, ANYONE?"

Sterling stood in the doorway from the kitchen to the dining room. Having not heard the inspector's last statement, he was unready for the shocked looks on half those at the table. He did not, of course, expect his employer to look as if caught unawares. Actually, the manservant was not certain such was possible, not as long as the Nameless One was with him even in spirit. With the personage no more than twenty feet away from his master, the idea was beyond comprehension to the butler. Still, knowing his place, he said;

"Realizing today might call for a particular type of planning, I thought slices of fresh pound cake, served with fruit, would best be in order. It's a very light cake, and served with but a dollop of frozen creme, there should be only enough sweetness to aid digestion, not stir the blood. Shall I set a self-serve—"

Ravenwood gave his man a signal the butler interpreted from long association. While the others were still staring at Legrasse, unable to put their minds to thoughts of further dining, Sterling began to clear their plates. Over the next few minutes, he would take away all traces of their luncheon feast and replace it with two trays of precisely cut cake slices, two pots of frosted creme and seven different containers of freshly chopped fruits in their own juices, and of course, coffee and tea for all. Those gathered did indulge themselves to some extent, but as one might expect, their attention was still fastened for the moment on the man from Louisiana.

The first thing that Legrasse did was to relate the entirety of his recent excitement in the swamps outside of New Orleans. He could readily tell from Quinn and Ellen's reactions that she was already aware of this menace while he was not. As he expected, when he finished telling the tale of what had lead him to New York City, the young woman now known to all gathered as the Domino Lady told hers. When she had finished, Legrasse commented, musing;

"Certainly sounds as if you and I saw much the same kind of monstrous phenomena. Different ends of it, of course. But then, your storm came long before you came across…" The inspector put his hand unconsciously to his chin, tugging at it, his words drifting off for several seconds until he suddenly snapped back, saying;

"Of course, well that's exactly it, isn't it?" As the others questioned his meaning, Legrasse explained;

"Some weeks ago the West Coast is pummeled by hurricanes. Ellen here goes out to this completely sealed off area and finds this overwhelmingly large infestation. My investigation, only days after the same kind of storm gives up the same type of infestation, but smaller. That occurs halfway across the country."

"And now, here in New York," snapped Quinn, "the rest of the way across the county, we just finished surviving the same kind of horrible storms—"

"The same kind of horrible, unseasonable storms," interjected Ravenwood.

"You think this thing… is what? Is here? Has stretched across the country, underground, underwater? What?"

"Calm yourself, Mr. Quinn," answered Legrasse. "If I knew anything further, I would have already placed it on the table. What happened to me in New Orleans was much in the vein of things that have happened to me in the past. I gave up police work so that I might study such phenomenon, to prepare for… for whatever it coming—"

"'What is coming,'" said Quinn. "That's why I'm here. During the storm the other night, I met a policeman—"

"Yes, Mark Thorner," interrupted Ravenwood. "Good man. Out of town right now assisting the mystic you came to New York to consult with, inspector. Elsewise I'd have him here—Old Knob's Gallows, I'd have them both here. But, it was the two of them actually that told me what was coming and asked me to fill in for them. When I said I would, Thorner sent you to me himself, Mr. Quinn." As the Black Bat nodded in agreement, Ravenwood turned to Legrasse, telling him;

"Inspector, they guessed you would be coming. Consulting the Nameless One gave me the train you were on, allowed me to intercept you, save us all some time. Sterling did the rest there, picking you up and all."

"And me," asked Ellen. "Is it more than a coincidence that I'm here as well?"

"I feel as if I should just hand out one of those oh, so convenient, little white lies everyone says are so harmless and tell you that coincidence is all there is, but..."

"What do you mean?"

"The Nameless One, when he pinpointed the inspector, he also mentioned that he had been gifted with a vision of your delemia while you were still in San Francisco. Seeing in your mind that you had heard of me, he dragged that memory to the front of your mind so you might head here and join us."

Ellen sat staring at Ravenwood, her eyes filling with a fearful apprehension. What she had seen, gone through, that had been terrible enough. But now, to discover that what she had thought was just a single, isolated incident could possibly have spread everywhere across the country, or maybe even the entire world, that the hideous unknown things that had slaughter two policemen before her eyes with such incredible ease could be everywhere—everywhere—that even her own mind was not safe from invasion—

"What in God's name are you talking about? Where are these things? What are they? When—"

"PLEASE."

All attention went to Ravenwood. He had spoken the single word sharply, but not loudly. Such had been necessary. Ellen, of course, being a woman, was far more in touch with the ether of the world than the others, more prepared to see the staggering implications of what they were discussing. Of course, this also meant she was the natural first one to be overwhelmed by such implications as well.

Legrasse, of course, like himself, had seen enough of the bizarre and the supernatural to maintain a level head, at least for the moment. But, Ravenwood could see that Quinn was only seconds behind Ellen in seizing upon the gravity of the situation. Unlike her, he had come across such mindless terrors as well in his time, but not to anywhere near the extent of the mystic, himself. Indeed, even the inspector had nowhere the understanding of the beyond Ravenwood possessed. All of this in mind, as the other three sets of eyes there at the table fastened upon him, the young occultist said;

"Allow me a moment to explain why evil is often so successful. Ellen, we three have all seen such things before. Mr. Quinn has seen and combated, as he told us, things beyond the ken of most human beings several times before today. His contacts have, it seems, been briefer and less intense than those of the inspector. As for me, my entire life for years now has been dedicated to such matters. And yet, I know that the time will come again when something so extraordinary, so far beyond my understandings, will manifest itself before me that I will fail to react in time."

"So, you're not saying I'm just some hysterical female," asked Ellen, not quite defensively. "I appreciate that because, I'll admit... I certainly feel like one."

"I think what he's saying," interrupted Quinn, "is that you are a hysterical female, but that some times it's okay to get a little hysterical."

"Actually, I believe he's means a bit more," added Legrasse. Turning to stare at their host, the inspector delivered him a look that demanded a comment. Ravenwood nodded slightly, and then gave him one.

"A bit more, yes," said their host in his even but forceful tone. "What I'm trying to say is that evil's main advantage in such matters is that often, by the time we finally understand what it is we're facing, we've run out of time. Say it's some sort of were-beast. If you've never seen someone transform into something else, by the time they're done changing, they can slaughter you and all the rest of the witnesses present, not because said witnesses are hysterical, but mainly because the poor unfortunates simply could not adjust to what they were seeing in time to react."

"Like the two policemen who had to die so I could live," Ellen added quietly.

"Not so you could merely live," Legrasse told her in a comforting tone. "So you could tell others what happened to them. So you could honor their heroism, so you could warn the world, help it survive, and to fight back. Take it from me, a great deal of a policeman's job is coming in once something has happened and then doing whatever can be done after the fact. It's no picnic, and it bruises the ego, but it comes with the job."

"But what about us," asked Quinn. "We're not the police. We're just a handful of people. Now don't get me wrong, I'm not one to back off from a fight, but I know when it's time to turn mother's picture to the wall and call in the marines."

"Not certain that's a good idea," answered Legrasse. "You've had to deal with the police quite often, haven't you, Mr. Quinn? Like Miss Patrick's officers, could they handle these things? Soldiers are certainly taught more than policemen to be prepared for combat, to be on the attack, but not to attack things such as we're discussing. Marines, I'm sadly afraid, would be just as helpless as the next man, without proper instruction, that is."

"But still," argued the man known as the Black Bat, "Maybe that's what we should be doing—telling the government and then perhaps offering that training? I mean, no offense, but you people are talking monsters. Horrors from... from... from where, for Christ sake? We're talking demons—things from Hell." Quinn took a deep sip from his coffee cup, then added;

"I don't want to sound like a coward, but then I don't want to end up a suicide, either. We're just four people, Ravenwood. Isn't what you're talking about a tad too big for us?"

"There's actually no way to know, yet," answered the young mystic. "We're going to have to do some investigating first to know the answer to that."

"What, where, when... that kind of stuff." Quinn's questions were meant to show eagerness, not fear or argument. Understanding, their host for the afternoon said;

"I arranged today to go as it did for all our benefits. None of us knew one another. We are, all of us, I believe very competent at what we do, our extra-curricular activities, as it were. Mr. Quinn, strong, proficient with multiple weapons, and, also in command of a small force of equally competent warriors, if my guess is correct."

"It is," answered the Black Bat with a nod. "But, let's also remember the liabilities—hard for me to explain daylight absences, and wanted by the police. If we all end up working together on this, any of you risk jail or even just plain being gunned down simply for being seen with me."

"You may have to risk those daylight disappearances just as we may have to dodge bullets along side of you," answered Ravenwood. "Inspector Legrasse may not have your youth, and thus not be able to match your physical prowess, but he has seen more than either of you, and is, from what I have read, a born tactician." When the inspector's left eyebrow went up in response to the younger man's words, Ravenwood explained;

"I knew you were coming, sir. I did my research. The same Lieutenant Thorner who sent Mr. Quinn my way also told me much of you, inspector. Those of us who live our lives in the worlds populated by magicians and monsters have our own libraries, our own magazines. Not that much has been written on your activities, sir, but you are well thought of in the circles."

"And me," asked Ellen. "What did you know of me?"

"Only that you were headed here to consult with me. Only that you were brave and strong and capable. I would not have sent for you to fight alongside me at this time, Miss Patrick, it's true—that was the Nameless One's doing. But, you have to understand, that is because I would not have sent for anyone. One does not ask the neighbors in when all the forces of a dark and evil Hell are about to come a'calling."

Sterling had begun clearing away the dessert settings and other paraphernalia minutes earlier. As he took away the last of the fruit pots, Ravenwood's voice went cold and quiet as he told the others;

"The Nameless One has known something terrible was approaching. Up until today I had little to go on. Now that we have spoken, much has fallen into place. I would still have to do some further research, but I believe now that we have all met and talked that I might be able to find out what we need to know by dinnertime tomorrow."

"What do you want us to do," asked Ellen.

"With the knowledge I have no right to request anything of any of you, desperation trumps good manners and I am forced to ask, could we meet again here tomorrow evening, at say seven o'clock? I could tell you all I've uncovered over dinner, and we could plan from there how we should proceed—would that be agreeable to everyone?"

Of course it was. No matter how cautious any of them might be feeling about joining forces with others, it was the coming horror over which they felt their trepidation that forced them to agree. Indeed, the heroes known as the Black Bat and the Domino Lady had already revealed their secret identities to total strangers— something even just the day before would have seemed inconceivable to them.

But, something more than inconceivable was coming—some thing beyond all human measure was approaching—was already in their world, already murdering innocent people across the country.

Of course they had to agree to stay, to return. To fight. Indeed, as they spoke of what was to come, it was the consensus of the entire quartet that if they could, they would like to tear into some-thing right then and there rather than waiting for even another moment.

And sadly, it was that noble restraint, that inspiringly brave and selfless attitude on each of their parts which would give evil its great opportunity to destroy them all.

Chapter 13

AFTER THE LUNCHEON MEETING FINALLY BROKE UP, THE ATTENDEES went their separate ways. Ellen, having numerous acquaintances throughout the city's social scene from her college days, and not having been in New York City for quite some time, decided to do some visiting.

"Looking up a number of the old sorority gang," she told the others, "getting a shopping spree going, it's all good cover for the society gal on the go."

The men all bid the young blonde a fond farewell, except for Quinn. Needing to get back to his own affairs, the lawyer offered her his escort to the building's lobby at least, and further if she would be willing to accept a ride from himself and his driver. When he assured her they could talk masked-avenger shop in front of his chauffer, she agreed heartily, wanting to ask him more than a few questions about himself, or more specifically, about the Black Bat.

Inspector Legrasse stayed behind to have a few more moments with their host. First off, the young magician had made an offer of cigars and a chaser from his quite well-stocked bar which the inspector found quite intriguing. And, since the only other people he knew in the city were absent from its boundaries, as a stranger to her doors he was well pleased to pass a few of the intervening hours where he was. As a fellow student of the mystic arts, however, he was quite extraordinarily pleased for the chance to meet further with someone who looked to know so much more about the beyond realms than he himself.

Indeed, snifters of brandy quickly lead the pair to Ravenwood's private library where the occultist and Legrasse spoke for so long into the evening that the inspector found himself quite embarrassed when Sterling entered after what seemed a quite brief interval and announced that dinner was to be served. Legrasse tried to beg off, feeling quite the fool, but Ravenwood would hear nothing of it.

"Ceremony be damned, old man," responded the younger gentleman. "Look, you know damn well that I'm as annoyed as you are that our discussion's about to be interrupted by something as ridiculous as protocol." The inspector hesitated, but Ravenwood pressed the issue. Standing before him, hands held apart imploringly, he said;

"But just think, if you stay for dinner, which I can assure you Sterling will have made to accommodate your presence, then we can keep right on working. In fact, you didn't checked in to a hotel in advance did you?" When the inspector admitted he had not, Ravenwood insisted;

"Good, then you'll stay here. I've got a lot more books in this place, the contents of which I don't know in the least. Frankly, I could use the assistance."

"He has a number of bottles stashed in the bar like that, too, sir," added Sterling with a wink. Legrasse smiled, both at the butler's humor, and also at the warmth with which both servant and master had shown toward him. As he made to answer, Ravenwood continued, saying;

"Anyway, you know as well as I do, inspector, that there has be be something behind these infestations, and if we can find out what it is, then we can find something that we can use against it... anyway, Sterling—"

"Yes, master?"

"Rearrange the dining table, the inspector at one end, me at the other. Set things up so we'll have plenty of work room. And then prepare one of the extra bed rooms for our guest here. Come, John, let's fill our arms and drag some of this musty library out into the fresh air." As the two busied themselves, Legrasse said quietly;

"You know, this is awfully decent of you. Ever since I retired...," The inspector went silent for a moment, his mind obviously elsewhere. The pause lasted only a few seconds, after which, looking a bit flustered, the policeman continued, saying;

"Let me rephrase that, before I was retired by a bunch of politicians..."

"Gravy train engineers not wanting the passengers learning there's something wrong with the bridge ahead," ventured Ravenwood in a questioning tone.

"What can I say? It was far too early for me to be leaving the force—so stupid, but there was no way to mix this kind of business with police work—not in my 'enlightened' city... oh no, they did not want any part of that. Fools—trying to shed the image of zombies and voodoo priests, even when they're hip deep in it—"

Legrasse suddenly jerked erect, cutting himself off from rambling. Looking at the floor for an instant, then the ceiling, he finally focused on Ravenwood again, then said;

"Look, the simple truth of it is, I pretty much need this kind of charity right now, and I'm grateful for it. And..."

"Oh, let's drop this line, shall we," answered Ravenwood. "You can't possibly be as grateful to me as I am to you." The words flooded out of the younger man so quickly, the following silence made it evident he might not actually have wanted to say them. As both men flushed, feeling more awkward with each other as every new second ticked by, Ravenwood finally cleared his throat, then said;

"Listen, the thing is, yes—I'm supposedly the big expert in New York City on the occult. I'm the Socialite Sorceror, the West Side Wizard, and all the rest of their hokum."

"Now, now," said the inspector with a bit of a chuckle, "don't forget the 'stepson of mystery.'"

"Thank you," answered Ravenwood with a wry smirk. Pursing his lips to one side, he added, "I wasn't feeling silly enough. Anyway, now, you and I both know Anton Zarnak is the real deal. I tell you, I was overwhelmed when he sent word that he was going to be gone, and that I should watch the store, as it were. Positively spinning. But then, then came the storm." Shutting the door, embarrassed to have his words leave the room, the young occultist confided to Legrasse;

"Any one with the slightest training could tell the storm we just had here wasn't natural. The West Coast storm had caught my attention earlier, of course, as well as your Gulf storm after it. When the weather went bad here I started studying, knowing something terrible was quite possibly headed our way." At that point, Ravenwood sat down, staring absently at one of his walls of books.

"You're worried about abusing my hospitality, embarrassed over the fact an insane and stupid world was too frightened by the truth to keep you on the payroll. John, please, hear me when I say, if I had known you were out there, I would have paid you to come to me."

"Is it all right that I don't quite understand," asked the inspector. Taking a seat next to the younger man, he added, "I mean, what would you need with an old war horse like me? I couldn't know half of what you do."

"Don't sell yourself short. Listen, yes, I've solved this and that little crime, cleared up a few insignificant mysteries for some bored millionaires, that kind of nonsense. But so far, my life could just be a series of cheap radio dramas. You, on the other hand, you've turned back invasions from other universes. Invasions—plural, as in more than one—from other universes. The fact you don't even see this as something special sends shivers down my spine."

"But, you've got this Nameless One fellow of yours to watch over you, don't you—to make certain everything flies smoothly?"

"He's been somewhere near by my entire life, John. And, yes, I know he has my best interests at heart, but so too did the God who gave us all free will and then stepped back and left us at the mercy of a dark and uncaring universe. Please just trust me when I say that I'm grateful to have you here at this time. The Black Bat brings us fire power and connections in the city we could find extremely useful. The Domino Lady, there's something about a woman's viewpoint, her emotions, feelings, and the such that I believe can be quite helpful in times like these."

"Oh, I agree," added the inspector heartily. "One time, Zarnak and I would've been finished if it weren't for the fact we had a woman with us. It was pure, raw emotion that saved the three of us, and nothing else. Add on that this Ellen, well, she's smart, tough, and if I'm any judge, she certainly seems willing enough to jump in and give it her all..."

"Yes, two excellent lieutenants for you," said Ravenwood. Raising his index finger, he turned it around to tap his own chest, adding, "And with myself as your third, we might just possibly live through all this."

"Me—you want me to run things?" Legrasse stared blankly. His first instinct was to assume Ravenwood was having sport with him, then to swing violently in the other direction to the assumption that the young man had no courage whatsoever. Finally, however, turning to face him, the inspector stared at Ravenwood unblinking, searching the younger man's soul for the answer he needed.

"You really think I'd be better in charge... don't you?"

"I really do. Understand me, John... Merlin knew a thousand times more about magic and the such than Arthur. Notice, though, he still advised from the background and left the being of a king to Arthur. Leading, especially in times of crisis, it takes someone who knows how to not only make a snap decision, but who knows how to live with those decisions once made. I, myself, I'd like to live through this thing. You take over command, you increase all our chances by 1000%. And, coincidentally, that just makes the odds better for the rest of the world, you know."

"And you know," said Legrasse in one of his long, pulled-out drawls, "what's coming is probably so damnably big and black and terrible that I'll probably be dead so quickly it's not even worth the discussion." Standing, Legrasse made his back iron rod straight, then clicked his heels, bowed at the waist, and offered;

"But good sir, since you insist, I shall accept your proffered hospitality. I shall dirty your sheets, eat your good food, smoke your fine cigars, help you and anyone else empty your decanters, and lead whatever troops you can find into whatever battle comes our way."

"Now," answered Ravenwood with a relieved laugh, "that's what I call a house guest. Let's go eat."

The two men threw open the doors to the library just as Sterling was approaching to call them to the table once more. Laughing, their arms filled with books, the two immediately began to chatter about which deity they might be facing, what cosmic alignment could possibly be provoking it into action, and what they could do about it.

In the meantime, the gathering darkness had plans of its own. Quinn, it knew, would be out striking fear into the hearts of the city's criminal element. Legrasse and Ravenwood would, most likely, be awake even later than the Black Bat. But, the Ellen creature, the blonde thing, it understood, had already retired for the evening.

Knowing her value to the team being assembled against it— far beyond what little they had realized it could amount to—that which watched from the shadows waited for her head to hit her pillow, and then it came to her, massive and reeking and as ready to destroy her utterly as anything it had ever eliminated in the past.

Chapter 14

"NOW WHAT EXACTLY IN HELL IS GOING ON HERE?"

Ellen looked around herself, eyeing the stateroom into which she had checked, wondering what was wrong—what was provoking her subtle discomfort. She had chosen one of the ritziest places along Manhattan's grand West 59th Street. That address automatically parked her among the elite of those visiting the city. It also gave her a view facing the lower boundary of Central Park just across the street.

Beside arranging a front view for herself, Ellen also made certain that her suite was situated as high as possible, thus extending her view of the park for a score of extra blocks. Despite her public worldly manner, Ellen Patrick was truly her father's daughter. The merest glimpse of trees and hills and bodies of water always gave her an extra inner peace no other experience could rival. Still, despite the hotel's grandly lavish amenities, as well as her breathtaking view, the Domino Lady's alter ego was greatly unsettled.

"Something is too wrong for words here," she muttered. "And it's going to make me crazy until I figure out what it is."

The blonde sighed at the thought of trying, though. Ravenwood had called himself an amateur detective earlier, but no one was more an amateur at that particular game than she. Finding clues, putting together evidence, building cases, that took a different kind of training than hers. It took a trained investigator, someone with a cop's mind.

That Inspector Legrasse might look like an old shoe, she thought, a giggle firmly in her brain as she pictured him, but I'll bet nothing gets by him.

So then, the voice from the back of her mind asked quietly, what is it exactly that's getting by you?

Ellen sat on the edge of the bed and tried to puzzle things out. What was it that was nagging at her so? What could have happened, she wondered. After all, all she wanted to do at that moment was to go to sleep. So—what was it she might have noticed on the way through her rooms that was giving her the unsettling, unnatural feelings she was then experiencing? Feelings so disturbingly bizarre she could not simply ignore them and get some much needed rest.

"Something just isn't right."

The blonde froze. Even the sound of her own voice was not right to her in her ears. The melody of it was missing, the color, the warmth. For a moment, she dismissed the notion, deciding that there must be some logical explanation—perhaps she simply had some phlegm caught in her throat.

If that's the case, the voice from the back of her mind whispered, try it again.

Still sitting on the edge of her bed, Ellen started to speak once more, but stopped herself. She knew the notion was silly, but what should she say? What words were right? Correct? Appropriate?

It's just an experiment, she told herself. Say something. Say anything—

But what?

The Gettysburg Address, your phone number, the dinner menu at La Plume, you idiot, say something!

"All right, all right, I'll say…"

And there it was, that same croaking, dried out sound the universe—for some reason she could not fathom—was attempting to pretend was her voice. Ellen's eyes went wide with horror. Not over the loss of her voice—the beauty of it—she was not so vain. No, it was something else. With trepidation, she began to look around herself, in every corner of the unfamiliar room, at the blank and silent walls—searching. Before she could help herself, the eyeing of her room became positively desperate, her gaze switching from spot to spot frantically because something was happening around her—she knew it. Something subtle was changing—shifting—and she needed to discover what it might be, before it was too late.

Too late for what?

With horror Ellen realized she had no idea how to answer her question. A different voice within her head, one she had never heard before, urged her to caution, to relax. She had gone through a terrible ordeal in San Francisco, then raced without pause straight across the country to meet with Ravenwood, only to find out she had been influenced by some unseen character in some unknown, mystical way to do so.

Who knows what else he might be trying to get you to do with those powers of his?

Ellen gasped. She had met Ravenwood, broken bread with him, talked to him at length, observed him interacting with others—there had been no trace of such duplicity. What was making her question him so?

Really, she thought, her mind filled with an unaccustomed confusion, he seemed so honest, so earnest, and in many ways, so much like a boy—trusting, honorable...

Was it honorable to have this unseen thing of his, this nameless other-worldly creature he keeps hidden behind that weird little door, to go into your mind and force you, against your will, to come here? To his city? His apartment? His—

"No!"

Ellen screamed the word in the dry, croaking, unfamiliar voice. Tears broke free from her eyes unbidden, and she cursed them. She was not this weak. She could not be. To fall apart, sitting in her hotel room, just asking herself a few simple questions. What was she going to do when they came up against something? How was she going to fight it?

Why bother to fight at all, the voice asked her again. As she sat shivering in the silent box of a room with its featureless walls, the calming whisper came to her sweetly, asking, Really, why should you fight at all? This isn't your job. It's too big—too all-encompassing. This is the job of the police, or the Army. After all, you remember what happened to those patrolmen. If big, strong men couldn't stop these things, what chance do you have?

It was true, she thought for a moment. Yes, she told herself, it was not like her to hide behind her petticoats, as it were, but really, how much was she supposed to do? Had she not avenged her father by this point? She had struck down every mobster she could find in the city—it was not her fault that now there were no more. If she was only honest with herself, she had to admit she had latched onto this, this... crazy monster hunt merely as a way to continue venting her anger—but why?

"Why are you still so bitter—so horribly angry?" Barely noticing the flat ugliness of her voice at that point, she continued to whisper to herself, saying, "if anything, these 'monsters' did you a favor. They killed everyone connected to your father's murder. You should be happy."

Happy?

Her mind threw the single word at the speech she had just made. Ellen laughed at the irony of it, as well as at the shambles her life had become. Happy—certainly. Why not? Hands drenched in blood, life dedicated to hate, now she could find some weak male to shackle herself to forever. And she had the nightmares from Hell to thank for setting her so wonderfully, deliciously free. So giddy was the trembling girl at that moment, she found herself thinking that if her room had a window she would hurl herself through it. And then, it hit her—

"If my room had a window?"

She was Ellen Patrick; her room always had a window. This suite had massive wall-sized windows! Throwing open her eyes, the desperate blonde looked for the dazzling view of Central Park that should have been directly in front of her, but she saw nothing. Indeed, no matter which direction she tried, she found no windows. There were no paintings on the walls, no furniture on the floor.

Nothing but the bed on which she was sitting.

The bed—

"Am I sitting? Am I?"

As her mind hurriedly retraced her steps, she followed her day from the airport to Ravenwood's to the hotel. Through dinner and back to her suite. She had come in, locked her door, taken a long and relaxing bubble bath… and then she had dressed for bed… read for a while… and gone to sleep. She was sleeping. No—

She was dreaming!

And with that terrible realization, the nightmare so desperately trying to snare Ellen Patrick within its clutches finally began in earnest.

Chapter 15

TONY QUINN HAD COME HOME EARLY, OR MORE SPECIFICALLY, THE Black Bat had returned early. A tip had reached him from an always reliable source that a certain segment of one mob family was about to move in on another. Normally this would have pleased the Bat to no end—gangsters murdering one another. And indeed, he had been inordinately excited at this bit of news. If the ambush of one faction by the other came off as planned, the death toll promised to be high.

He had gone out as the Black Bat merely to make certain that the mayhem did not spill out onto the public. The assault was planned for the docks, and late into the evening. That meant as little civilian traffic as possible. The Bat had liked that aspect of things. It meant he could show up, watch as the two sides slaughtered each other, and then he could step in and wipe out those remaining.

It was one of those times when he would not make use of his Black Bat insignia, not reveal his presence to the police and the world at large. So far he had been very clever about when he utilized the marker he carried and when he did not. First and foremost, if he were to use it that night, when scores of mobsters could end up dead, it could make him appear to be a crazed executioner.

Executioner, he smiled, that's okay. Truth in the title and all that. But, we wouldn't want the press to start adding "crazed" as an adjective.

No—that, he thought, wouldn't do at all.

Tony Quinn was extremely careful about letting people know exactly what the Black Bat was up to and when he was up to it. For instance, his recent sweep through Vincent Nelfadamo's mansion—he knew word of his involvement would never reach the public. That time it was a warning to the police, that he would not tolerate such monsters in his city, a hint that if they did not do their jobs that he would do it for them. He knew there were those in the police force, both the honorable and the corrupt who would understand the deeper message implied, that if the Black Bat had to keep doing the police's job, that someday he might consider cleaning up the police to be his job as well.

Bloody right, I might, he thought.

Most of the time, when he did use the stamp he used it to let the people know he was out there doing his job—performing what he considered his sacred mission. Appearances of his that were bound to make their way into the media always met with a few foreheads being emblazoned with his blood red calling cards. It never hurt to let the public know who was protecting them. It could help bring pressure on the corrupt police officials as well as the network of judges and politicians he so far had often found beyond his reach.

His accurate public image as a protector of the little guy also had helped him at those times when he got himself in over his head. These were few and far between, but they happened. When they did, it was not a bad thing to know that many a decent civilian would throw open their home, or their car door, to shield him from his enemies—even when that enemy some times proved to be the law.

"Yeah," he muttered to himself, there in his study, "ain't that a kick."

The idea made Quinn go cold for a moment. In rapid succession, he remembered those times over the past year when such had been the case. Little old ladies, lying with the most innocent of faces to the police hunting him that, no, they had not seen the Black Bat, while all the time he hid in the shadows directly behind them—wounded and desperate and trapped without their help.

People of all sorts had come to his aid, and the honesty and gratitude of it had warmed him—kept him going when common sense said stop before it was too late. Time and again, mailmen, truck drivers, housewives, high school students, people of all races, all religions—

But why not, came a thought into his head, they love you, you know. The man in the street, he knows who's on his side and who isn't. You should think about that some time.

Quinn walked back and forth in between his dresser and bed, his stride becoming more and more purposeful. He had been keyed up—agitated—ever since he had left the docks, his thoughts drifting away from the present and onward to the future. He had been wondering for several months what might lie in store for the Black Bat, to what purpose Quinn might best put his alter ego next. There was, he had realized recently, little point in merely racing about town beating up bad guys.

"'Bad guys,'" he quoted his thoughts aloud. "I'm beginning to wonder if I even know what I mean with those words."

Who were the "bad guys," really? The question plagued him, assaulted him. As he rolled the notion over in his head, he examined it from every angle. The idea of it had been ringing in his mind ever since the docks, ever since he had decided it was time to really start making things happen.

After all, look at all this magic mumbo-jumbo, a voice within his mind asked him. What do I know about things like that? What should I want to know, what do I even care?

Continuing to move back and forth, wall to wall, Quinn unconsciously wiped his dripping gloves on his vest once more, bringing the images of Ravenwood and Legrasse clearly forward within his mind. They were the occultists, the magicians, the damn voodoo priests… let them deal with whatever it was that was headed New York's way. He had enough to do.

His mind kept taking him back to the docks earlier that night. Not wanting to shove the vision aside once more, the Bat allowed a repeat of the glorious violence of it to refill his brain. It had been something to see—an overwhelmingly violent battle which pleased the Bat to no end. After all, he had been partially responsible for it.

It had been his invasion of the Boot's mansion and his slaughter of the gang lord along with many of his higher echelon players that had inspired the Brumalli family to move in on the Nelfadamo smuggling interests at the docks. With their top brass dead, the killing of the lieutenants in charge of the docks would allow those aligned with the Brumalli clan to pick up both a trained work force and an illicit import operation for the price of a few bodies and several boxes of bullets.

But, such an outcome did not please the Black Bat, and so he had been there to set the mobsters straight, to set all of the city straight, the world—after all, that the Bat did what was best. Without hesitation, after the Brumalli family's attack squad had subdued the dock bosses, before the two sides could argue or come together, he had taken aim and fired from his rooftop vantage point with the sniper rifle he had brought for just such a purpose. As the leader of the Brumalli forces had fallen, the criminals set to attacking each other once more in an intensely wild frenzy. The criminals all feared for their lives since neither side knew who of them had fired first.

Dozens had died in the opening seconds of the first barrage, and when enough of them had been slaughtered that those with cooler heads, and lesser aims could finally attempt to stop the carnage, that was when the Bat had stepped in and taken matters into his own hands. He had killed all he could find without mercy, moving between them, tricking them into shooting each other, emptying clip after clip into the rest. And, when his own personal blitzkrieg had finally come to a rest, still did he walk up and down the docks, placing a bullet in the head of every gangster he could find.

"Let me see them cause any more trouble."

Quinn laughed at the notion hidden within his words. None of those he administered to that evening would be causing any more trouble for anyone. The Black Bat smiled as he brought the scene back within his mind. It had been wonderful, the dazzling, liberating freedom of it. The pure, wondrous joy of sending bullet after bullet through the gangsters' heads—the spraying blood, the shattering skulls.

Feeling practically faint over the powerful recollection, Quinn tore off his mask, radiating in the power of the memory. Blood from his glove leaving a ragged trail acros his face, the avenger reveled for a moment in the glory of his triumph, the smell of crimson on his fingers delighting him to no end.

"And," he seriously asked his reflection in the mirror, "Why shouldn't it?"

Yes, he thought, why not, indeed?

He was, after all, the real power in New York City. It was the Black Bat who was the hero the man in the street respected, the one the women all adored. The police were next to nothing—incompetents, fools, most of them. Criminals the rest, accepting bribes to turn the convenient blind eye whenever it was needed. The thought of such men wearing the uniform of protectors made him boil with outrage. He could wipe them out himself—he knew he could. And if he were wrong, if he was not strong enough to do so alone, then the people would rise up with him and wipe them out.

"Wouldn't they?" Staring into his mirror, he answered his reflection in all honesty;

"Of course they would."

And then, the Black Bat laughed. Although he had never thought such outrageous things before—that did not mean they would not work. As he moved back and forth in his room, he thought on the ease with which he could conquer the police, and then the rest of the city, the state—indeed, who knew how far he might be able to take such a daring plan.

"Who cares?"

Exactly, he told himself, it was a glorious idea, a worthy one, a notion that should be made a reality, no matter how long it took, how much blood it spilled, what the man in street thought about it. Who could care how scarlet he painted the world, if it freed it from tyranny. Let history judge him, and let the judges be damned.

Quinn laughed again, and then once more—a harsh and terrifying sound less of a family with comedy than with madness. He could see it all now, clearly, as if waking from a dream. It was all so simple.

He would make himself king of the United States, no, of all North America—no, of all the Americas. It was his destiny. No one better deserved such a role.

Why stop there?

The voice in the back of his mind was right. Why, indeed? Why stop there? Why stop at all? He would sweep the globe, topple all empires and crush those that resisted beneath his booted heel. The brightest engineers would be gathered, and rockets would be built. In his lifetime the moon would be taken, Mars, Venus—the solar system, the galaxy. All would be his.

"All of it!"

More than all. He would have everything he wanted. He would slaughter any who stood in his way, and then—yes, why not? He would make Ellen Patrick his queen. Once he had swept away all the evil in the world, he would deserve her, and he would have her.

"There's nothing," he told himself smugly, "like a plan that works."

And, as that last horrible thought curled its way through the Black Bat's head, at long last he stood up out of his arm chair, the one in which he had sat down into almost immediately upon returning from Ravenwood's home. Yes, he had meant to go the docks that night, but when he had closed his eyes to think as he relaxed in his easy chair, a potent and masked sleep had grabbed hold of him and twisted at him until he had been manipulated into something the nightmare approaching the world could not only understand, but use to its advantage.

"Well then," he said to himself. "If this is going to work, there's no time like the present to get it started."

Pulling his mask back on, throwing away his weapons, the Black Bat headed for the front door of his home. In his mind he saw himself going out to destroy the police force of New York City and then moving outward and onward to unite the world under a never-failing banner of peace.

And, in the background, the force the Bat had sworn to help destroy only hours earlier roared in unstoppable laughter. It had the fool of a woman in its clutches. In a matter of minutes it would break her. Now, it had him as well. It would force her to kill herself soon enough. Then, it would sit gleefully back and watch the destruction of this one as well.

Chapter 16

John Raymond Legrasse stretched his arms out to their full extent, head tilting downward, eyes closed.

Good Lord, he thought, only slightly amused, I haven't done this much studying since high school.

Stretching, straining, pushing muscles one against the other, he did what he physically could to force himself awake. It was not a terribly difficult thing. After all, with his years of experience as a police officer, he was used to having to sit for long periods, simply waiting for something to happen. He was also quite used to sitting and studying diverse facts and clues trying to arrange them into some sort of recognizable pattern.

Well, he thought, his eyes finally opening once more, that certainly describes tonight, doesn't it? Endlessly looking at a lot of random bits of this and that in the hopes it adds up to something, when actually all we're doing is sitting around waiting for something to happen.

"Not really, old man," said Ravenwood absently. "I mean, we might find any number of things that could help us with whatever is coming our way."

"Excuse me," said Legrasse, his head turning toward his host, eyes rimmed with suspicion. "Were you talking to me? Answering something I said, perhaps?"

Ravenwood looked up from the dust-smeared book through which he had been digging his way with effort, partially because it was written in a dialect of Latin not seen in some twelve hundred years, partially because he was beginning to suspect it had nothing of value to aid his current needs within its pages. Looking away from the text with pleasure, he thought for a second about what the inspector had asked, then said;

"I'm not certain I understand what you mean."

"It seems to me that I asked you a perfectly ordinary, straight-forward question," responded Legrasse. His eyes suddenly narrowing, his police instincts smelling evasion, he went into an official manner he had not had occasion to use for several years. Unconsciously drawing himself up, pulling the muscles of his chest and shoulders straighter, he told the younger man;

"I was thinking about the great deal of random flotsam and jet-sam we've been sifting through in the hopes it adds up to something, as well as the fact that all we really seem to be doing is sitting around waiting for something to happen. At that point, you answered my thoughts as if I were talking to you instead of think-ing to myself."

Ravenwood looked across the table at the inspector, his face positively stunned. Not knowing how to answer, what the answer possibly could be, he offered weakly;

"Coincidence?"

"I'm thinking not," answered Legrasse. One side of his mouth curling upward, his palms sliding across the table top toward each other, he added, "I'm thinking there's something going on here. Something that none of us regular Toms, Dicks or Marys aren't going to find too keen when it arrives."

"I'm not certain I appreciate your tone, old man."

The inspector reared back slightly, pushing himself against the back of his chair. Moving himself and the piece of furniture away from the table, chair legs digging into the carpeting, he answered;

"Oh, you don't? Huuuummmm—well now, let me get this straight. You muck about in my mind without permission, then pretend no knowledge of doing so, then decide you're the offended party when such is pointed out to you. You've got an admirable stockpile of brass, son—I'll give you that."

"You're bordering on the insulting, inspector."

"And you're bordering on getting catalogued as someone who needs to be dealt with," snarled Legrasse. "You've got quite the way about you, don't you, Ravenwood? You mystic types, once you get lost in your spells and potions, we regular folk—we're all just puppets to you, aren't we? Just little bits of monkey meat for you to jerk around on strings."

"Now wait a damned minute here, inspector," retorted the younger man. Growing visibly agitated, the occultist's muscles began to tense as he growled, "you're getting pretty cheeky for someone who's supposed to be a guest."

"Another clever bit, I'll grant you," snapped Legrasse. "Gather us all together, find out what we know, then throw us back into the streets, or should I say, throw back the two in whom you don't have any further interest."

Ravenwood sputtered, the breath literally snatched from his lungs by the older man's pointed accusation. Finally standing from his chair, he jammed his hand across the table, index finger extended outward toward the inspector and, raising his voice, he shouted;

"Here's ego for you. You tired old relic, you get lucky, survive a few encounters with some minor creatures, learn enough to keep yourself from getting eaten, and suddenly you're someone I should find 'interesting.' Well, Methusala, why don't you tell me why I would ever find you 'interesting?' Ehhhh, tell me."

Standing up, suddenly Ravenwood became quite animated, his arms moving about wildly, not so much as if he were trying to use them to underscore his point, but more as if he were a baby bird making his first awkward attempts at flight. Keeping the large dining room table between them as he spoke, he pointed at Legrasse once more, snapping;

"Yes, tell me something, you fossil, you relic, tell me why someone with my knowledge of that which lies beyond the veil should even consider working with an old fool like you? The other two, they've at least got strength, guts... but you, you're a has-been. An also-was. This is what happens when you start feeling sorry for the elderly."

And, as Ravenwood hurled those words, Inspector Legrasse came up out of his chair, threw himself onto the table, rolled over it, and landed on his feet directly in front of the younger man. While the mystic's eyes bulged slightly, Legrasse—still in motion—delivered a savage roundhouse right which knocked Ravenwood head over heels into one of the couches in the living room. Without hesitation, the inspector followed his advantage, moving into the room at a fast clip, grabbing the younger man up by his collar and dragging him back to his feet.

Ravenwood attempted to mutter a hasty spell of protection, but between the shock of the attack and the blood filling his mouth, he was unable to do so. Nothing, however, prevented Legrasse from following up his attack and slapping the younger man across the face with the back of his large and quite solid free hand.

"What do you think now, Mr. Ravenwood, couldn't you possibly find some way I might be of use to the great and powerful you? If only I had the strength or the guts of the others!"

The inspector followed his first blow with another, and then another, backhanding the occultist into near senselessness. Legrasse stopped for a moment to catch his breath, Ravenwood dangling from his iron grasp, blood running down his face, over his chest and arms. The younger man had been caught totally off-guard by the unexpected assault, and now was completely at the mercy of his attacker.

Indeed, Ravenwood, barely conscious, could not even think clearly. His already swelling face was alive with pain. His left eye had been bruised, several of his teeth had been dangerously loosened within his head. Lifting the much lighter man higher to where their eyes could meet, Legrasse looked his opponent over for a moment, watching the color of the younger man's dazed eyes shift as he attempted to focus his vision. After a moment, however, the older man simply sneered;

"You're pathetic."

And, so saying, the inspector brought his free fist around violently and slammed it into Ravenwood's bowels. The young man's wobbling eyes flew open, his body doubling up into a tight spasm even as his mouth jerked wide to give his dinner ample room to escape. Covered in vomit, Legrasse laughed loudly, then pulled Ravenwood closer to him, whispering in his ear;

"Clever attack. Make me too slippery to hold onto you. Nice try—stepson of mystery. But now, I have an idea. You magicians are always so clever... let's find out something together—"

And then, dragging Ravenwood across the room to one of the massive floor-to-ceiling windows which made the entire apartment appear so wonderfully open, the inspector snarled;

"Let's see if you can fly!"

And, so saying, Legrasse picked the younger man up bodily and hurled him through the penthouse window with nothing between him and the street twenty-some stories below except air!

Chapter 17

ELLEN PATRICK SCREAMED AS SHE HAD NEVER SCREAMED BEFORE. The sound began deep within her, flowing upward through her body, searing her throat, hurting her own head. Tearing a membrane in her nostril, a trickle of blood ran down to dribble across her lips. The scream did no good. The young woman had been hoping to wake herself up, but the breath-taking cry was not up to the challenge of freeing her from her torment.

And then, as she gasped and choked trying to regain her breath, the beautiful blonde saw something coming for her in the dark recesses of her mind. It was some type of unfathomable body, a thing that held more shapes than the eye could follow, a thing of smells so revolting one could not begin to catalogue them. In some fashion Ellen could not understand, the approaching horror was many differing sizes at once, all of them covered in arms and claws, beaks, gills, legs and appendages of all manner.

"Stay away from me..."

But, it was the monstrous form's misshapen, terrible eyes that were more terrifying that anything else.

"Please..."

The wretched apparition began to reach through dream for

Ellen and she found herself unable to do naught but scream once more. As the first of its misshapen, grasping lengths came in contact with her skin, she smacked the oily, blue-haired appendage away, but it merely doubled back along with a half-dozen others. Sounds came from all the grasping, fleshy members then, a bubbling low drone like the sound of bees in a hive.

"Keep back," Ellen demanded, but her voice was weak and feeble. She knew she was dreaming, but also that she was stuck in no ordinary nightmare.

And then, suddenly, before she could think, before she could breathe, five more figures were approaching her, then twelve, and then in seconds they were virtually without number, reaching off into the infinite void in all directions, moving forward with a cold and horrid indifference, their intent wicked and terribly obvious.

"No…"

As Ellen's eyes went wide and her blood went frigid, she opened her mouth and screamed as a billion, billion blind and groping tendrils came flopping for her, a surrounding crop so oppressive that they blotted all light and sucked the void clean of air.

✠   ✠   ✠

The Black Bat walked into the police station nearest to the home of Tony Quinn. At first, for a remarkable second, maybe two, no one within the building seemed to notice. Then, before he could say a word, suddenly an officer spotted him. The patrolman was an alert individual, so much so he noted that the man standing in the lobby of the precinct house had no .45s in his holsters. Poking a friend in the arm, he said;

"What's this guy sellin'?" When the fellow officer jerked in surprise, his friend pointed out the missing firearms, chiding his pal by saying, "Yeah, com'on—it's gotta be a gag."

"Yer right," agreed the other. "Like the Black Bat would walk into a police station without his guns. Yeah, sure—and Congress is going to declare it illegal for politicians to steal from the public."

The officer's witticism brought roars of laughter from those who heard it. The desk sergeant, however, although close enough to have heard the line, did not think much of it. Instead, he demanded;

"All well and good, Fitzroy, but even if this couldn't possibly be the real Black Bat, as you say, perhaps before he walks himself straight into the captain's office, we should be askin' him what his business is here—what do you be thinkin' of that idea?" The patrolman gave his sergeant a cursory salute, then walked over to the Black Bat. As he approached, he asked;

"So, Mr. Black Bat, is it? Could I ask what it is you'd like of us this fine night?"

"You will all kneel to me now. You will, the every one of you, prostrate yourselves in good and decent obeyance, or I shall see you properly punished."

While pleasant laughter went up all around the lobby, the desk sergeant began to scowl. Fitzroy caught the look and, knowing that the figure in the costume would be in for a time of it if his superior officer's apple got even a slight amount more cooked, the officer took it upon himself to approach Quinn. Sticking out a friendly arm, he told the Bat;

"All right, any other time we'd be most appreciative for this opportunity to rid the city o'da Black Bat, don't you know? But you've come just now at our shift change, and the paperwork that would be created is just tremendous, so I'm thinking, why don't you be a good little boy and scoot along now?"

The officer moved on Quinn to show him to the door. So confident were all that this was the end of the costumed man's entertainment value that to a man they returned to what they had been doing previously. As the patrolman approached, the Black Bat focused on his outstretched hand, saying;

"All right, as long as you're certain it would cause too much paperwork if I stayed..."

And then, the Bat grabbed the man's arm at the wrist, snapped it forward, then turned it in a rapid circular motion. The officer's eyes went wide with pain as bone pressed against bone, finally snapping. At the same time, the Black Bat started the patrolman moving in a circle so that at the moment his wrist shattered he would be sent flying violently into the largest group of his fellows.

Suddenly, the fellow in the Black Bat costume was again the center of attention, some beginning to wonder if he might not be the real Black Bat, most not caring, simply wanting to take him down because of the principle of the thing if nothing else.

Laughing, Quinn caught hold of another policeman, spinning him around, bringing him forward at top speed into his gloved fist. The officer went down like a sack of flour, hitting the floor with a dull thud. As the desk sergeant roared orders, the Bat screamed;

"Now, will you all bow down to me as ordered, or are further demonstrations necessary?"

"For God's sake," came the sergeant's voice in response, "he's just one guy. Take him down, you bunch of sissy Marys—and I do mean now!"

All around the lobby, police officers released the restraining straps on their weapons. Drawing the service revolvers from their holsters, in seconds a full fifteen men had their weapons pointed at the clearly insane man they had surrounded there in their lobby. As Quinn continued to bellow, hammers were cocked, then triggers were fired, and at least a score of bullets went flying, all of them dead-targeted for the Black Bat's chest!

☩   ☩   ☩

Legrasse blinked. In that split-second, Ravenwood had fallen another half-story. As he watched the young occultist draw further and further away from him, the inspector's mind suddenly snapped clear. Instantly he could see where and when he had fallen into sleep—where and when his mind and his actions had fallen completely under the guidance of another.

No, not another, the back of his mind whispered to him, not some one, but some thing!

Wasting not another moment, the inspector wheeled about, his eyes moving from door to door within the apartment. In less than two full seconds, he spotted that for which he was searching, a door off to the side. It was the one he had spotted earlier, the one thinner than the others in the penthouse—the one made of wood not cut from any tree that ever knew Earthly soil. Staring at it, knowing he had found what had to be that for which he was searching, he shouted;

"Nameless One—help us!"

For a terribly long and frightening movement, nothing happened. Then suddenly, as the inspector's mind began to snap, twisting madly over what he had done, suddenly the silver-inlaid knob began to turn, and a wave of energy splashed forward from the unseen bedroom.

The door opened, and then, for an infinitesimal moment, time stopped everywhere, and the Nameless One came into the world!

Chapter 18

"PAUSE..."

At the utterance of that single word, combined with the proper hand gestures, the requisite controlled breathing and the force of an all-powerful will, across all the bubbling depths of the vast multi-verse linear progression skipped a beat. It was a solitary pulse, a hiccup in time, unnoticed by most of the universe, but it left one lone, paralyzed sphere amidst all the other countless worlds—weightless and timeless. In less than a moment, of course, everything would begin to move forward once more, but for that one unbelievably short instant, all of space and time stood as but playthings for a single individual—the Nameless One!

From behind the bizarrely thin door within Ravenwood's suite, bent and wizened, came that hoary being. The white-bearded man-shape moved with a slow majesty for a dramatic several seconds—and then suddenly, while Legrasse watched, the ancient figure shattered, splintering into what seemed nearly a half-dozen separate forms before completely dissolving into nothing more than an ephemeral memory. The inspector's body collapsed under him then, sinking to its knees while its owner struggled with all his will merely to remain conscious.

"What's happened to us," he muttered, shame beginning to wash over him as he began to realize what he had just done—or more correctly, the sinister, horrible truth as to how he had been used, made to perform the terrible act he had just completed.

At the same time, however, in spots close together according to one type of mathematics, but unfathomable amounts of light years distant from each other according to another, the Nameless One's various shades threw themselves to the task requested of them by Legrasse.

In the first shard of time it entered, one segment of the Nameless One's being plucked free Tony Quinn from his madness, and his central location within the lead storm closing on him. The ancient one's wraith-self had to move impossibly quickly, of course, for even with time nearly-lassoed as it was, still were some of the bullets dangerously close to the Black Bat's body. Indeed, the segment of the timeless sage there in the police station lobby had barely replaced Quinn's form with his own when the lead began to strike.

Dimensions away, a further segment of the venerable master caught up to Ellen Patrick. She was in the center of the dreamplane, a world barred to most, and even then only reachable while one is asleep. Ellen had been tricked into entering and, since she thought she was merely asleep, could not be returned to her world merely by waking her slumbering self. Thus, having no choice, the aspect of the Nameless One which had reached the desperate blonde formed a protective barrier around her fleeing form, taking the thousand and one poisoned hits coming for her all too-human frame.

While, at the same time, just above the streets of Manhattan Island, yet another phase of the white-haired old wizard appeared just below the body of Ravenwood as the bloodied and unconscious magician continued his downward fall. As the young man passed through the elder's insubstantial form, he suddenly appeared back in his suite, settling gently on the living room floor before a stunned and grieving Legrasse.

Separated by oceans of actual moments, but at what seemed the same time, Tony Quinn and Ellen Patrick also appeared in the suite, there in the living room near the inspector and their young host. As each shouted out in turn, Sterling came staggering out of his own room.

"Mr. Sterling," mumbled a still quite damaged Ravenwood weakly as his consciousness slowly revived itself, "so good of you to join us. Sorry my being pummeled into gravy seems to have disturbed your slumber." Giving the older man the weakest of smiles, he added;

"Do accept my apologies."

"My goodness," answered the butler in complete dismay. "What's been going on here? Master, what should I—"

"Your master will require immediate bed rest and visit from his physician."

All heads turned at the voice, each of them surprised to see the slight, white-haired figure of the Nameless One coming from the kitchen with a turkey combo sandwich in one hand and a frosty cold bottle of Coke in the other. As the four who had just been placed so much into his debt made to speak, the ancient sage cut them off with the wave of his hand. Taking a bite of his sandwich, he settled into a seat at the dining room table making the most distinct "yummy" noises, then said;

"Yes, yes, I saved your lives. Yes, yes, again—you were all under influence of terrible power from beyond. Forcing you to give into fears or desires or suspicions you have never been able to deal with successfully in your pasts. Do not ask of it, for there is no explanation I could give which you do not already know. You were attacked by one who used your own fears against you—you were, as Mr. Moe Howard might say, smacked in face with your own pies."

With a weary sigh, the Nameless One turned from the others and took a large bite of the sandwich in his hand. His teeth began happily grinding away, tearing into the turkey, tomato, bacon and Swiss cheese with the ravenous frenzy of one who had not eaten in months. As the others tried to crowd the ancient sage with questions, Ravenwood croaked;

"No. He's just died... how many times? He's strained to the limit. Let, let him... let him eat."

Sterling and Legrasse helped Ravenwood onto a couch, one overflowingly large enough to serve as a bed, at least until the young man's doctor could arrive. While the others had been talking with the Nameless One, the butler had already placed a call to his master's physician and secured an assurance that the man would be there in less than a half hour. While attending to the young mystic,

Legrasse continued to apologize for what he had done to him. Waving away the policeman's penitence, Ravenwood explained;

"Yes, I came out of the conflict the worse for wear... true enough. You're quite the dangerous man, inspector—take my word on it. But please, save your apologizes..."

"But, good God man, what I did—"

"You did nothing, don't you understand? We were, the both of us, under an influence from beyond. I was a fool not to foresee such an attack, and," his voice grew darkly bitter as he added, "and a fool not to recognize it once it was here." Turning his attentions to the others, Ravenwood did his best to raise what remained of his voice to where he could be heard by everyone else, then said;

"Listen, all of us... judging from what played out here between the inspector and myself, as my master said, it would seem that our enemy played off our greatest insecurities to get us to cripple ourselves for it. Would have succeeded, too, if my faithful watchdog hadn't come to our rescue..."

"Do not thank me," said the Nameless One in between bites. After washing down a quite large one with a long pull on his cola, he explained, "old Legrasse here realized truth in what seems to me amazingly brief period for you human types, and called for me. I had been attempting to pierce veil behind which this monster hides, was not watching as closely as I should have been. Time in real world goes by so quickly, unimpeded, like vapor in teeth of gale—when I am not actually in it, it often slips by without my notice."

"That dream I had," asked Ellen, her voice somewhat hesitant—shaken. "It wasn't really a dream—was it? I was actually in some... in that place, wasn't I?" The Nameless One nodded, his mouth once more too full of sandwich to answer. Taking the news as well as possible, Ellen asked;

"Is that the kind of thing we're going to be facing?"

"Ummmmmm, could be... yes," answered the ancient sage with a nod. "All of that... and much worse."

"The way it play with me, twisted my mind," added Quinn with a shudder. "I mean, I was completely awake. And, I can't lie about it—I knew what I was doing. But, it all felt so good, seemed so right. And in the meantime, all this thing had done was send me off to die."

"You were asleep long enough," corrected the Nameless One. "Just one moment where eyes fall heavy, and this one can invade. This type of attack, however, is one-time thing. You will know now when it comes. You had no defense against it before, but not to worry. Now you will recognize feeling of invasion if it ever comes to you again. Much like allure of certain women. What boy does not know, man remembers."

"Hey," interrupted Ellen, slightly put out, "that no one way street, you know."

The Nameless One spread his hands in opposing directions, the one holding his sandwich closest to Ellen. The young blonde leaned over and took a large bite out of the turkey combo, making a nasty face at the ancient sage. The white-haired old wizard pretended to be greatly shocked, then let his eyes twinkle in the girl's direction. She made a small, grateful smile in return, feeling halfway back to normal merely from the simple bit of teasing banter.

"So, what happened then," said Legrasse, trying to piece together what he had seen, "we've come under the notice of whatever this thing is coming after our world. And, even though we haven't done anything yet, don't even know who or what it is, it seems to consider us threat enough to try and eliminate us."

"Swell," growled Quinn. Feeling foolish and almost a trifle helpless, having been forced to throw away his guns and march off to his doom as if only a puppet, he said, "so the old guy here took the bullet for each of us. I'm guessing you can't keep something like that up for terribly long. Yes? No?"

"You are correct to suspect such, young man," answered the Nameless One, a trace of regret in his timeless voice. "When inspector here called, I entered his mind to discover what prompted his summons. Immediately I sent my spirit selves to rescue you all. Their destruction does not concern me overly at this time, however."

The elder continued to eat, starting in on a bowl of fried steak and rice brought to him by Sterling. As he complained about the butler's cooking, Ravenwood told the others;

"The Nameless One is about the best guardian a brash boy like me, and now you three, could ever hope for. He's a wonderfully loyal and courageous fellow, but he's not stupid to the point of foolishness. He made certain he kept enough of his essence in reserve… to be able to reform as he has here. A few dozen more meals and he'll be as good as new." Ravenwood coughed violently for only a moment, then added;

"Quite good as new."

"Then," a terrible and wicked voice passed through the room, "there shall be no more meals."

All heads turned in first one direction, then another, attempting to both discern what was happening, then formulate a plan. Was the voice coming from outside the building, sounding inside their heads, the communications of an invisible person, or coming to them in some other manner at which they could not even guess? Panicked, the group focused their attention on the Nameless One, which was exactly for what the thing from beyond had been waiting.

"Thank you, humans. I could never have found the annoyance myself."

And then, using the eyes of the five others there in the room, the still unknown force which had so far that night toyed with them all with such ease, pinpointed the location of the Nameless One. The ancient sage made motions as if to protect himself, but if so the attempt was a thing far too little, and far too late. As the other watched helplessly, green and purple fire fell from the ceiling, engulfing the Nameless One.

"NNNNoooooooo!"

Legrasse restrained Ravenwood as the crippled mystic tried to leave the couch. Indeed, all wished to help. Considering what was at stake, there was not a person in the suite who would not have traded places with the old man without hesitation. But, it did no good to mourn their terrible luck, or to batter themselves with recriminations. Their best chance of seeing the monster eliminated early had just been taken from them.

The Nameless One was gone, nothing remaining but a wisp of charred smoke, and a single spoonful of rice.

Chapter 19

MINUTES PASSED IN PAINFUL SILENCE. RAVENWOOD, BLEEDING, BROKEN as he was, crawled from his couch at the moment of the Nameless One's disappearance to the spot at his table where the wizened old man had been sitting.

"It can't be, can't... just can't..."

Delirious, unaware of his injuries, uncaring of the further damage he was doing to himself by moving about so, the young mystic clutched the slightly smoking chair desperately, his look one of a jilted lover, or a lost child. His eyes were wide, staring, drained of color. He was a man suffering a mortal wound who had no more blood to offer.

"I don't understand what happened," said Quinn. His anger and frustration reaching the breaking point over the way all of them were being used with such ridiculous ease, looking to Legrasse, he said,

"I mean it. What the hell was that? What the goddamned hell was that? There's the damn spook-town voice, then all of a sudden a fireball blasts the old guy and he just disappears? What was that?"

"Something found him," answered the inspector quietly.

"Something that wanted to get him out of the way, to deny us his abilities as a resource."

"'Deny us his abilities as a resource'," Quinn repeated the words slowly, examining them as one might do a phrase from a foreign language they almost understood. "Well, pass out the medals, general... could you be any colder about the situation?"

Legrasse bristled somewhat, the way any man accustomed to giving orders—to be deferred to—would when treated with insolence. Pulling the loose reins of his anger in tightly, he spoke in a low growl, saying;

"Now, you listen to me, counselor... the Nameless One apparently was the real target of this thing we pledged to destroy the entire time. We were, the four of us, pawns for its move against him."

"Then why did it try so hard to kill us?"

"Why not," answered the inspector. "It had to make its play look real, and it certainly wouldn't spoil its plans any to have us dead along with the Nameless One."

"It makes sense," said Ellen who was doing her best to comfort the grieving Ravenwood. "Remember, it had the advantage of knowing we were being pulled together to stand against it. It knew us, maybe all about us, but we didn't know it. For that matter, we still don't—do we?"

"It's true," croaked Ravenwood. Tears still falling unbidden from his eyes, he lifted his head, saying to the others, "But, we can't let that matter. Please, listen to me, we can't lose faith with each other now. We can't."

The mystic held one hand aloft to make a point, but found himself still too weak to support his own weight thusly, and began to collapse. Ellen caught him, heedless of the fact that doing so smeared her lace nightgown with crimson, excepting that it made her finally aware of the fact she had been transported to Ravenwood's suite in her night clothes.

"Tony," she said, her voice pleading, "we're all distraught, but we can't turn on one another. Remember what he said, this thing, whatever it is, it could find us, plant suggestions within our heads, toy with our dreams. We didn't know what it was, we thought what we heard within our minds was our own thoughts. It can't trick us again."

"It, it had that one punch," Ravenwood gasped. Falling into the chair from which the Nameless One had disappeared, he struggled to stay conscious, ignoring his pain as he added, "it saved it, like any good fighter, using it at just the right moment to try and cripple our efforts as best it could."

"It's made a good attempt—"

"Goddamnit!" Ravenwood slammed his fist against the table, droplets of blood flying from his hand, his clothing. The length of his arm from his elbow to his fist left a sticky maroon imprint on the polished wood. Staggered by his injuries, but not willing to let things fall apart, as his face drained even whiter, he spat;

"Ellen—"

"Yes?"

"Allow me first to say that you look positively fetching in your night frock, and I apologize for decorating it, but I am leaking. Second, would you be so good as to reach to your left and smack Tony in the head?"

Turning around, the blonde gave the Black Bat a light but firm open-handed blow to the back of the head. Gasping for air, Ravenwood struggled to hold on as he said;

"Thank you. Now, would you all please pay attention as I'm sure to be passing out soon. Sterling, do be a good man and get me an ice pack."

When so ordered, the servant pulled such into view, saying that he had made it while calling the physician and had been trying to deliver it for several minutes. The young occultist smiled, accepted it, and then asked the butler to wait for the doctor and to let him in as soon as he arrived. Finally, turning back to the others, he told them;

"Now, you all listen to me. I've just lost the equivalent of a father, grandfather, big brother and favorite teacher all rolled into one. None of the three of you have any idea what this kind of loss is like. In fact, considering the shock I'm falling into, I'm certain I don't even know myself. I can tell you this, though, it hurts like bloody hell, but I'm still moving forward—with or without you. Any of you—all of you if I have to."

Ellen brought a comforter from a side couch which Ravenwood accepted graciously. As he allowed her to drape it about him, drawing it close to himself, he continued, telling them all;

129

"We've learned a great deal tonight. First off, we now know the storms were no accident. This is nothing natural, but something planned. This isn't some monstrous thing released by an alignment of the stars. This is something that was called down upon us on purpose. It's an attack, an invasion, and there's intelligence behind it."

Ravenwood suddenly had a coughing fit, one that expelled a black and ugly wave of sputum up out of his bowels and across the table. Spitting the last clinging strands away, he ignored the episode as best he could and continued once more, saying;

"It considered the Nameless One it's greatest enemy, most likely because he was the only one of the world's masters actively looking for it."

"Naturally," interrupted Legrasse. "Makes sense if this isn't some random nastiness, but the opening salvo in a coming war. After all, in war, you don't want to destroy every army in the world, just those poised against you. And the best way to put any army into disarray is to kill its generals."

"Kill the Nameless One," said Quinn, his emotions finally under his control once more, "using us as its tools, and it cripples the major force trying to stop it. Not only by taking away our leader, but by setting us one on the other because of our guilt."

"It takes enormous energies to do what this thing did," Ravenwood told the others. "To... to reach out from the other side, to watch, to kill..."

Before he could go on, Sterling entered the room, informing his master that the young man's physician had arrived, and was on his way up from the lobby. Nodding, feeling slightly dizzy from the effort, the young occultist ordered the doctor be brought straight in when he arrived. Turning back to the others, he was just about to continue when Ellen cut him off, asking;

"This thing, whatever it's up to, it's all going to come together very quickly... isn't it?"

"What makes you say that," asked Quinn.

"Think about it, Tony. If it feels it's a good idea to throw most of its energy into taking down the Nameless One—if it's willing to reveal that the storms were being guided by an intelligence, and to sacrifice the element of surprise... that sounds like something you do when you have all your pieces in place on the board and you're feeling that it pretty much doesn't matter what the other side does."

As the sound of the front door to the suite being opened came to them all, Ravenwood nodded his head in agreement, saying;

"I'd say she's right. What do you think, John?"

"I think I'd better get back to work in those books we started in on, see what I can find."

"That might be a good idea."

As the doctor entered the room, all went silent as the man gasped at the sight of Ravenwood. His eyes going immediately to Legrasse, scanning his bruised and bloodied knuckles, the doctor was about to demand the appearance of the police when suddenly he noted the presence of Ellen in her nightgown, and then the Black Bat. Looking down at Ravenwood, he said;

"Another one of those nights I'm just supposed to conveniently forget, I suppose?"

"Seriously," croaked the young mystic through his swollen lips, "what ever would I do without your keen powers of observation, doctor?"

Making a wry face, one that screamed out that the physician wished he could know more—knew that he never would—the doctor ordered Ravenwood be moved back to the couch. While The Bat and Legrasse did so, Sterling brought Ellen a robe, apologizing for not having thought to do so earlier. Grateful as she was, the blonde made her best attempt at laughing, letting the butler know if it were truly that important she would have done something about it herself.

As they crossed the room, then lowered Ravenwood down onto the couch, the inspector guaranteed the young occultist that he would get back to work immediately. Ravenwood nodded weakly. Then, bubbles of bloody foam flecking his mouth, he added;

"We'll win through, John. We'll make up for it all."

And then, his last reserve of strength run through, Ravenwood's eyes rolled backward up into his head and he passed mercifully into unconsciousness. While the Black Bat helped the doctor arrange the young occultist's body, the inspector headed immediately back to the table where he and Ravenwood had left their stacks of books. Calling Sterling to his side, he told the butler to find something from Ravenwood's wardrobe that would do Ellen more good than a simple robe.

"She's tall, he's slender, make it work. After that, fetch me a new pad of paper and put the coffee on. I remember reading something earlier… if I could find it again…"

"Can I help," asked Ellen sincerely.

"You go with Sterling," answered Legrasse, already pulling all the books on the table together, trying to organize them. "Wash your face, cry a little if it helps, have something to eat if that helps because, oh yes, you'll be helping, and our friend in black as well." Turning from the table for a moment, he gave the blonde a determined grin, telling her;

"Whatever we're up against, or maybe whomever, they've made one enormous mistake. They thought we were weak and stupid. Well, I resent that, and I don't fancy letting them get away with that. How about you?"

Smiling back, not just reacting in kind, but suddenly feeling an inner strength she had not been able to find in quite some time, Ellen said;

"Not in this lifetime, Johnny boy."

Legrasse raised an eyebrow to the young woman's comment, then watched her walk away to join Sterling with more than a touch of appreciation. My God, he thought warmly, his eyes lingering on her well-shaped form longer than he would have believed any woman could hold his attention, that is one hell of a girl. Got me feeling like an idiot teenager.

And then, as the door to Ravenwood's bedroom shut behind Sterling and Ellen, and the sight of the blonde was finally cut off from the inspector's view, he blinked hard, suddenly realizing how intently he had been watching her despite himself. A small part of his mind chattered at him to act his own age. But then, a different thought occurred to Legrasse, one that made him slap his knee with fury and break into spasms of uncontrolled laughter.

Indeed, so great and purging was the force of his glee that he could not help but lose moisture to tears, or to attract the attention of the others still conscious. No longer needed by the doctor, the Black Bat crossed the room to the table where the inspector was just beginning to recover himself. As he approached, the masked hero asked;

"What was all the clamor about?"

"I suddenly realized something about the human condition just then."

"Yeah," asked the Bat, intrigued. "And what was that?"

"That it shouldn't be taken lightly." Smiling undecipherably, Legrasse handed Tony a pad and pencil, saying;

"Here, take this. And let's get ready to kick this thing's miserable ass!"

Chapter 20

THOUGH HOURS HAD PASSED SINCE THE ARRIVAL OF THE DOCTOR AT the Ravenwood penthouse, nothing new or important had yet to be learned. For the young mystic it had been a time of rest and recovery. His physician had pronounced him "extraordinarily battered," but essentially undamaged. He had not lost so much blood that he would need a transfusion and, despite his lingering pains, he had managed to come through his battle with Legrasse without any broken bones.

"How could you pound on that guy with those giant paws of yours," asked Quinn, using the words to help stifle a yawn, "without breaking something is beyond me."

"Maybe part of you was managing to hold back," suggested an equally weary Ellen. "It's possible that since you know something about these voodoo things, you subconsciously knew you didn't really want to hurt him."

"I would very dearly like to believe that," answered the inspector earnestly. "Whether or not you are correct, you are certainly a kind young woman to toss an old fool such a graciously large life preserver to cling to." Pushing himself back from the text he was reading, Legrasse rubbed and pressed hard against his eyes, trying to force their ever-increasing bluriness to hold off just a while longer.

"I like the boy well enough to feel pretty damn bad even still, though," he added. Looking up at the others, the inspector confided, "I mean, you two only have to feel stupid over nearly messing things up for yourselves... I was clever enough to get dragged quite a deal further along. If there's a king of the fools in this room, I think we know who it is."

"Don't be grabbing for that scepter yet, your majesty," answered Quinn. "You forget about the Nameless One. We were all in on that one."

"Oh, let's just forget last night," suggested Ellen. When the others turned to stare at her, she added, "You know what I mean—not forget it, just put it aside, stop letting it drag us down. Ravenwood fell for that one himself, and if it slipped past him, I say we've got better things to beat ourselves up over." Legrasse closed the book before him and let out a clear and noisy yawn. Smiling with appreciation, he said;

"I'm always amazed how women can do that—" When Ellen shot him a semi-burning look, the inspector put his hands up in mock defense, saying;

"Don't misunderstand me, my dear; I'm on your side. I've always found men to be far more the romantics in this world, women far more practical. I think Tony here will agree we'd all be better off if we did what you said and..."

Then, as Quinn and Ellen looked on, Legrasse suddenly stopped talking and began staring blankly off into space. For a moment they both worried that he might be under another attack from beyond, that the same sinister force was trying once more to take over the inspector from afar. But, quickly they both noted his hands moving, making the gestures of one trying to recall something. As Legrasse's left hand moved to his face, pulling at his chin, making motions before his eyes as if trying to jump-start his memory, Quinn joked;

"Calling all cars, calling all cars, be on the look out for a missing inspector. Last seen looking completely dazed." Pushing the Black Bat aside, Ellen asked with concern;

"What is it, John? Are you all right—what is it that's got you fading out on us here?"

"Ohhh, Heavens, forgive me," said Legrasse, suddenly pulled back to reality as he was. "It was what Ellen said, it got me to thinking about the practicality of women. Then, that reminded me of something, I even think I might have mentioned it, I mean here earlier, yesterday…" Tapping the fingers of one hand before him on the table, the inspector looked at the other two there and told them;

"There was an African woman, saved both Zarnak's and my bacon a while back… lives here in the city. She's, oh, I don't know why I didn't think of this before."

"Think of what?"

"Think of bringing her in to help us with all of this," said Ellen. "Right?"

"Yes, yes," agreed Legrasse abstractly, still trying to recall the name for which he was searching.

"Good," answered Ellen with a small sense of triumph. "I was getting tired of being the only girl around here."

"Madame, Madame… Madame Sarna La Raniella," the inspector suddenly shouted with a vigorous tone of triumph. "Yes—that was her name. I'd stake everything I own on it. Quinn, could you find Sterling, please?"

"No problem. I think he said he was going to sleep."

"Well, get him in here. He's sure to know where to find this woman. Ravenwood would have to know her—know of her, at least. We get her up here, we'll get somewhere. I'm certain of it."

The inspector watched the Black Bat as he rushed off to roust the butler. The hero was still moving with a casual ease, but he was the only one. Ellen, far younger than the inspector, was still much more robust at that point, but was beginning to fade. Legrasse, he had to admit, he could barely read the pages in front of him he was so tired. No, if there was anyone who could help them, it was La Raniella.

And if she can't help us…

The thought trailed off in the inspector's mind, forced to silence by what was left of his iron will. They had to succeed, he told himself, unwilling to listen to any other alternative. They had to.

No matter how much more logical certain other, less optimistic options might seem.

✠   ✠   ✠

"LEGRASSE," THE WOMAN'S VOICE WAS DARK AND HUSKY. AS STERLING ushered her into the room, she continued, saying, "you far from home once more, ain't you now. But you not so stiff no more. Not so white, either. You learn to walk de silver path, I'm thinking. Impressive."

The woman moved into the room as if making her way through several inches of snow. Her movements were fluid, but heightened, and even Ellen caught herself watching the slow, rolling motion of the woman's advance. As the immaculately attired black woman was led by Sterling into the dining room, she spoke to the inspector once more, saying;

"So, you tough ol' patch of weeds, you done some big violence in this room recently, didn't you? Real bang-bang, skull knocker—wasn't it? The smell of it's coming off your hands, out of your brain, thick, like the taste of fried pork dancing with garlic and blood in the air. You hit this guy up real bad, didn't you?"

"Lovely as ever, aren't you," answered Legrasse gruffly. "And how's your dear husband?"

"Still happily married, don't you know? You find anyone brave enough to take to your bed, or you still climbin' poles all by yourself at night?"

"Suddenly it occurs to me why calling you immediately did not spring to my mind. Perhaps if we could get down to business, this need not be any more unpleasant than possible."

"Dey always hope in de world, isn't dere?"

La Raniella moved to the table and sat down in an open seat. Despite the early hour, she seemed completely fresh, appearing impossibly immaculate. Her blue silk dress hung low, almost to her ankles, but there was little of the Sunday school teacher to her look. From her highly polished pumps to her black-lace veiled pill box hat, she was dressed as if on her way to a box at Carnegie Hall, the glittering but tasteful strands surrounding her neck, obviously from Tiffany's and quite properly proclaiming that this was a lady.

Quinn saw it before Ellen, his heightened senses noting much about the black woman. She was definitely not one to allow race to bar any doors through which she needed to pass. There was a smile hidden within the corners of her lips, one he sensed could be unleashed as a reward or a punishment depending on its target. Ellen, coming from society, knew the goods when she saw them. La Raniella had the poise to hold her own, it was obvious. Indeed, dressed in men's clothing as she was, the blonde was feeling almost inadequate in the new arrival's presence.

In a few quick minutes, Legrasse brought Madame La Raniella up to speed with all that had happened from the first storms in California, all the way through to the destruction of the Nameless One. When she asked what the inspector desired of her, he informed her that he hoped she could tell them what it was they faced.

"Oh," she said, "is that all?"

Smiling, the woman dragged a small, but thick stone dish from her bag, as well as an opaque bottle. Pouring a thin line of a mercurial purple liquid into the dish in an ever reducing concentric circle, she struck a match and lit the innermost end of the spiral. As it began to slowly burn, sputteringly traveling along the circle with a hissing blue flame, she pulled back the light veil of her hat, then removed the stylish decoration altogether.

"You and you," she said to Legrasse and Ellen, "you've been in de presence, put eyes to that what's coming. Give me your hands, so I can see as you have seen, and maybe follow these things back to their homes."

As the three held hands around the table, even though she had not been introduced to him as anything but the Black Bat, La Raniella told him, "Tony, there's an uneasy stirring somewhere in the ether."

"Which means what?"

"Which means, sweet man, that I'm going to ask you to not pay so much attention to us as to the world around us—could you do that, please? It might be nothing, on de other hand, it might keep us all from ending like poor, broken little Ravenwood. Or worse."

The Bat, still not used to his secret identity meaning nothing to these mystics who were piling up all around him, nodded his head and pulled away from the table. He did not know what it was the woman expected, but he pulled a set of his .45s, made certain they were ready, and started to prowl the apartment, grateful he had called for one of his men to bring him a new brace of weapons.

In the meantime, La Raniella looked deep into the sputtering fire, and then blew on it softly, extinguishing the flame. The action replaced the oddly-colored fire with a smoldering billow of exotically scented smoke. As its bluish tendrils drifted toward her, the woman breathed it in deeply, her eyes rolling upward into her head. Her body sagged backward in its well-cushioned chair, her head lolling against the high back. Her hands, however, still held the other's tightly, showing she was very much still in charge of her senses.

The mystic held her pose for a number of minutes, then began to swim back to consciousness. Releasing her hold on the others, she told the one-time inspector from New Orleans;

"You made a good choice to call me. You told me this thing you face, it's been playing with your minds—yes?" When Legrasse agreed, she told him, "More than you know. All along, the force you oppose, it has been placing ideas in your mind, making you think this is some menace from a great beyond. It is not."

"Well, it's been doing a very believable impersonation so far," offered Legrasse.

"As you have often done one of an investigator," countered the dark-eyed La Raniella, "but these you face had your number long before you became involved."

"You know what's happening," asked Ellen.

"I do." So saying, the mysterious black woman took one of Ravenwood's smaller books from the table and used it to scrape clean her stone dish. Heedless of the glances of the others, she poured the contents of a different vial into it and ignited it as she had the other. As it began to billow, she told the others;

"Breathe… take a deep, strong pull. Get de smoke down into your lungs. Feel it in you blood." As the others did so, she told them;

"Dese things you faced, dese things what hunted our old swamp coon here, that will soon be sprouting along the beaches on this coast, they are not some curse filtering their way here from some long-sealed-off dimension—they were sent here by men."

"By men?"

"Yes, inspector," answered La Raniella. "By men. And I will tell you something else, dey be sending more. Another storm will soon be felt, one that will stretch from Lake Superior across to Montana. What's that tell you, Legrasse." The inspector thought for a moment, then said;

"This plague, it's not going across the country, it's going around it!"

"That's right, old gator, this country, it's got some powerful wicked enemies. It's got one wants to see it disposed of, put out of its way. It's got some plans, you see." And then, the mystic suddenly went quiet. After several incredibly long seconds, she whispered to the others;

"And, my friends, it seems those plans include getting rid of all of you—right now."

Madame Sarna La Raniella had just enough time to give the others that smallest bit of a warning when suddenly the suite burst with excitement. Before any could react, all the windows were shattered by the arrival of various types of grenades. As Ellen pulled La Raniella down under the table, Legrasse stood, pulling his ever present service revolver from the holster under his right arm.

"It's gas!" The shouted warning came from Sterling who had never returned to bed. As he moved into the room, Legrasse shouted to him;

"Stay with Ravenwood—protect him at all costs."

"It's more than gas," offered the Black Bat. "There's smoke mixed in there as well."

"And people…"

La Raniella's comment confused the group for only a moment, and then the first dozen of the black-garbed figures swung in through the already shattered windows.

Chapter 21

"Everybody down!"

Taking quick aim, the guns of the Black Bat barked remorselessly, raining slaughter on the invaders. Stepping from the dining room to the living room and then back again, in less than ten seconds the masked avenger snapped off fourteen shots. The action left nine of the invaders dead, three wounded—two mortally. The last man, the Bat caught from behind, coming upon him through the smoke and gas like a silent wraith.

"Excuse me…"

Quinn actually tapped the man on the shoulder and when the invader spun around, he found a speeding hand smashing into his throat. The two fingered thrust broke the invader's Adam's apple, clogging his windpipe, leaving him to choke to death in a matter of painful seconds.

The others would have applauded the deadly grace of their companion, but there was no time. Their unknown enemy knew who and what he was up against, and had sent what any logical odds broker would figure to be an overwhelming force to deal with those remaining. On the heels of the first wave, another score of the black-garbed invaders swung through the windows. At the same time, a second assault front came through the front door of the penthouse.

His weariness fading instantly, Legrasse pulled his old service revolver and fired through the mounting smoke. He could not see in darkness like the Black Bat, but something within him directed his arm, lining up target after target. With a confidence he knew could only come from his occult dealings, he forgot mortal constraints and allowed his senses to guide his shots. His heavy handgun barked repeatedly, spitting thunder and death.

Beneath the table, Ellen made hand signals to La Raniella, indicating that the witch woman should remain hidden. Seeing in the black woman's eyes that she had no intention of leaving the relative safety of her hiding place, the blonde nodded to her, then slipped out from under the table and into the fray just as Legrasse emptied the last of his chambers. As two more of the black garbed figures rushed for the inspector, Ellen stood up in their path, screaming to be heard over the endless echoing of all the gunfire.

"Reload," she shouted to Legrasse. "These two are mine."

As the figures approached, Ellen shrugged off the last of her normal personality, slipping into what she thought of as "Domino mode." She knew those approaching were men, could feel it through the air. Smiling, ignoring the long curved swords they held to the ready, she stood on the balls of her feet, one foot forward, hands at her side, palms up.

"All right, boys," she said in a light and breezy tone, not caring if they could hear her or not, simply needing to release her character, "let's see who's good the goods to play with baby tonight."

One of the men charged, bringing his sword down from the left. The Domino Lady ducked, not bending over to do so, but dropping her knees until they were practically touching the floor. As the man's blade passed over her head, his surprise at her ability to dodge his attack left him open to hers. With quick precision she reached upward even as she snapped one long leg forward. The result was the shattering of the man's knee even as she caught his sword hand at the wrist.

With a quick turn, she forced his hand open, capturing his weapon as it fell from his fingers even as he toppled sideways, his crushed joint no longer capable of supporting him. Pushing herself upright on the toes of her one foot still in contact with the ground, the blonde brought her other leg back down even as she took her new-found weapon into the palms of both hands. As she did so, the second attacker had already begun to move forward.

He brought his sword in from the right, bringing up a second, shorter blade with his other hand. Ellen blocked the sword with her own, dodging the second weapon by twisting to the side. As she did, she ran her sword down the length of her opponent's blade, slicing violently through his weapon's hilt, cutting through his leather glove, chopping away two of his fingers. As the man cursed, his words muffled by his mask, four more of the invaders moved forward on the Domino Lady.

"You boys sure know how to make a lady feel appreciated," she purred. Taking a solid stance, she held her blade aloft, daring the others to move forward. Expert that she was, Ellen knew she was in trouble. She was tired and had been through hell. The sword in her hands was an unfamiliar style of weapon from the foils and cutlasses to which she was accustomed. Still, she grinned at those approaching as if a giant making sport with a band of children.

"Okay," she said, her voice as gentle as her stance was rigid, "who wants to try and dance with me?"

Two of the invaders moved forward, one swinging from the side, the other making a straight lunge. Ducking far too the right, the Domino Lady allowed the forward thrust to glide by her while she brought her sword up and over its angle, bringing it back down on the other man's blade, knocking it into the sword of his fellow. As their weapons clashed, the blonde kept her own blade in motion, sliding it across the throat of the closest, and then into the chest of the second.

The maneuver worked perfectly, except that the second man jerked backward when pierced so violently that he ripped her blood-soaked weapon from her hands, leaving the Domino Lady defenseless as the other two moved forward. Seeing no way around the inevitable, Ellen snarled;

"This is like attending a cotillion in Alcatraz!"

Hoping to take at least one of the pair with her, the blonde made ready to throw herself into one of them. Glancing at each other, the pair silently agreed as to how they would attack. Then, they both moved forward, swords held high, only to have their heads exploded by flying lead as Legrasse unleased four newly loaded rounds. Blood and gore splattered the Domino Lady, but her attackers went down to either side of her, both dead before they hit the floor.

Stepping out of the finally dissipating smoke, the inspector apologized for his delay. Barely able to understand him over the ringing in her ears, the blonde merely waved him off, laughing as she told him;

"Better late than never, Johnnie."

And, as she grabbed up another sword from one of the newly slain, the Domino Lady suddenly realized that the attack appeared to be over. Warily, she and Legrasse both studied the rooms around them, only to find nothing but black-garbed corpses. As Ellen helped Madame La Raniella to her feet, Legrasse called out to the Black Bat. The inspector felt a wave of relief as the masked man entered the room looking hale and unharmed. A smoking .45 in both hands, he glanced around at the bodies everywhere, then noted;

"Nice work, you two. We should go into the wholesale slaughter business. We'd clean up."

Legrasse understood the callousness of the Bat's remark. Having been sorely used by the opposition, he was feeling a bit repaired now, being able to fling some of their unseen enemy's contempt for them back in their faces. Merely nodding, the inspector asked the Bat to find Sterling and to ascertain as to his safety as well as Ravenwood's. After that, he turned to La Raniella and asked;

"So, tell me, how much of our survival there do we owe to you?" When she feigned ignorance for a moment, Legrasse rolled his eyes, then said, "I doubt severely if we have time for games of any kind, madame. I'm tired and as you might suspect, have never been one much for mysteries even when I'm not. So, if you would, kindly admit to helping us, accept our heartfelt thanks and let's be done with it, shall we?"

"Only you, Legrasse," answered the black woman sharply. "Only you could make gratitude feel like de reprimand." La Raniella stared at the inspector tight-lipped for a moment, her eyes narrowed and harsh. Then suddenly, her mouth broke into a delightful, thin smile as she admitted;

"Yes, we all live thanks to my intervention. It is true. When I felt the attack coming, I had no solid idea of its nature, but those voices that whisper to me, they told me to burn de wax o'air. I admit I did not understand, but it is by obeying the voices, not understanding, that one survives."

"The smoke you had us breathe," said Ellen, her quick mind translating La Raniella's words, "it gave us oxygen somehow. Counteracted the gas mixed in with the smoke."

"That explains a lot," said Legrasse. "Our friends here expected easy kills. Thought we would be unconscious, or at least hacking up our dinners, choking on their smoke. Blinded by it." Nodding to himself, the inspector turned to the witch woman. His face its usual grim mask, he stared at her for a moment, then told her;

"I can see why you wouldn't want us to know you aided us. After all, information such as that might soften some of the animosity that swirls the air whenever you and I share it. And, well heavens, you wouldn't want that, would you?"

"No, not really, old weed," she said, the sarcasm in her tone offset by an intertwining charm. "I find you so very much fun to torment, it would be sad if we were forced to become friends."

Legrasse shook his head slightly, adding La Raniella's answer to the storehouse of information he possessed which continued to convince him he would never understand women. Suddenly feeling extremely tired, he made his way to a chair, sitting down with a solid thud. His senses telling him the attack was definitely over, he found his defenses shutting down, what little energy he had remaining to simply keep him awake. He knew there were numerous things he should be doing, but he needed a moment, at least one, to pull himself together. As he did, the Black Bat came into the room, dragging one of their attackers behind him.

"Sterling and Ravenwood are aces," he told the others. "And, I'm assured by our quick-thinking butler that the place is soundproofed to the hilt. We won't be attracting the gendarmes with our gunplay, although the hotel detectives will be here in a few minutes."

"What makes Mr. Sterling so quick-witted," asked Legrasse.

"Seems when the attack started," the Bat answered, "he simply threw shut the bolts in his master's bedroom then hid under the bed. Cool, collected—reasonable. I like a man who knows his limitations."

"What are yours, Tony?" The Black Bat smiled at Ellen, answering her;

"I've been making a life long quest to discover the answer to that question. Something tells me you might be the woman who could help me find at least a few of them, but before we jump to trying to discover them, I'm thinking we might want to indulge ourselves in a different game." As the others waited for the Bat to explain himself, he brought his arm forward, flinging the invader he had been dragging into the center of the room. As the body crashed in between them all, he said;

"I mean, as interesting as it would be to see if I actually have any limits, maybe we should try to answer a few other, possibly more pressing questions first."

"You mean..."

"That's right, John," answered the Black Bat, a cold and harsh smile on his face. "I noticed this one standing more in the background, giving orders." As the black-garbed figure on the floor groaned, the Bat added;

"That's why I let him live."

Chapter 22

DRAGGING THE INVADER UP FROM THE FLOOR, THE FIRST THING THE Black Bat did was to slam the man into a chair, then restrain his arms behind its back with a pair of slender cuffs of his own design, one of several he always carried when in costume. Not satisfied, he then took a coil of light-weight but incredibly strong cable he carried in his belt and lashed the man's waist and legs to the chair as well. After that, the invader was finally unmasked. That simple action told the quartet much. Indeed, wondering if what they learned then was a fluke, Legrasse reached down and unmasked several more of their would-be assassins.

"Orientals," mused the inspector. "The lot of them."

"Japanese, to be exact," added Ellen. When the others turned to her, she explained, "We get a lot of different Asians in San Fran... you learn to tell the difference."

"Well," said Legrasse grimly, intertwining his fingers so he could crack all his knuckles at once, the result being a deep and nasty sound, "let's see what we can learn from this fine young gentleman."

Grabbing up the cup of coffee he had been drinking, the inspector splashed it in the man's face. The man blinked several times, then finally opened his eyes. A look of uncomprehending defeat glistened within them. There was to it not so much of anger or defiance, as their was sadness. Indeed, to those assembled, it appeared the man was broken already. Suspecting some trick, Legrasse was just about to voice his suspicions when suddenly he realized;

"You know, I wonder if any of us can question this fellow. I don't know about the rest of you, but I myself don't speak Japanese."

One by one, each member of the group had to admit they had no skill in that area. There was the feeling among them that Ravenwood might have some passing familiarity with the language, but none present thought it worthwhile to awaken the badly damaged mystic on the off-chance he might know a touch of the assassin's tongue. Before they could go any further toward questioning their prisoner, Sterling entered the room once more.

"Forgive me, but I thought I should alert you," he told those assembled, "I have taken the liberty to call in some of Master Ravenwood's, ah, 'associates.' They are, how to put it, ah... specialists he knows, and they have proved quite useful in the past, removing other small messes which have proved, shall we say 'inconvenient' from time to time here in the penthouse. I just wished to assure you that they are an extraordinarily tight-lipped bunch, and that none of you need worry over their presence."

"Maybe we should check the bodies for any clues they might surrender before they're removed," suggested Legrasse. As he began to reach for the corpse closest to him, the butler made a gentle hand gesture which indicated he should not bother, explaining;

"Those on their way will strip the bodies of any effects for your examination. I have witnessed their work in the past, and they seem a quite competent, and extremely honest, group. I believe if there is anything to be discovered thus, they will be up to the task."

Grateful for being able to relinquish at least the one chore, Legrasse thanked Sterling for his thoroughness, then turned back to the problem at hand. A sense of futility washing over him, the inspector rubbed his eyes, looking to banish some of his ever-increasing fatigue. Finally, knowing he was not going to be able to improve his condition any further, Legrasse sat down in a chair in front of the prisoner and asked him;

"Well, let's go another route. Do you understand English, you heathen bastard?"

"I have my own gods," the man answered sullenly, but in only lightly-accented English. "And I know both my mother and father. Is there anything else upon which I might correct you?" The inspector nodded his head several times unconsciously. Looking at the others, he said;

"I'm not certain if this makes things easier or not." Then, turning back to their prisoner, he asked, "All right, so why don't you tell me, my blood-thirsty friend, just how inhuman am I going to have to be to get something resembling the truth out of your murderous hide?"

The prisoner tilted his head upward. It was evident to all in the room that he did not do so to look at Legrasse. His eyes were indeed aimed in the inspector's general direction, but they were not focused on him—were not focused on anything. As the man stared off into space, Madame La Raniella tapped Ellen on the shoulder, saying to her softly;

"Come, let us leave the men to do what they must. We shall do what we do best." As the witch woman lead Ellen to the kitchen, the blonde said with a touch of annoyance;

"You know, the place comes with a butler. There's no need for us to run off to find some 'women's work.'"

La Raniella waited until the kitchen door had been closed behind them before answering. Opening the refrigerator door, she busied herself with finding something easy to prepare that would replenish everyone's spirits without dulling their wits. When Ellen again protested being "dragged away from the action," the black woman told her;

"We are not needed there."

"But we are needed here," snapped the blonde, her tone somewhat annoyed, even a shade angry. "I guess we should kick off our shoes, too."

"If it makes you more comfortable," answered La Raniella. As Ellen bristled, the older woman took sympathy on her, saying softly, "But comfort is not your problem in dis matter, is it?"

"What do you mean?"

"I mean, you have all been through de most terrible ordeals tonight—yes?" When the blonde nodded, La Raniella nodded as well, telling her, "I know. You have been stripped of dignity and self-image both. Legrasse, he is fine. Dat ol' bucket of a man, you can pour and pour the horror of de world into him, he never overflows. He has de balance. He is not why we are here."

"What do you mean?"

"I mean de boy, Tony. He is feeling most used, most foolish. He slaughtered many of your foes tonight. I watched his soul, reaching out from him, guiding his bullets. He was the right hand of death, and it was awesome to behold. But violent and thorough as it was, it was not enough." As she placed a number of fresh vegetables and pieces of fruit on the table, La Raniella turned to find a cutting edge as she continued.

"He needs to feel a man again, needs to feel triumph. Dis boy, even ol' Legrasse, dey are good men both. But, dat is dey key—dey are men. Dey will not wish to play dey savage before you. But savage they will need to be to loosen the truth out there." Ascertaining that the celery she found had already been washed, she tore several stalks free from the rest, then began to slice them down into roughly quarter-foot sections. Handing one to Ellen, she said;

"You, you think you have much to prove because God fashion you a woman. Tell me, sweet child, who is it you think needs this proof you so often feel you need to offer?"

Ellen stood silent, staring down at the black woman before her. Her immaculate clothes now torn, blood-spattered, she sat calmly at the table, her hand still extended. Numbly, the blonde took the proffered stalk and sat down next to La Raniella. The blonde had held herself together throughout the evening as horror after horror had assaulted her—rose to the challenge when the only way to remain alive was to strike down all who approached in cold blood. Now, her face and clothes, her entire body streaked with the scarlet of her survival, she felt the weakness she had dreaded ever showing begging for release.

"We are alone here, my child," came La Raniella's gentle voice. "You do not have to be de Amazon now." When Ellen looked over at the older woman, La Raniella opened her eyes wide, letting all the sympathy she had within her pour out freely as she whispered;

"Did you think little Tony was de only one who needed healing after dis terrible night?"

And then, feeling a sudden, terrible urge to unburden herself,

Ellen Patrick finally opened the door to her emotions which she had slammed closed the day she had received the wireless notification at sea that her father had been murdered. Since that horrible morning, she had worked, toiled, enslaved herself to only one goal—the relentless, remorseless destruction of evil. She had pretended to grieve for the sake of show when first she had returned to America, all the time seething inside, coldly planning her revenge.

Since the day she had stepped off the boat, no matter what her face told the world, inside she had felt nothing but hatred. She had dallied with men only as part of the act she needed to perform, feeling no joy or pleasure during any part of her existence except when dispensing death. Now, suddenly, having been driven to the brink of despair by a hatred so massive it dwarfed her own, she felt the gelid barrier she had stretched across her heart shatter, her need for revenge melting away like fog in sunlight. Nodding to her, La Raniella whispered;

"It's time, my sweet. Let it go."

And then, Ellen Patrick, her insides crumbling, reached out for the woman next to her. The celery stalk tumbling from her fingers, she grabbed onto La Raniella as if the woman were a life preserver, clutching her as if not doing so would send her to her doom. Tears held in for far too long exploded from the blonde, erupting from her as her body convulsed from the terrible fury of her violent sobs.

Holding her quietly, understanding her need, Madame Sarna La Raniella merely whispered quietly, giving the desperately crying woman in her arms the comfort she needed. When the long-expected screams finally erupted from the dining room, neither woman seemed to notice.

Chapter 23

THE SUN HAD RISEN AND STILL THE PRISONER HAD NOT TOLD LEGRASSE and Quinn anything useful. Eventually, both men had succumb to the need for sleep. Rather than ask Sterling to guard the would-be assassin, the Bat had brought in two fellows in his employ. Norton Kirby, an older gentleman whom everyone called Silk, and a large and ranging truck of a man known to the world as Butch O'Leary, had been called in to help keep the apartment complex secure. Far better rested than the others, and both appearing highly professional, they inspired enough confidence among those who did not know them to allow them to catch a few unworried hours of sleep.

Sterling surrendered his own quarters to Quinn so that he, himself, might sleep on the couch in Ravenwood's room, in case his master might need him. Legrasse, of course, retired to the room already made up for him, while Madame La Raniella made certain Ellen got back to her hotel safely. With all of her belongings still down at West 59th, it was decided she should gather them up, get some rest, and then rejoin the others for lunch. The witch woman, who seemed to the fellows had become quite protective of the blonde, assured the worried crew the Domino Lady would be returned in time to break bread.

"Do not look so worried, Mr. Sterling," La Raniella said, cupping his cheek delicate with her gloved fingers. "You tell me, would I ever miss a chance to cross fork with knife if you are de chef—could such be possible, mon cheri?"

The butler had swelled with pride at her words to the point where the others did not think it wise to argue. Besides, they agreed, if Ellen and La Raniella could not take care of themselves, who could?

By noontime all the men in the penthouse were both awake and alert. When they went to survey what damage might remain, Legrasse and Quinn each marveled at the degree to which Ravenwood's penthouse had been repaired. Except for their prisoner, all of the dead assassins had been removed. The broken furniture and shattered windows had been replaced. Most of the blood stains had been completely eradicated and even the majority of the bullet holes in the walls had been repaired, although it was too soon for those areas to be repainted.

Legrasse set immediately to going through the personal effects of the invaders. His efforts, sadly, came to little effect. The men had been professionals. The sashes they wore as belts had contained what the Black Bat recognized as throwing weapons, and their sleeves had contained hidden pockets filled with other oddities, such as flash powders and the such, but none of them had so much as a matchbook that might indicate their source of origin.

Knowing that the inspector's investigation was certain to be thorough enough, the Black Bat instead turned to looking for clues in another direction. Assuring his men that he and a rested Legrasse could look after the penthouse for the time being, he sent them to search through their various contacts to see if they could discover anything about the assassins. It was a very-small-needle in an extremely-large-haystack kind of assignment, but both men were extremely loyal to Quinn and desperately wanted to help. It would give them something to do, and as the Bat told himself;

Who knows, it's a long shot, but with a little luck they might even find something.

Waiting for lunch to be served, the inspector and Quinn sat at the dining room table. Neither had spoken for quite some time for the simple fact they had nothing to say. With the Nameless One removed from the picture they were feeling vulnerable—naked to their enemies. With their host incapacitated they felt direction-less—alone.

To the one side of the table were the ragged piles of books, pamphlets and manuscripts Legrasse and Ravenwood had been reviewing earlier. To the other side were various piles of the assassins' belongings. Absently playing with one of the invaders' devices, a flat, star-shaped piece of metal with highly sharpened edges—ones he suspected might be coated with poison due to a slight discoloration at their points—Quinn finally broke their deafening silence, offering;

"All right, so far we have nothing. Or at least, we're thinking we have nothing. What do you say, why don't we stop feeling sorry for ourselves and put all our bits and pieces together and see if they come out to something?"

"I've already jotted down a list," answered Legrasse, his tone weary, annoyed—not with Quinn, but with himself. "Doesn't seem to be much there, though. But, maybe that's merely your so correctly-labeled self-pity talking. Perhaps if I were to read what I have aloud, you know, sometimes hearing a thing jogs different parts of the brain."

"True enough. What have we got?"

"Well, we know our happy house-breakers were all Japanese. We know they were all male, that they called themselves 'ninjas.' whatever that might be…"

"Oh, I found the answer to that one, at least," said Quinn. "Sterling pointed out one of Ravenwood's books, A History of the World's Secret and Hidden Societies. Thumbed through that for a while and finally found an illustration in the section on the Orient that matched up perfect. They're Japs, all right. Silent killers—part assassin, part magician. Not real magic, stage stuff. Trained in all sorts of fighting techniques—supposed to be pretty dangerous fellows, actually."

"Well, we certainly made short work of them last night."

"True," agreed the Black Bat, a trace of a smile crossing his lips. Sighing, though, he added, "And, as much as I'd like to pat myself on the back and just let it go at that, I think the truth is we caught them off-guard."

"It's the truth, all right," agreed Legrasse. His tone, shifting to something less than agreeable, he added, "They swung in here expecting to find us choking, or even unconscious. By the time they found their gas and smoke were useless, they were already dead."

"Correct me if I'm wrong, but you don't sound happy about the fact we lived."

"Oh, well, of course it's not that, Mr. Quinn," answered the inspector. "Obviously. It's just... how can I explain... ever since I found myself being pulled into this voodoo, witchcraft, sorcery... whatever you want to call it, I've longed for... how do I say this without sounding the complete fool... just a good clean fight. Does that make any sense to you?"

"More than you can imagine, brother," said the Bat, nodding as he did so. Taking a sip from a glass of water he had brought out with him, but so far not touched, he went on, saying;

"I mean, I can't compare with you when it comes to this stuff, it seems, but I've had my own run in with some of this other-dimensional, come-from-outer-space, spit-out-of-Hell crap and I... I didn't like it."

The two men looked at each other then, saying nothing, simply staring. The Black Bat studied the inspector's face, his gaze tracing the deep lines set across his brow, around his eyes. The masked avenger read the weariness in them, the fatigue. He found no fear—at least, not that of a coward. He saw not fear of death, or even pain. No, what he saw in Legrasse's eyes was the fear that humanity might be exterminated, the fear he might not be able to hold the line, to keep back the soulless terrors clamoring to swallow all of mankind whole.

And, as the inspector stared back, he saw much the same thing in his counterpart. Without his hero's mask, or even his dark glasses, Tony Quinn's face was a horror to behold. He was, it had to be admitted, a quite handsome man, every part of him, except his eyes. Those were surrounded by hundreds of black and ugly scars, spider webs of ruined flesh that bespoke a terrible physical agony upon which Legrasse did not wish to dwell. The thought of it made him more than a little uneasy, knowing that the casual young man across from him had once had such done to him on purpose.

Even when laboring to extract information from their prisoner, the pair of them had certainly made the man feel pain, but neither of them had done him any permanent damage. It simply was not in their nature to do such, despite the stakes. Indeed, as the comparison curled its way into the inspector's mind, he suddenly coughed, breaking eye contact with Quinn, saying;

"Damn it all, you see, that's what comes of dwelling on these horrors. The two of us, grown men, feeling the hebe jebe jitters like school children walking past a dark house with broken windows."

"When it's all said and done," asked the Bat quietly, "Isn't that what we are right now? I'll admit, it's how I feel."

"Well then, gentlemen," interrupted Sterling, coming in from the next room, a newly arrived Ellen and Madame La Raniella behind him, "might I take your mind off such gloomy notions and interrupt to say that luncheon shall be served as soon as I can clear the table." As all gathered sounded their approval, the butler added;

"Oh, and I feel I should mention, your prisoner in the other room..."

"Yes, tight-lipped Tom," growled Legrasse, his voice still weary. "What about him?"

"When I asked him if he would like some lunch, he told me he wanted to speak to you."

"What about?"

"Apparently," answered the butler, his attention focused on his task of clearing the table more than anything else, "he wants to tell you who sent him."

Chapter 24

SOME FIFTEEN MINUTES LATER, EVERYONE IN THE PENTHOUSE WAS seated around the dining room table except for Sterling. Although invited to join the rest, the thought of eating with those he was to serve was simply too foreign a concept to the manservant for him to be able to handle. Ravenwood, although barely able to leave his bed, had insisted on being present during the further interrogation of the prisoner. The others had not argued with his decision if for no other reason they valued the young mystic's occult abilities. If the prisoner tried to lie to them, their host was certain to know the truth.

To either side of Ravenwood sat Ellen and La Raniella. Next to the Domino Lady sat Legrasse, next to the witch woman was the Bat. This allowed the men to position their prisoner at the opposite end of the table from Ravenwood, with one of them to either side of him—just in case.

It had to be admitted, however, that none present thought the man could be planning anything. He seemed far too subdued, too intensely thoughtful, as if he had come to some sort of major decision. Ravenwood, after studying the would-be-assassin for several moments, both physically as well as with his extra abilities, finally declared he wished they might eat first and then move on to the questioning. As he put it;

"I'll be blunt. Everyone here is hungry. If we delay eating, it's quite possible we might believe some falsehood simply because we wish to dine. Or that our guest might agree to something said which isn't true, simply because he wishes to dine."

"Oh, yes—I've seen that happen," said Legrasse. Nodding, Quinn added;

"I was D.A. in this town—believe me, truer words were never spoken."

"There you have it," said Ravenwood quietly. "Besides, in times of crisis Sterling always seems to come through with the most amazing creations. I believe he thinks food has the power to distract people from their troubles."

"If he believes that," said Ellen, "then he certainly knows more about women than any man should."

The fact that everyone around the table, outside of their prisoner, at the very least smiled at the blonde's comment gave Legrasse a great deal of encouragement. They had all been through terror, and the blackest of evils, each one of them enduring far more than they had ever known previous. La Raniella and Ravenwood, of course, had seen much of the black and grasping horrors which could snake unbidden from around the loose corners of the beyond.

"Which," the young mystic mused, "could be why our foe arranged for me to be removed from the picture by a physical assault."

The Black Bat had once had his own run in with one kind of eldritch terror, a story he told the inspector earlier when the two had been searching through Ravenwood's books. Legrasse had told him a tale of his own to reciprocate. Some may have thought it a waste of time, but it brought the two, perhaps not closer together, but at least to the point where they could understand one another better.

It was Ellen upon whom Legrasse centered the bulk of his concern. She had been abused by their foe the worst, he felt. Perhaps she merely touched some previously unknown paternal instinct in the old warhorse, but whatever the case, he was grateful to hear her joking once more, the sparkle in her eyes letting him know that it was not merely just some brave front she was maintaining to put the others at ease. She had been knocked off her pins, but had climbed right back up and was ready to take more. Staring at her, he heard a voice from the back of his mind whisper;

If only we were twenty years younger, eh?

The inspector blushed at the thought, embarrassed that there was a part of his brain which could even entertain such notions, especially considering all that had happened. And all that was probably still to come. Hoping no one had noticed his moment of discomfort, Legrasse turned his attention to the afternoon meal's first course which Sterling had just begun to serve. The butler had brought in a soup of which he said;

"It's a Chinese specialty of mine, a light but hearty broth with chunks of well-boiled beef joints, several oriental vegetables, and carrots. It's good for the throat, and marvelous for whetting the appetite. The bowls are small, but the tureen is big. Help yourselves to more, but do remember there is more coming." As he filled Ravenwood's bowl, he whispered to his master;

"I thought I should start with something that didn't require a knife or fork. Our 'guest' at the other end of the table, all the throwing weapons that were found on those people... it seemed prudent, sir."

Ravenwood simply nodded, impressed as always with the range of services Sterling continued to provide him. He also realized the broth was probably all he would be able to consume, considering his injuries, and that by serving it first he was allowing his master to graciously turn down anything heavier, thus saving Legrasse any further embarrassment for the beating he had handed the young man.

The meal was one of the butler's usual spreads. Following his no-sharp-utensils policy, platters of pre-sliced turkey, chicken, roast beef and duck followed, served with platters of sliced tomatoes, celery and peppers. Each person had their own set of four dipping sauces along with a personal tray of pickles, olives and other finger-appropriate treats. Dessert was another spoonable affair, strawberries in syrup poured over ice cream and pound cake. By the time it came, half those at the table were begging Sterling for mercy.

As the butler cleared away the last traces of the meal, looking as please with himself as any man could, the others turned their attention to the lone assassin left alive from the previous night's assault. The man had not eaten anything after the broth, although he had allowed himself a second bowl of that. It did not seem to any of the others that he was depriving himself, it simply appeared to be his way.

Not actually caring to any great degree if he had gotten enough to eat, Legrasse was the first to thrust aside what few pleasantries the group had shown the invader in favor of getting down to tactics. Turning toward the ninja leader, he said to the man;

"Very well, we've established that you speak English. We also proved to ourselves that you're quite a hard nut to crack, and by that I mean, we put you through the mill, and you told us basically nothing." His head tilted at an odd angle, the inspector moved forward on the man, his voice crackling with a dark edge as he growled;

"Now, after taking what we had to dish out and giving us not so much as a note, suddenly you decide you want to start singing arias to us. Call me unappreciative, but if you don't mind, I'd like to know why."

The man turned his head toward Legrasse slowly. As one might expect, the assassin had kept to himself during the luncheon, neither speaking to anyone nor even making eye contact with them. He had sat his place quietly, sipping his broth and simply waiting for the moment which had finally arrived.

Now, as he raised his head to Legrasse, the inspector studied the invader the way any policeman would any prisoner during an interrogation. Legrasse had done so when the man had stoically taken all the physical, verbal and mental abuse he and the Bat could dish out. During his years on the force, the inspector had been present when hundreds of different hard cases had finally decided to talk over the years. Such was nothing new to him. Murderers, rapists, robbers, mental defectives and every other type of gutter scum had reached that moment in his presence, and he thought he had seen every reaction they were capable of generating.

As he looked into the eyes of the ninja leader, however, Legrasse was somewhat startled to realize that the old adage about there always being something new under the sun to behold might actually hold water. In the past he had seen such men's eyes show him plenty of fear, much of doubt and greed and every other emotion connected to venal self-interest which had ever manifested itself in the human condition.

This was the first time, however, he stared into the face of such a cold-blooded killer and found shame.

This, thought Legrasse, is about to get very interesting.

As to how correct he was, the inspector had no idea.

Chapter 25

"My name," began the assassin, "I know, is not important to you. But still, as a thing I would like to believe might again know honor, I will tell it to you. It is Koji Matsuriki. I am a soldier in the Japanese imperial army. I will tell you why I and my men were sent here, what our mission was, what our leaders hope to accomplish—all of it. I will also tell you why I have decided to do so. When I am done, if you all agree that you believe my words, you will grant me one request."

Those seated around the table remained silent, not certain how to answer. After an awkwardly long moment, however, Ravenwood finally answered the man, telling him, "If it is something reasonable, something we can grant in good conscience... I don't see why not."

"I would tell you something," added Madame La Raniella in a threatening tone, "not to save you pain, but to keep us from wasting too much time—we will know if you are lying."

"I suspected as much," Matsuriki assured the woman. "It was one of the main reasons I decided to work with you people. Please to understand... this has nothing to do with any desire on my part to help you specifically. I do so for my own reasons."

"That's fine," growled Legrasse. "Just hurry up and do it, if you don't mind?" The former assassin looked down to the table, hiding his eyes. None thought he was about to attempt an escape, or to continue the earlier hostilities. For one thing, only his hands had been freed for the meal. As he began to speak once more, the tone in his voice was even more assurance he meant no further harm.

"Our countries, Japan and the United States, will soon be at war. It is only a matter of time. Trust my words on this matter. It is a thing of fact, not opinion. With this to consider, my superior, General Hiramashi, is determined to enter into such a conflict from a position of strength. Most of the imperial staff are in complete agreement with him."

"Never a reporter around when you need them..."

The Bat had only meant his quip for his own ears. When several of the others turned and stared at him, the masked avenger put up his hands sheepishly, making silent apology for his interruption.

"As in any war, it is thought best that the crippling, or even the destruction of your country without the necessity of any troops or large scale invasion would be the most desirable. To this end, the high command has turned toward magic. The storms circling your nation, they call forth a terrible growth. I do not understand how this is done, but I know what is happening."

"You mean the vines," asked Ellen. "Tentacles, whatever they are?" Matsuriki nodded.

"They are extensions. Somehow, the storm allows a monstrous, mindless fungus of some sort to leak into our world. It is growing beneath your country now. Those first searching grapples, they are nothing. When the circle is complete, they will be everywhere, and they will be endless."

"You mean there's a giant... what, a big mushroom," asked Quinn, "growing under the country? And these snaking things, they're, they're what?"

"They are your doom."

"This guy's like a radio drama," snapped Ellen. Trying to get the proceedings back on track, she asked, "So whose big idea is this all?"

"Our German allies..." Matsuriki said the last word with a clear disgust, his tone angry and yet deeply sad at the same time. So great was his emotion he was forced to pause for a few seconds before finally continuing, saying;

"They wish America eliminated as well. They see the clear threat you pose. They are also at this moment combing the world for ancient means to make battle against their enemies. One such means they traced to China. Since this backward land is under our sway, they gave the information they had to us, the agreement made that if successful, if what they suspected to be there was found, that it would be used against America."

"Look, I graduated college so I wouldn't have to deal with any more lectures," said Ellen. "Could we get this down to the important details?"

"All is haste to you people." Matsuriki gave his answer with more pity than rancor, but he also took the blonde's meaning. With a quite humble nod in her direction, the one-time assassin said, "Some one hundred years ago, two Germans journeyed to a monastery high in the Chinese mountains, looking for a certain book. They..."

"Oh, no." Everyone's gaze turned toward Ravenwood. The young man, face blanched white with horror, stared accusingly at their prisoner as he said, "Friedrich von Junzt, Gottfried Mülder... you're saying the Nazis have read The Secret Mysteries of Asia—" When Matsuriki nodded sadly, Ravenwood added in a terrified whisper, "you're telling us that those murderous... they've got their hands on the *Ghorl Nigral!*"

"The—the *what?*"

"The *Ghorl Nigral*, inspector. *The Book of Night*. The ancient legends say it was actually discovered by a wizard of another world, that he stole it from the creatures who wrote it and hid it away. It's long been believed that somehow a copy of it made it's way to Earth, was hidden in the city of Yian-Ho..." The young mystic's eyes glazed over for only a moment, then he snapped back to reality, spitting his words with all the energy he could muster.

"This is how they have played with us so easily. This damned thing is what they're using to attack the country... the storms, the burrowers beneath..." and then, his eyes locking onto the black-garbed assassin at the other end of the table from him, Ravenwood cursed;

"This is how this goddamned bastards were able to destroy the

Nameless One... it all makes a terrible sense. I couldn't understand it before... thought we were only up against men, men using magic, but common magic, reasonable... but, but now... oh my God... the *Ghorl Nigral*..."

"This is bad, I take it?"

"Mr. Quinn," answered Ravenwood, "You have no idea. None. If these monsters learn all..." the young mystic laughed at his own words, realizing even he was not comprehending the full enormity of what they had been told. Cackling, his voice straining, he shouted;

"All? All? If they master even a tenth of what that cursed scripture is feared to hold, there is no telling what evils they might..." And then, Ravenwood stopped, his mind retreating from the fantastic to the mundane. Again eyeing Matsuriki, he demanded;

"How did you get the book from the monks?"

"We took it."

"I can't believe it," replied the young mystic angrily. "Those men had a sacred trust to keep that book safely guarded, out of the hands of vile and corruptible humanity. There's no way they would simply let you take it."

"You are correct in this assumption," answered the prisoner quietly. "My men and I were made to parachute into the mountains. Only our superb ninja training allowed as many of us to survive as did so. When we entered the city, we went straight to the head monk—demanded the book. He refused us."

"And you killed him," offered Legrasse.

"Yes," replied Matsuriki. "I delivered the stroke myself. It was distasteful, but I believed this demonstration would prove we were not to be dismissed. The old monk's second, he walked up to me. I truly believed he was going to take me to the book at that point. When I demanded it from him, the man took the end of my sword and moved it, positioning it against his heart." Staring directly into Legrasse's eyes then, Matsuriki explained;

"I did not want to murder this holy man. There was no need. It was just a book—" At that point a lone tear broke from the prisoner's eye. His voice close to shattering, he swallowed a deep breath, and then in a tone far-away, one haunted with pain, he told those gathered;

"The monk threw himself onto my blade. He pushed his way

onto my sword, then stood there, his blood bursting forth from his body, splashing me, rolling down the length... soaking me, the ground. He stared, he just stared... until he fell, dragging my sword from my hand."

Another pause followed. There was no question among those at the table. Even without Ravenwood's intuitive abilities, they would have believed him. Before any of them could comment, Matsuriki continued.

"My sword shattered when it hit the ground. I was frozen with horror at what had happened—at what I had caused. My men, seeing this occurrence differently, took the breaking of my sword as a terrible offense. They put all the monks to death, then ransacked the city until they found the accursed book. We were welcomed home as heroes. The book was immediately set upon by the imperial council and the priests they brought in to... to put their plan into operation."

"That second monk," offered La Raniella, sadness and hesitation mixed in equal parts in her voice, "he, that really was not your fault."

"Yes," the assassin answered. "It was. All men are responsible for their actions, even those things which they allow to happen through their own... lack of action... inaction. Is that the correct word?"

"It's close enough," answered Legrasse quietly. Taking a deep breath, letting it out slowly, the inspector asked, "well, that tells us about the storms and the such. But last night... what was that all about?"

"After they succeeded in eliminating he whom you called the Nameless One, they lost the ability to study you from afar. Some kind of supernatural interference. The problem was not explained. We were merely given our orders by radio to... you must understand, my superiors... they fear you."

"Little ol' us," asked Ellen in a mock southern accent. "I do declare you'll turn my head."

"We were stationed here, in your country... in case a more physical force was needed to help their plans along. We received our instructions last night. We were ordered to attack immediately... to kill all within. My men—so young, so... eager... foolish—"

"All right," said the Black Bat, rubbing his hands together. "We know 'who' and we know 'why.' We've even got a good idea of 'how' and a handle on 'when.' I think if our boy here gives us 'where,' we can maybe do something about all this."

"If you mean from where is the attack being launched, the base for the operations is in the Tokara chain, a string of small islands running out from the southernmost tip of Japan. It is a lump of rock to the south of Yokoate, so small it was never named. But, you could not hope to do anything to stop them."

"Why not?"

"Because, the last storm will begin tonight. The island is thousands of miles from here. And, even if you could reach it, it is nothing but one large military complex. There is nothing there but soldiers, weapons and the priests. You could not possibly make it there in time. And if you did, you would only be killed. It is impossible."

"Bah, impossible," spat Madame La Raniella. "As dey Wonderland writer said, 'sometimes I believe six impossible things before breakfast.' It is already past luncheon. I think your impossible could maybe be put to the test."

Noting the strong sound of hope in the witch woman's voice, all eyes turned to stare at La Raniella, their owners silent in anticipation of whatever she might say next. Feigning ignorance of their excitement, the black woman made a show of pulling the wrinkles free from one of her gloves, then "noticing" the eager looks on the faces of all the others, she asked;

"Oh, you were thinking I might have an idea. Oh my, I would be so sorry to disappoint you... so I will not. I believe I have the answer to how you might reach dis island."

Chapter 26

THE TRIP TO LOWER MANHATTAN TOOK LESS THAN HALF AN HOUR thanks to Sterling's superior driving skills, coupled with the butler's intimate knowledge of the city's traffic light patterns. Madame la Raniella had instructed the others to pack for battle—to prepare themselves as if they were going to be at the island Matsuriki had described within a few hours. After that she had left for home, giving the others her address, telling them to be there at 7:00 that evening.

"What I have in mind, it works best between de phases of the sun and moon, de light and dark. I will also need time to make some preparations—and to find someplace where I can send my husband for the evening."

"Why's that," asked Quinn. "He not comfortable around all the supernatural stuff and the such?"

"Oh my, no," answered La Raniella, her lips forming a delightful smile. "He is not comfortable around our dear inspector. Is he, mon cheri?"

Legrasse colored, his face settling into a dark and unamused scowl. None bothered to ask to what the witch woman was referring. Each decided on their own idea of what the tension might be

8

between the two men. It seemed the wiser course than asking about it. Instead, the team set about making the preparations La Raniella had suggested.

All that needed to be accomplished was done so without a great deal of effort. Legrasse and Ellen merely had to pack the bags they had brought to New York City to have everything they owned in that part of the country within reach. Noting their extreme lack of firepower, Quinn offered to beef up their armaments. Both were happy to accept, thus when he called his man O'Leary to bring him the supplies he himself wished to carry, he added their requests to the shopping list.

Ravenwood, it was decided by all, including the young man himself, was simply in no shape to accompany them. Though none of his bones had been broken, he could not move without at least a cane due to several quite severe sprains. On top of those, Legrasse had also rattled the young mystic's brain against his skull so severely that he was still suffering from a persistent ringing which refused to dissipate very quickly. As they prepared to leave his penthouse Ravenwood, his face ill-concealing his obvious disappointment, had confided to them;

"I feel somewhat the fool, not going with you. I gathered you here, placed you in this danger..."

"You prepared us," Ellen corrected, "for the danger descending on all the country. You kept us from stumbling in the dark, from going up against all of this on our own and simply being wiped out. And let me tell you, cutie, a girl appreciates things like that." Running a single nail playful under his chin, the blonde cooed;

"You are rich—right?" While the others chuckled, Legrasse took the young man's hand, shaking it as he said;

"Again, sorry I wasn't able to resist that—"

"Please," Ravenwood cut the inspector off. "There was nothing any of us could do then. The only thing you have to apologize to me for, my friend, is doing such a bang-up job of cleaning my clock that I can't come along and help avenge the Nameless One's passing."

"Speaking of the Nameless One, you're sure about what you said, right," the Black Bat asked of Matsuriki. "I mean, these friends of yours we're going to be dropping in on, they got no idea we're coming to party—yes?"

Matsuriki nodded. Since Madame La Raniella had left earlier and the group's questions of him had ended, the one-time assassin had sat quietly in a corner. To those who bothered to consider his mood, he seemed to be wrestling with some sort of decision. Needing to answer the Bat's question, however, brought him back to the present. Finally lifting his head, the ninja rose from his chair and said to Legrasse;

"Sir, may I take it you are pleased with the answers I have given to you?" When the inspector said that he was, the one-time assassin nodded, more to himself than anyone else, saying;

"Good. Then before you leave, I would remind you of that which I said earlier, that if you found my answers to be as you wished, that I would make a request of you."

"We do have to be off," the inspector reminded him, "but if it's something quick... or that young master Ravenwood here might be able to handle—"

"No, this would take a stronger arm than his." Crossing to the side table where his, as well as the weapons of his comrades still remained—he had been allowed the freedom to move after his earlier confessions—Matsuriki pulled two of the swords piled there free. He chose one short and one long, checked their cutting edges, and then returned to where Legrasse stood waiting. Handing the longer one to him, hilt first, he said;

"By not refusing to slaughter helpless monks, I made a mockery of all I hold dear. I allowed my men to follow me down that path, and then led them clumsily here to their deaths. There is only one way I might regain my honor now." And then, the former assassin knelt on the floor in front of the inspector, facing away from him.

"After making the symbolic entry cut, it is the rare individual who still has the strength to complete... it is customary to have a second who, if he feels honor has been satisfied, will grant a quick release."

As Matsuriki prepared to disembowel himself, what he was actually asking of Legrasse became shockingly clear to all gathered. Ellen and Ravenwood both shouted for them to stop, Quinn somewhat torn as to how he felt. Long blade in hand, the inspector touched it to the ninja's shoulder, and then spoke to him quietly.

"Listen, I'm not going to argue custom with you. Who am I to tell you what to believe? Besides, in New Orleans, I've seen every kind of pagan, hoodoo ritual ever created. Your beliefs are your beliefs, but I'm going to ask you to give me a moment before you start bleeding all over what I'm certain must be a very expensive rug."

Matsuriki did not respond verbally, nor turn to look at Legrasse, but he did cease moving. Sensing that was the best he was going to get out of the man, the inspector continued, saying;

"You feel you've been badly used, and I agree. You feel you've been a tool used to commit atrocities, and I won't say you nay on that count, either. Because of all this, you're now thinking that the only way to make up for the blood you've spilled is to spill some of your own, and I'm not certain I can find an argument against that notion."

"Legrasse!" Ellen's voice filled the room, but so did the inspector's violent retort.

"Quiet," he shouted at the Domino Lady. "This doesn't concern you—this is between men!" Legrasse lowered his head and closed his eyes, squeezing their lids hard one against the other. He needed the moment to calm himself, indeed, to even figure out what it was he wanted to say. Knowing he could not wait long, though, he opened his eyes again, practically hissing;

"Now—you listen to me. You want to gut yourself, take the easy way out, fine enough. All I know of you so far is that you're murderous scum, and that the world would be better off without you. But, I also say, if you really want to make things up to the universe, then show the goddamned universe you really mean it."

The ninja's hands wavered at Legrasse's words, his head turning to look into the inspector's eyes, to see if what he might find there was as true as what he had heard.

"Come with us," Legrasse offered. "You want to spill your blood, do it showing those sons of bitches that ordered you to become a monster that you're a man—your own man—and that you'll do as you please. You want to die, die getting that terrible book out of those goddamned bastards' hands." As a new light came into Matsuriki's eyes, a new idea the likes of which he had never seriously considered before rushing through his mind, the inspector thundered;

"Help us. You know this island. If we have one chance to succeed, it rests on you, on you being man enough to bear the pain of your shame long enough to shove it down the throats of those who gave it to you!" Legrasse, unblinking, his face as stern as a Baptist preacher in his pulpit, sucked down a deep breath, then spat;

"Then, by God, after we've wiped them all off the face of the planet, if you still want to knife up your guts, I'll be happy to chop your damn head off of your shoulders."

Matsuriki remained on the floor for a terrible long passage of time. None present could guess at its length, none thought to check their timepieces, or to consult one of the many clocks all about. It would have been too rude, too intrusive on the moment, as if saying it could possibly belong to anyone other than the man kneeling on the floor with the sword pressed ever so firmly against his abdomen. Second after second passed, all eyes focused in one direction, all breaths held as one. And then, finally, Koji Matsuriki, chief of assassins, master ninja, rose from the floor and bowed respectfully to Legrasse.

Silently, he moved to the side table where his weapons and those of his fellows were stacked earlier. Swiftly he refilled the many hidden pockets of his costume. Then, finding a pair of swords he found suitable for what awaited him, he slid them into position behind his sash, saying;

"If you please, let us attend to the wiping out of all 'sons of bitches' off the face of the planet. I believe I might be man enough to bear the pain of my shame after all." As the others relaxed, the warrior smiled grimly at Legrasse, telling him;

"Besides, if I still want to knife up my guts, I know you'll be happy to chop my damn head off of my shoulders."

And then, the ninja turned on his heel, walking off to join the others at the doorway leading to the penthouse's elevator. Standing alone in the dining room, Legrasse closed his eyes, squeezing off the slightest prayer to his Maker. Then, opening them once more, he found himself smiling, grinning actually, from ear to ear, as he said aloud;

"Now. Now we have a chance."

Chapter 27

"OKAY, MATES," SAID THE CAPTAIN, HIS VOICE LOW, EYES FIXED HARD, trying to penetrate the ebony gloom all about them. "I think we're almost ready for you four to gather your kits and prepare to make an exit."

The zeppelin tore silently through the dark night sky over the Pacific. Beneath it the water appeared calm, though it was too soon for anyone to be able to tell for certain. The moon was barely a sliver, thus cutting the light it could reflect to a bare minimum. Nor were there many stars visible that night, either. Thick, ominous clouds had begun to gather when their voyage was not even half completed, and had continued to thicken the entire time.

"Hope you four can make landfall before this storm hits," the captain mused. His eyes constantly scanning the view before his ship, he did not like the feeling he was picking up from the surrounding atmosphere. When they had launched from Australia the weather forecast had called for clear skies and smooth sailing. Granted, meteorology was still for all intents and purposes an infant science, but normally those predictions the captain received from the national board were usually at least somewhat close to the mark.

Closer than they were that night, anyway.

"You and me both, skipper," answered the Black Bat. Making a last check of all the various pockets and pouches his costume contained, satisfying himself that each was tightly sealed, he said, "This is going to be a tough enough night without having it rain, too. Right, inspector?"

Legrasse did not answer. He was not ignoring Quinn so much as he was ignoring the world. Not so much tired as simply contemplative, he sat with his head nestled against the gondola wall, palms resting on his knees, eyes closed. Outwardly he appeared calm, almost peaceful. Such was not the case. Within his mind, he had drifted back to their departure from New York City, an event that had left him somewhat shaken.

I'm not certain I'm ever going to understand all of this damn hocus pocus, he thought bitterly, only his iron will keeping his limbs from trembling. Sweet Jesus, the deeper I delve into all of this, the more I attempt to learn...

The inspector paused for a moment, not wishing to complete his thought. A part of his mind, chuckling at such a desire, snarled at him contemptuously, growling—

Oh, just admit it, you're an old fool who's never going to survive this madness. Ravenwood, La Raniella, Zarnak... these people are bloody magicians, for Christ's sake. You, you could study all this for the rest of your life and you wouldn't know a tenth of what any of them know.

Legrasse frowned at that thought, not so much over the agreement he felt toward it, but the fact it was quite possible his life might not last more than a handful of hours from that point, anyway. When he and the others had arrived at the brownstone home of Madame La Raniella, he had been totally unprepared for what she had in store for them all. Taking them to a particularly dark corner of her building's basement, she lit several candles. One by one they illuminated a space on the floor some four feet in diameter. It was solid, bare cement—unblemished, unadorned. Moving into the area, the witch woman took down a handful of curved pieces of bamboo from a nearby shelf.

The sections of dried grass proved to fit smoothly one into another, making what appeared to be a perfect circle. La Raniella placed the circle on the floor, then returned to the shelf from where she had taken the bamboo to fetch forth a highly polished gray-green stone. Placing this in the center of the circle, she told the quartet with her;

"What I have created here is what is called, 'dey Dollins Circle.' Those standing within one can move through time and space to wherever they might find another such device."

"Wha—what?" Ellen's raised eyebrow and short exclamation only expressed what all present felt. Before more such sentiments could follow, La Raniella explained;

"True, dis be an ancient, and dangerous magic. But tell me true, after all dat which you have seen dese past two days, what is one more little oddity? Listen and accept, for time is running down dey slender thread of opportunity for all of us. What action can be taken, must be taken now."

"And this will take us to Japan," asked Matsuriki, his tone torn between disbelief and wonder.

"No. It can only take you to another such circle. I have contacted people sympathetic to our cause in Australia. By now dey should have completed assembling their own circle." Closing her eyes for a moment, the witch woman said softly;

"Dey have. Can you not feel it, vibrating in the air. Their Dollins, it calls to this one, waiting to guide you to it. Its creators, once you have all passed through, dey will take you to an airfield where transportation of dey more conventional type will take you to your island."

Of course, it had taken all of those assembled a while to comprehend what they were being told. The enormity of the idea was in some ways almost too callosal for any of them to comprehend. In some ways, as La Raniella had told them, it should have been nothing much, simply another wild insanity about which they might wrap their heads. But for Legrasse, it had been the spine-shattering straw which had collapsed his camel-like fortitude.

As the witch woman had explained the sensations they would feel and the such during transit, how to avoid being seen by other travelers moving through the dreamplane at the same time, et cetera, the inspector had failed to take note of much of anything she said. Within his mind, he found a growing panic whirling his thoughts about, hurling them against the walls of his brain, shattering them one after another.

When does it end, he wondered. When do you finally get some

handle on it all? When can you close the book, knowing you've finally reached the goddamned end?

The unbidden thoughts filling his mind disturbed Legrasse mightily. Had he seen too much, been tested too often? He had no way to answer his own question. He was certainly no coward. That had been proved too many times over to be considered. But bravery, he knew, came from the individual's ability to measure themselves against whatever it might be they were to go up against.

And when, he asked himself tersely, do we ever get the opportunity to do that anymore?

Staring down at the bamboo circle on the floor, the inspector found fear drifting across his mind, radiating out of his skull, down his spine, filtering outward into his other limbs, a paralyzing whisper creeping through his nerves and flesh and blood. It passed as quickly as it arose, filtering outward through his skin as if pushed free from his body by some separate, intervening power.

So shaken was Legrasse by the experience, he insisted on stepping through the circle first, claiming that if he showed everyone how safe and easy it was, it would put them more at ease, and that if it did not work, tearing him into bloody pieces or stranding him in some unsuspected limbo then the others could be saved for some even more horrible fate.

"And that's what we love about you, John," Ellen had teased. "You're sunny disposition."

The inspector grinned at the blonde's comment, her charms as intoxicating to him in the dark and mysterious cellar as they would have been on the gayest of dance floors. As he gathered up the back pack of supplies he had elected to carry and stepped one foot into the circle, La Raniella caught hold of his arm. Stopping him gently, she said;

"Listen, you old weed, dis world not done needing you yet. You don't get foolish on it, not come back. You got big work ahead of you, John Raymond. Don't be thinking there be others ready to fill your shoes. Feet your size only come so often."

A proper woman, as well as a married one, La Raniella did not hug the inspector to her, or make any other type of overt gesture. Rather she simply tightened her grip slightly, stared into Legrasse's eyes for a moment, and then released him to finish moving inside the circle. Seconds later, he found himself in a oddly-shaped room in Australia where a plump, leathery-faced woman asked the inspector if he would care for a cup of tea. Before she could pour one for him, Matsuriki appeared in the circle, then the Bat behind him. The delay between his arrival and then Ellen's seemed a trifle longer than the others, but considering all that awaited them he chose not to bother questioning it.

Let sleeping dogs snore, he told himself. We've got enough to worry about.

Within minutes of their arrival, a friendly middle-aged man answering to the name Mulberry ushered them outside to his waiting vehicle, an unusual half-bus, half-truck kind of affair, the origins of which the quartet could only guess after. In less than twenty minutes he had them at the airfield where Madame La Raniella had arranged for their transportation. The zeppelin captain and his crew were willing to undertake the mission thanks to both their desire to see Japanese encroachment contained, as well as the substantial retainer the witch woman had made certain Ravenwood wired to them.

After that, the four adventurers were in the air in less than an hour from having stepped through the gateway. Only a handful of hours later, they were within sight of their destination. Matsuriki had assured the captain the lights in the distance were the island they were seeking. On his word the skipper had his crew make ready to drop the over-sized inflatable rescue raft his passengers would be using to try and reach the island unseen. The ninja insisted on following the raft out the exit door, explaining that he had been trained for such things, that he could recover and inflate the craft before the rest of them were in the water.

All had agreed with his assessment. After that, the Black Bat had taken the plunge into the dark waters below, followed by Ellen who touched Legrasse on the arm as she made ready to jump, telling the inspector;

"Now don't leave me down there by myself with that naughty Quinn too long."

Giving him her most girlish giggle, the Domino Lady then turned and hurled herself and her bags out into the night. Hearing her faint splash, Legrasse stared out into the darkness, his eyes locked on the island fortress far off in the distance. A strange, and as far as he was concerned, quite unexpected calm came over the inspector at that point. Tapping him on the shoulder, the captain asked;

"Ready to take the plunge, sir?"

"No," answered Legrasse honestly. "But then, when has that ever stopped me?"

And, so saying, the one-time inspector of police for the city of New Orleans stepped off the edge of the gondola and plunged into the black waters below.

Chapter 28

IT HAD TAKEN THEM FAR TOO LONG TO GET TO THE ISLAND. TOO LONG for the four of them to get their bearings, to find the raft, find each other, get dry enough to not start shaking, store their gear, assemble their paddles and start making their way toward the faintly lit pile of rock that looked impossibly far away.

Far too long.

Matsuriki and the Black Bat laid claim to the paddles, both insisting that Legrasse and Ellen rest. Neither had any qualms about taking the pair up on their offer. Sitting in the back of the raft, huddled against one another for warmth, Legrasse said quietly;

"It's puzzling, but I must admit I never would have thought the ocean could get quite so cold in the evening." Laughing lightly, the Domino Lady replied;

"That's because you're too used to the temperatures back in the Gulf. Things are always warmer in your neck of the woods. I grew up with the Pacific. It can get plenty cold this time of year."

"Ummmmmhummmm," was the inspector's only comment. Not knowing what else to say, he suddenly found himself in an unexpectedly playful mood. Making his tone one as innocent as possible, he pointed toward the others rowing silently, adding, "I noticed for once you didn't have much to say when the men offered to spare you a chore."

"Well, they're big strong men," she responded in a cartoon caricature of a voice, "and I'm just a helpless little girl. But, what's your excuse?"

"Me?" He said the word with surprise, suddenly realizing how deeply he had thrust himself into a joke which could be so easily turned upon him. Taking the shot he had to admit he roundly deserved, he answered;

"Well, what would you expect, child? Look at me, old and tired, a doddering old relic, worn out, cast aside... why, it's all I can do to drag myself out of bed each morning." Legrasse emphasized his joking by releasing a long, depressing yawn, then gave the Domino Lady a puzzled look, saying;

"Actually, I don't know what makes you... ohhhhhh, wait... now I understand. You're upset because you think I was upbraiding you shirking your responsibilities because you're a woman, not because you're young. I see. You're not upset with me, you're just insecure."

A wicked smile crossed Ellen's face, one perfectly matching the fire flashing in her eyes. Pursing her lips, barely able to contain herself, she answered the inspector.

"Oh, you're good. You must have all the local Scarlet O'Haras lined up around the block. A whole harem of O'Haras probably."

"If I did," answered Legrasse, his voice low, his gaze smoldering, his intentions all too obvious, "not a one of them could compare to you."

And suddenly, all of the playfulness drained out of the two. Ellen, cradled against the inspector for warmth, found herself feeling a touch uncomfortable. It was not because she found the older man objectionable in some manner. Her shift in feelings came more from the surprise of his forwardness. However, if the Domino Lady was caught off guard by Legrasse's statement, she was not the only one. The inspector immediately released Ellen's hand, thoroughly embarrassed by his actions—behavior he could not only not justify to himself, he could not even understand what had made him do so.

Yes, Ellen Patrick was obviously a beautiful, accomplished, marvelously intelligent and highly desirable woman. Perhaps the most magnificent member of the opposite sex he had ever met. Still, they were years apart in age, and about to throw themselves against an overwhelming force of well-armed men. The fate of the entire world was at stake, and for some reason he could not even begin to adequately explain, Legrasse found himself acting like some adolescent.

That's what love does to people, you know.

The inspector shuddered at the thought. Could he be falling in love with the Domino Lady? It was possible, he supposed. It was not as if he was immune to feminine charms. But still, it was also not like him to show interest in a colleague, especially at such a time when there was so much at stake.

Well, he told himself, she is a fairly spectacular colleague.

"John..."

"Yes, dear lady..."

"You've gotten awfully quiet."

"I know," agreed Legrasse in a quiet, hesitant tone, "that's true. And, if you don't mind, I think perhaps it best if I remain that way for a while."

Yes, he told himself, before I say something I regret even more than that which I already have.

Ellen nodded, her look one of gratitude. She did not appear uncomfortable with the idea of Legrasse thinking of her as more than a fellow warrior. Deep down, she had to admit it had taken him so long to act like a normal, ordinary male around her she had begun to wonder if she were losing her touch. After all, even though he acted as if he were some stodgy old grandfather, he was only in his late thirties. And, having watched him battle ninjas, let alone knowing that he had demolished Ravenwood, as well as all his other exploits, Ellen was well aware that John Raymond Legrasse was far from over the hill.

No, if the Domino Lady was grateful for anything, she was feeling the emotion mainly over the fact that his chivalrous treatment of her allowed her the time to compose herself. Because, she found herself flushing from head to toe at the thought, she knew perfectly well that when the inspector had said what he had, had looked into her eyes when he did, that if he had followed through and bent to kiss her, that she would have grabbed onto him and kissed him back—hard.

And not let go.

In fact, she thought, one of the things he seems to like is our independent streak. Maybe I'll just—

"Get ready everyone." Matsuriki's voice was barely above a whisper, just enough to be heard over the lapping of the gentle waves against the side of their raft. "We have arrived."

The Black Bat and the ninja pulled their paddles inside the raft, allowing the craft to drift forward to the jagged shore line. Tossing a line up over a convenient outcropping, Matsuriki pulled the raft in close to shore, then tied it off. Pulling himself up over the rocky edge, he disappeared from sight for several seconds, then leaned back into view, making a hand signal that the others should follow.

The Bat indicated that he would go next. His exit from the raft, up and over the outcropping, was as silent and swift as the ninja's before him. Moving forward carefully to the front of the raft, Ellen and Legrasse handed up all of the equipment the quartet planned on taking with them. Then, as the Bat and Matsuriki separated the gear, Ellen made ready to pull herself up to join them. Her hand on the rope tying the raft off, she first turned to the inspector, simply looked at him for a long second, then whispered;

"You, mister, had better not die up there, because we have got some unfinished business." Taking a single second to allow her words to sink in, she added, "I expect a cup of coffee and your life story when we get out of this."

And then, without waiting for a reply the incredible blonde, maybe even more beautiful to Legrasse in the men's boots, trousers and jacket she had chosen for the assault, pulled herself upward and disappeared into the darkness on the other side of the rocks. Not knowing how he felt about anything that had happened between them, indeed, wondering how such a thing could possibly happen to him, Legrasse merely sighed over the absurdity of the situation. Then, knowing there was no time for such reflection, he pulled himself hand over hand up onto the unnamed Japanese island, saying under his breath;

"Ah well, if nothing else, it is always good to have something to live for."

Chapter 29

THE FOUR MOVED ACROSS THE ISLAND AS QUICKLY, YET QUIETLY AS they possibly could. It had been agreed on the journey over the ocean that their main, their only concern was to get their hands on the *Ghorl Nigral*, or more specifically, to get the horrid thing out of the hands of the trio of wizards who would be using it to cast the last segment of their spell that night—who for all they knew were already bent over the nightmare tome, practicing their evil art.

"If we deny them the book," Matsuriki had assured the others, "then all is over. If the circle is not completed, then the rest will wither."

"So," the Black Bat had commented, "we just have to destroy the book and we're finished. Doesn't sound too hard."

"You don't think they might have made themselves a copy of the spell," asked Ellen. "You know, for a fall back position… just in case."

"I do not believe that would help," the ninja told her. "What we were told when we were sent to recover the book is that it had to be brought back intact. And that above all we had to make certain we had found the original. It seems that many of these magical books are a part of the spell themselves." When Ellen asked what he meant, Matsuriki explained;

"I mean, that if the book, the real book, the one written by the sorceror himself, is not at the center of the casting, then things will not work. It's supposedly why so many people know about magic, but so few can use it."

"Rings true to me," Legrasse had noted. "I admit to not having any great storehouse of knowledge in these matters, but from what I have learned that sounds on the money."

"Then we're agreed," said the Bat. "We find this damn book, burn it, blow it up, get rid of it somehow, and then trot ourselves out of here and celebrate over coffee and doughnuts or whatever we can find."

No one raised any arguments. Legrasse went so far as to name the type of cruller he would prefer and the others agreed, even though in their heart of hearts none of the four thought there was much chance of them living through the night. Matsuriki had drilled them, both on the zeppelin and while they paddled to shore, on the island's defenses—and to the various problems they could possibly face.

The dangers the island held were not the worst part of the entire affair, however. What worried the ninja the most was the fact that they could not be certain where the book would be when they arrived. Which meant they had several hundred men through which they had to make their way, with no clear idea in what direction to carry the battle. Making his best guess, the ninja had told them it was quite possible their objective would be found in the chamber which had been used to cast the first three segments of the spell.

"But," he also observed grimly, "as I assume you all realize, 'quite possible' is not at all a certainty."

That thought was uppermost in all of their minds. In the quiet, making their way through the darkness and light drizzle which had begun to fall, each of them rolled the idea of their mission over in their heads. And, the closer they came to the buildings which just minutes earlier had seemed a dozen miles away, the more ridiculous their position became to all of them. A small army stood between them and their goal, one that would fight to the last man to stop them. Indeed, the idea was coming close to paralyzing some of them when suddenly Matsuriki raised his hand sharply, indicating the others should stay back.

Standing straight, he walked forward, calling out in Japanese. As the others watched from hiding, they saw what the ninja must have heard, some ten soldiers leaving from one building headed for another, marching in a tight formation. The ninja, whom they had learned earlier held the rank of captain, watched the men as they marched by as if he were performing a parade ground inspection. So stern was his visage none of the men dared make eye contact with him. Their job was to stare straight forward. With Matsuriki watching them they were more than happy to do just that.

As the officer in charge of the small squad came up behind his men, the ninja spoke to him for a moment. The officer did not seem reluctant to speak, only to falling out of step with his men. Matsuriki nodded to the officer as he increased his speed to stay in line with his group. Waving the others forward, the ninja started the quartet running immediately as he told them;

"I asked if I was in time to witness the casting of the last spell. They said the wizards are already in the temple."

"What does that mean," asked Ellen, her voice tight, almost shrill. "Is it too late?"

"I do not know," was the only answer Matsuriki had to offer. Breaking into an open run, the ninja headed straight for a large ebony bulk off to their left. As the group came closer the others could see that the shape was three trucks parked next to one another. Lightning unexpectedly split the sky, followed by a deeply ominous thunderclap. Matsuriki set to working close to the rear end of the middle vehicle, ignoring the increasing fury of the storm as he told the others;

"I am going to create a diversion. Once I am finished, we will have some thirty seconds before this truck explodes. With luck it will take the other two with it."

"And what's the plan?"

"I am thinking, Mr. Quinn, that you should head to the left now, engage every one you meet—and kill them. You, Miss Ellen, should go to the right and do the same. The two of you should slay as many as you can, as quickly as possible, and most importantly, as nosily as possible."

"And yourself and myself, sir?"

"We, inspector," Matsuriki answered, his hand pointing off into the distance, "will be heading that way, up the middle."

185

"To the temple, I presume?"

"Unless," Matsuriki turned his head toward the others, a sly grin spreading across his face, "you had a better idea?" Legrasse stared at the ninja for a moment, trying his best to come up with a humorous rejoinder. After several embarrassing seconds of failure, compounded by Ellen giggling in the background, the inspector finally answered;

"Oh, just light the damn bomb."

Matsuriki nodded, striking a match against a rough spot on the truck's side, shielding it from the growing downpour with his gloved hand. As he touched flame to fuse the Black Bat and the Domino Lady both took off in their designated directions. On his feet, the ninja ran at top speed, barely catching up to Legrasse when the first truck suddenly exploded. Shrapnel and burning fuel filled the sky, and when it descended back to earth the blazing fragments set fire to the canvas canopies of the other two trucks. Instantly sirens began to sound from every corner of the island.

"You run pretty fast for an old man," joked Matsuriki.

"Why, didn't you know," answered Legrasse, "learning how to run fast, and knowing when to do so is how you get to be an old man."

Voices began to sound loud enough to be heard over the sirens. The inspector did not need to understand Japanese to recognize their meaning. They had been spotted. Pulling one of his revolvers, he said;

"Well, let's send the bastards to Hell." Pulling free his sword, his eyes twinkling with a wild ferocity, the ninja nodded, answering;

"At the least."

And then, gun fire began to ring out from multiple directions, and the pair were forced to meet the enemy.

Chapter 30

ELLEN WAS THE FIRST OF THE FOUR TO ACTUALLY RUN INTO ANY OF THE enemy troops. She had thought it might feel odd, going into battle in men's clothing, but the notion fled her quickly as combat began. She had turned a corner and suddenly found herself in the middle of six Japanese soldiers—four of them carrying two boxes of belted ammunition between them, the other two moving a large machine gun.

Throwing herself into the cluster, Ellen tackled the quartet carrying the ammo. Stepping in close, she smashed one soldier in the bridge of his nose with her elbow, another with her fist. Both men dropped their burden, wounding their companions as the heavy boxes crashed against them—slamming one on the foot, the other in the knee. While those four shouted out in pain, the other pair lowered the weapon they were transporting to the ground, desperate to defend themselves, but they were too slow. As they fumbled slipping on the rain-slick pavement, the Domino Lady's left hand shot forward twice, crushing the throat of one, blinding the other.

Without stopping, she then twisted around, pulling the pistol strapped to her side at the same time. With four well-placed shots she slaughtered the first soldiers she had disabled. Then, sliding the pistol back into its holster, she reached behind her to one of the two packs she had on her back. Pulling out one of the incendiary grenades the group had been given by their Australian hosts, she overturned the ammunition crates, spilling their contents into a pile. After that, the blonde pulled the grenade's pin, dropped it into the center of the belts, and ran.

Across the way, the sudden explosion followed by what seemed endless gunfire was just the distraction for which the Black Bat had been hoping. As the noise stole the attention of a column of troops heading in the same direction Legrasse and Matsuriki had taken, the masked Avenger threw himself into their midst, a .45 in each hand.

Able to see through the surrounding gloom and pelting downpour as if it were the stroke of cloudless noon, the Bat struck down target after target, slaying fourteen of the soldiers before any of them were even aware of his presence. Holstering the spent pair of automatics with practiced precision, he reached behind himself, easily pulling free the second pair attached to the back of his belt and began firing again. He finished off the column before emptying his second brace of pistols.

Replacing the second set of .45s, the Bat pulled the first two free once more, jamming a fresh clip into each. Then, he headed off in the direction of another set of soldiers, whispering into the darkness;

"As long as I can see you guys, and you can't see me, who knows? We might all survive this thing yet."

At the same time, Legrasse and Matsuriki had reached a point from where the temple was in view. Only some three hundred yards away, the ninja had pointed it out just before he and the inspector had run into an entire squadron of soldiers. With the advantage of surprise, the troops still under the impression the island was being bombed, not that it had been invaded, the pair were able to wade into the startled soldiers, laying waste to them.

Legrasse emptied his first pistol, and then a second. His need to reload at that point might have been the end of him, but Matsuriki threw himself into the attack, slaughtering all in his way. Using the confusion in the air and the close quarters to his advantage, his arms were a blur as he used both his swords at the same time. The ninja made no attempt to bring any sense of form or grace to his attacks. That was for younger men, a thing one saved for competitions. This was a matter of survival—not the preservation of his own life, but of the entire world's.

Matsuriki fought as he did for he had become fully convinced that there was no controlling what was being unleashed beneath America. The wizards in the dark concrete bunker so close at hand were bringing a thing into being that would be thousands of miles in length. Their purpose was to have this monstrosity devour hundreds of millions of people.

How, he wondered, did men incorporate into themselves the thought they could control such a thing? That a beast with an appetite to consume flesh and blood in such hideous quantities could be told "enough," and then locked away like some lapdog?

Bringing his left sword around, he took the arm off one man even as he brought his right up into the groin of another. His slices were crude and his chops were savage. The soldiers he battled were shown no mercy. They were merely wounded to the point where they would fall down and stay out of his way. It pained the ninja to fight so, to use his long-practiced skills in such a barbaric manner, but he had no choice.

"All that is made," he shouted in Japanese, his swords still singing, "can be unmade. All that is lost can be found once more!"

Legrasse did not understand his comrade's words, of course, but he was grateful for the man's presence. So violent were the ninja's attacks upon the soldiers surrounding them that they had lost all interest in the inspector, giving him the precious seconds he needed to reload. He had dropped to one knee to do so, making himself a smaller, less obvious target while filling his pistols. Once he had finished he rose once more, aiming at several soldiers charging from their right. Before he could fire, however, Matsuriki touched the inspector's arm with the edge of one of his swords and shouted;

"No! Save your ammunition. Head for the temple. Leave these to me—they are unimportant. All that matters is stopping the ritual!"

Legrasse did not hesitate. There was no debate within his mind. Matsuriki was right—the ninja's life did not matter. None of their lives mattered. All that was important then was getting inside the temple and stopping the ritual any way possible. To make things easier on the inspector, Matsuriki slid one of his swords into his sash and then reached inside his sleeve. Pulling forth several small envelopes, he dashed their contents against the ground. Immediately there was a blinding flash, one filled with a fiery, reflective smoke which left many of the soldiers about them dazed.

Matsuriki wasted not a moment, his blades flashing, opening arteries, taking off hands, slicing faces open across the eyes of those around him. That they were his countrymen he shoved from his mind. The soldiers were no longer his brothers, cousins, life-long friends. They were no longer even human. To the ninja they were merely inconveniences that had to be dealt with harshly. Finally.

As the screams of the blinded rose all about Matsuriki, the inspector took advantage of the precious seconds that had been purchased for him with blood and ran for the temple. He tried to stay within the shadows, grateful for the growing storm's additional cover, feeling the coward the entire distance. Behind him, somewhere in the darkness the Domino Lady and the Black Bat were searching out soldiers and bringing the battle to them simply to distract all attention to them. They were throwing their lives away for him. The same way Matsuriki was.

All of them, he thought, fighting while I don't. Making themselves heard and seen simply to protect me.

No! The word screamed within his mind, forcing all other thoughts to dissipate. They do not sacrifice themselves for you, but for the same reason for which you sacrifice yourself. Now, shut up, you fool, before your idiocy causes them to do so in vain.

Properly chastised, Legrasse kept moving forward, hiding while others battled, avoid conflict while others fought and bled in his stead. Reaching the temple, the one-time policeman found a doorway that was unguarded and hurried inside. As he moved indoors, he patted his pockets, making certain he still had the grenades he had resisted using so far. Then, hearing voices ahead of him, he pulled one of the hard green eggs free, getting ready to find it a target.

Moving carefully, he did his best to find his way to the section of the bunker being used for the ritual. As the voices he was following grew stronger, he focused on pinpointing their location. Then, when he was certain he had found the right chamber, he grabbed the doorknob before him, turned it and was just ready to throw himself inside when a rifle butt was brought down savagely against the back of his head, knocking him forward into the room, spilling him across the floor and directly into the hands of his waiting enemies.

Chapter 31

LEGRASSE DID NOT PASS OUT FROM THE SAVAGE BLOW, BUT HE WAS dazed beyond his ability to defend himself. Although part of his mind remained crystal clear, knew exactly what was happening all about him, it could not rally his limbs. As the inspector's body plunged headlong into the main area of the temple, soldiers rushed forth, seizing him immediately. Searching his soaking clothing roughly, but efficiently, they stripped him of his weapons, then thrust him forward toward the altar in the middle of the massive room.

Stumbling awkwardly, barely able to maintain an upright position, Legrasse came to a halt a few feet from the cold gray block. Bent over, his hands wrapped around the back of his head holding his throbbing skull, he thought;

Well, you old jackass, I don't think this is the way you were supposed to do this.

"Mr. Lee-gruss," a Japanese man dressed neither as a soldier or priest said, attempting to pronounce the inspector's name. "I am impressed. You found us. Reached us. I must admit, as... police, your skills do you credit."

The speaker was tall for a Japanese, well dressed, his suit obviously made expressly for him, and by a tailor whose shop commanded the most important clientele. Legrasse almost made a comment on how poor the man's English was compared to Matsuriki's, then thought the better of such an idea and remained silent. Considering the scarlet claws of pain still inching their way into his brain, it was not that hard a task to accomplish.

"I knew when air raid sound, it was you. Had to be. Since guns not stop yet, I believe Domino and Bat here, too. Hoping to have them here also. Alive. Makes all better."

"Don't... don't understand."

The agony within his battered head had leveled off, begun to recede, but it was still commanding nearly all of Legrasse's attention. For a moment, the speaker thought perhaps that the inspector was ridiculing his English. Studying him for a moment, however, he let the perceived slight pass. It was obvious to him Legrasse was simply in too much pain. Speaking more slowly, the man said;

"You know why we here. To remove America from path of Japanese destiny. Your country to be destroyed. Last piece of spell tonight. Book say, good to have witness—those not wish spell succeed. Emotion powerful part of these magicks. You hate me, all of this, make spell strong. Fear for loved one, shame over failure, any emotion good for..."

Then, the speaker suddenly went silent—his focus diverted elsewhere. Trying to straighten himself, Legrasse turned weakly to attempt to discover what had taken the man's attention. He spotted the source of the interruption without problem. The soldiers had captured the Domino Lady and the Black Bat. Ellen was still able to walk, although her clothing was torn and covered in blood. Blinking several times to clear his vision, Legrasse noted that the blonde was actually limping, and that she had taken a number of fierce blows. She was, however, in no where near as bad a shape as the Bat.

The inspector could not even determine if Quinn was still alive, so still did his body hang in the grip of those dragging him across the temple floor. Yes, Legrasse realized, he might be playing possum, preparing to strike at the first moment attention was turned away from him, but he did not believe it so. Such would make things too easy, too convenient—like some infantile Saturday afternoon serial. The speaker shouted out to those bringing forth the prisoners, his tone one that bespoke satisfaction. Indeed, the man seemed so pleased, it made Legrasse realize;

They don't know about Matsuriki...

As the thought passed through the inspector's mind, one of the trio of wizards standing behind the altar turned to stare at him, his eyes narrowing. The colorfully garbed figure did so for a handful of seconds, then called out to the speaker. Turning back to Legrasse, the man asked;

"What has so brightened your spirit, Lee-gruss?"

"Ellen..." even saying the single word made the inspector's head throb. "You didn't kill..." The speaker smiled, believing he knew what had inspired the sudden hope the wizard had detected within Legrasse. Giving the men behind the altar a waving hand signal meant to allay their fears, he said;

"No. As I said... alive, you help our cause. Who knows? You may even be present to emperor. There is always time for death— later."

The Black Bat's body was dumped unceremoniously on the poured cement floor near to Legrasse. Ellen was then thrust forward toward him as well. She managed to neither trip over Quinn or stumble into the inspector, but just barely. Other soldiers followed the first group, bringing the bags and weapons belts they had taken from their captives. These were deposited in front of the altar, far out of reach of their owners.

"And now, all are here," said the well-dressed man. Smiling with a deep and abiding satisfaction, he turned to the wizards and nodded. The main figure amidst the trio acknowledged his signal and then pulled away a dark purple cloth which had been covering the top of the poured concrete altar. As he did, Legrasse's eyes went wide as a terrible peal of thunder shook the entire building.

The *Ghorl Nigral*, the inspector realized. *The Book of Night!* Desperately Legrasse looked about, helpless to discover any means at hand through which he could halt the hideous ritual about to take place. If he could not, it meant at the very least the destruction of his country. If Matsuriki was correct, the berobed fools before him were about to destroy the entire world. But, he wondered frantically, what could he do? He was surrounded by armed soldiers. He had nothing but his fists, if he could even walk forward far enough to use them. Ellen and Quinn were worse off than he was. And, with the cessation of screams and gunfire from outside, he was forced to assume no help would be coming from Matsuriki. Bitterly, he thought;

Well, you tried. Rest easy... at least you died with your honor intact.

And then, a voice sounded within Legrasse's head, one that had been with him for some time, but which had not revealed itself for fear of detection.

The ninja is not dead

Flabbergasted, unable to understand, thrust beyond his capacity to simply believe, Legrasse pushed his way past minor concepts such as rationality, grasping desperately at faith as he asked within his mind—

How?

Never look at the magician, it whispered. Always keep you eye upon the assistant

And as those words sounded within his head, John Raymond Legrasse began to laugh. When all heads turned toward him, his revery became the jubilant exultations of a madman. All had suddenly been made clear to the one-time inspector of police, not just what was happening to him immediately, but degrees of the possible which he had never imagined. As he continued to howl with a cleansing, near-frightening glee, the speaker demanded;

"What prompts you, Lee-gruss? What makes you dare thus?"

"Happy to tell you," laughed the inspector. Bent over, his hands holding onto his knees to keep himself at least semi-erect, he tilted his head upward so as to be able to see his counterpart. His eyes gleaming insanely, he spat;

"You bastards are finished."

And then, the air thickened as a green radiance burst forward from deep inside Legrasse, hundreds of thousands of tiny rays of emerald streaming outward from the inspector's pores. The blinding display flew upward toward the ceiling, then curved, racing back down toward the barren floor. Several nervous soldiers fired weapons uselessly into the light. Far more ran for the exit.

The wizards, frantic behind their altar, yelled back and forth furiously, trying to interpret the phenomenon before them. The main sorceror consulted the stolen tome before him, flipping pages desperately, searching for some explanation to that which he was seeing. As he did, the brilliant green trails began to weave themselves one into another, rapidly building a shape there in the center of the room. As this happened, Legrasse's attention was split in a dozen separate directions. Somehow at the same time he realized that...

Matsuriki was alive—

That he had gained entrance to the temple—

That the Black Bat was breathing, reviving, regaining consciousness—

That Ellen had begun inching her way toward him, making ready to help him to his feet—

That the wizards had lost all interest in himself and the others—

That they, as well as all their soldiers, had become completely spellbound by the shimmer before them—

That not all of the shining verdancy was manifesting into the form growing before him—

That some was leeching along the ground, making its way toward the pile of packs and weapons—

That the temperature in the room was rising greatly—

That all pain had left his body—

That all artificial lights within the temple had been extinguished—

And...

That as dimensions shattered and logic twisted, strained beyond any accountable reason, sanity wrung from its fibers, the dazzling emerald shower finally solidifying before him could mean only one thing... that the Nameless One had returned!

"You minor annoyances," the ancient, white-bearded man-shape hissed. His hands moving in unearthly patterns, he made a sudden gesture which caused the air around him to thicken. While all eyes attempted to focus, the brains behind them not able to think fast enough to comprehend what they were seeing, three shaft-like protrusions began to erupt from the front of the twinkling shield all about the Nameless One.

At the same time, Matsuriki had managed to reach the pile of packs and weapons unnoticed. Much to Legrasse's surprise, he only snared one of Ellen's bags, and then pulled back, making his way around the soldiers crowding forward. Reaching the Domino Lady, the ninja slipped her the bag, even as two of the wizards finally regained their senses. Shouting in panicked tones, the men obviously were directing their guardians to attack, but the orders came too late. A number of the soldiers took aim and fired upon the Nameless One, but to no avail. Bullets struck the shield covering him and simply disappeared, the force of their attack absorbed, their physical forms dissipated.

Legrasse struggled to make sense of all that was happening around him. While those of the enemy that had not fled the temple focused on the Nameless One, Matsuriki had already reached the Black Bat, was helping him to his feet. Next to them, the Domino Lady had opened the bag the ninja had brought her—the one given her by La Raniella just before they had walked through space and time to Australia. In front of him, as more bullets struck the ancient mystic's shield, the wizened figure said;

"Thank you for your violence. It shall be put to good use."

And, before the Nameless One had finished his sentence, the three protrusions manifesting themselves within his shield suddenly tore free from him and extended violently forward, spearing the three wizards at the altar. The soldiers all about reacted in horror, many beginning to empty their weapons upon the Nameless One. Still more fled for the exits, stumbling over each other as they did so, crushing one another, screaming mindless oaths. Within his protective barrier, however, one only being made stronger by the scores of bullets being flung against it, the ancient guardian continued making his mystical gestures. Taking an instant to turn and stare into Legrasse's eyes, he returned to his casting even as his voice sounded once more within the inspector's brain—

Go—now!

Looking to his left, Legrasse realized that what Ellen had pulled from her bag was a set of curved pieces of bamboo identical to the ones La Raniella had used to send them to the Pacific. As the Domino Lady placed a highly polished gray-green stone in the center of the circle, Matsuriki thrust the Black Bat inside its boundaries. When Quinn disappeared the ninja indicated Ellen should go next.

At the same time, the entire temple had begun to shake, its concrete walls splitting, moving closer together. Massive sections of the ceiling began to crash downward, rain and hail splattering in behind the falling rubble.

"Legrasse," Matsuriki shouted, "come on!"

The ninja disappeared into nothingness. The Nameless One raised his arms to the sky. Thunder barked overhead. Legrasse stepped forward. The ancient mystic's arms came down, pointing at the altar. Legrasse moved a foot inside the bamboo circle. The Nameless One spoke, lightning flashed, Legrasse brought his other foot inside the circle, and then—

Epilogue

THE QUARTET LAY SCATTERED ACROSS THE FLOOR OF MADAME LA Raniella's basement. Their clothing, the Dollins circle which had remained there waiting for them, even the immediate floor and ceiling of the cellar were charred and smoking, the result of the backlash of the Nameless One's attack upon the *Ghorl Nigral*.

Later, they would discover that when the ancient mystic had shattered his physical self to rescue them all, that he had hidden one of his aspect selves within Legrasse's mind. Recognizing the source of their enemy's power, he had chosen to act immediately, letting the wizards believe they had removed him from the playing field. The wizened mage had known he could not defeat a trio of sorcerers who had the *Book of Night* at their command. Not in a frontal attack, anyway. Thus, he had decided to hide himself from their eyes, to allow them to think him destroyed, and to count on the four brave souls who were willing to risk so much to get him close enough to the *Ghorl Nigral* to destroy it once and for all.

Such knowledge would come later, however. At that moment, those who had been counted upon to accomplish so much began to howl hysterically, unable to believe they had survived. Patting his arms, his legs, Tony Quinn shouted;

"Look at me, I'm in one piece!"

"I believe we are all in one piece," offered Matsuriki. "How that was managed…"

"I'll tell you how it was managed," said Ellen, pushing herself up off the floor. Her clothing now burned as well as torn, soaked through with blood and sweat, her hair filthy, matted, her face bruised and blackened, she limped over to Legrasse, then took his left arm by the wrist and raised it over his head, shouting;

"It was because of the once and future ass-kicker of all time and space here!"

As the inspector flushed slightly, Quinn and Matsuriki began to applaud and shout agreement. Dropping Legrasse's arm, the Domino Lady joined in with the cheering. Raising his hands in protest, the inspector managed to get the others under control. As they quieted, he said;

"You're a very kind group of romantics, but I believe we'll find that the Nameless One was pulling all our strings from the background. If you're going to start buying rounds of drinks, they probably should be the kind preferred by long-lived old Indian mystics."

"As soon as I have learned how one with my, shall we say, unique abilities can earn a living in this country," added Matsuriki, "I will be happy to buy drinks for any who are thirsty."

"You know," said the Black Bat, "after hearing that guy on the island, I have to ask, why is it your English so good?"

"I have a degree in comparative languages," the ninja answered. "I earned it at your Princeton University."

"Ohhhh, a Jersey boy," teased Quinn. "That explains a lot."

Madame La Raniella arrived in her basement then, shocked at the damage from the amount of the explosion which had followed the four through the Dollins Circle—glad, and even somewhat amazed, to see all four of the recently departed returned and alive. Immediately she demanded details on all that had happened. As the Black Bat and Matsuriki began to answer her questions, Ellen pulled Legrasse aside. Staring into his eyes, she said;

"Now, where were we?" More than a little flustered, the inspector said in a substantially lowered tone;

"I believe I understand a great deal now. It was after the Nameless One sequestered himself within me that I, well… I mean, all that flirting I was doing with you, it really wasn't like me. I think..."

"John Raymond," said Ellen, placing a single finger against his lips to silence him momentarily, "I know what I saw in you before and after the Nameless One's 'death.' So I'm only going to ask you one question. When you almost kissed me in the raft, did you want to, or were you being forced to?"

Legrasse stared into Ellen's provocative brown eyes, feeling his insides melt. His defenses deserting him one after another, a voice from the back of his mind whispered, you've faced all manner of hell things without a second's hesitation, and yet you stand here flustered before this girl? As the voice chuckled within his brain, the inspector said;

"In the boat? I wanted to kiss you the first moment I saw you. But..."

"Oh," she said with a throaty sigh, her finger sealing itself across his lips once more, "you foolish, foolish 'old weed.' Let me make something clear, you are a man who owes me a cup of coffee and a life's story. I am a woman who collects the debts owed her. Do you understand?"

Smiling despite himself, Legrasse nodded, then bowed in the direction of the exit. The two looked at each other for a moment, then crossed the room to where the others stood, still chattering about recent events. Straight-faced, the inspector interrupted, thanked La Raniella for "a marvelous time," and then headed for the stairs. Following him, Ellen simply turned and said;

"I have to go with him. He owes me a coffee."

Watching the pair leave, or more specifically, watching Ellen leave, the Black Bat poked Matsuriki in the arm, pointing at the Domino Lady's all too feminine gait, and quipped;

"And that, my friend, is what we Americans fight for. What do you Japanese guys fight for?"

"For the emperor," answered the ninja. Rolling his eyes, Quinn chuckled lightly, then said;

"Man, that's what comes from being educated in New Jersey, all right." Turning to La Raniella, Quinn thanked her for all she had done as well, then said he had to take Matsuriki to the nearest bar and begin his reeducation. As the men mounted the stairs, the witch woman said nothing. She understood their need. They had offered all to fate, suffered greatly, and somehow survived the impossible. If any four people anywhere on the surface of the planet deserved to find a moment of peace in the face of the coming storm, it was them.

La Raniella knew things were not finished. The *Ghorl Nigral* might be destroyed, an entire island raised up and crushed about it, all of it then sunken beneath the waves, but that would not be the end of things. The Japanese would attack again; it was in the cards. War would come, and America would stand on the brink once more, all too soon.

But, that was to come. For now, she had a Dollins Circle to put away, a floor to clean. The impossible had been accomplished. Once more.

For the moment, it was enough.

THE END

ONLY AN HOUR
A New Tale of the Black Bat

*"If our imaginations were filled from waking to
sleeping with a sense of the evil in the world, we
should scarcely be able to work or eat our meals."*
–Robert Lynd

"I'M TELLIN' YA, PAULIE," WHISPERED THE SHORTEST OF THE FIVE MEN
in a shaking whine, "I'm still worried. I don't give a dead dog's ear
what'cha say."

"It's a little late ta be rethinkin' tonight, Frank," answer the
man closest to him, the compact unit's obvious leader. "Besides,
yer juicin' yerself crazy over nuthin'."

The quintet of dark figures were making their way carefully
but swiftly along the Brooklyn docks with a familiarity that fairly
shouted they were no strangers to the rough and low area known
as Red Hook. Two of the company carried nondescript sacks of
some weight. The other three were burdened only by weapons.
Two of the trio wielded handguns, the last of them a double-
barreled shotgun which he kept only barely concealed beneath a
frayed and open overcoat. Their target was, surprisingly, not one
of the massive freighters berthed along the miles of Brooklyn
dock front, there in the light of the midnight moon, but a far more
subtle vessel.

Practically hidden from the world's view in between a massive
fruit hauler up from South America, and an even larger freighter
carrying a cargo of rare woods from the shores of Eastern Africa,

sat the yacht, Paglo's Venture. Mr. Leonardo Paglo was a local legend in that area of New York City. He was a self-made millionaire, an immigrant's son who had worked the docks with a fierce energy and a keen mind, moving upward in the world of shipping bit by bit, year after year, until finally he came to either own or lease half of the entire Brooklyn waterfront.

His travels from utter poverty to riches had taken nearly sixty years, but he had loved every minute of his climb. Certainly he could have kept the Venture stored at any of the exclusive docks to be found along the shores of Long Island, or those up the Hudson outside the city. Paglo sneered at such ideas. For him, to have his sleek beauty close at hand was not only efficient, but a snub to those with whom his station demanded he interact—all the society swells who respected neither the size of his work ethic or his dedication to his shipping line, but only that of his wallet.

"Don't hand me no banana oil," whispered the nervous Frank. "Don't be tryin' to tell me the Bat ain't nuthin'."

"Jiminey Christmas," hissed one of the gunmen, "youse guys know it's bad luck ta say dat name."

"Oh, what a team of sissy Marys," snapped Paulie. "I hope the shadows don't get too dark, or you pansies'll all be soakin' yer drawers."

The crack shamed the more worried pair into silence, but not without bringing to Paulie's mind the one thing no hoodlum in New York City wanted to think about ever—the Bat, or as he was more officially known, The Black Bat, the masked vigilante who for the past year had been making things so incredibly difficult for those with a criminal bent. In only slightly less than twelve months the mysterious figure had brought crime to a virtual stand-still. He had toppled the heads of several criminal families, leaving their organizations in amazing disarray. Not interested in only the masterminds of the city's misery, he had also pursued jewel thieves and counterfeiters, loan sharks, bank robbers, and even the occasional freelancer, the crazy inventors and the such who were always coming up with this or that mad weapon of destruction.

Those of a criminal bent could take some small comfort in the fact the police were almost more interested in stopping the Black Bat than they were actual wrong-doers. Some said it was payola—that a number of those on the wrong side of the tracks were actually paying the police to keep the heat up on the Bat. Others said it was simple jealousy, that the Black Bat made the cops look so bad they simply had to put him out of business. The official line coming out of city hall was that the Bat, like any who took the law into their own hands, had to be stopped like any other lawbreaker. It sounded good coming out of a stuffed shirt like Commissioner Warner, but any smart guy knew it was simply a load of applesauce for the masses.

Paulie knew it for sure. Working to keep his crew in order, he demanded they simply trust him as they always had. In the meantime he patted the revolver hidden beneath his jacket, knowing in his heart he, himself, could never trust anything except a good, old fashioned lead-spitter. And, he told himself, he was not even going to need that much for their work that night. Leaning on one of Paglo's sailors, one with an unfortunate habit of losing big at craps, Paulie had discovered the shipping magnet's fondness for using the Venture as a bank. Yes, he had a large, sturdy safe in his offices, and second story men had blown it open and looted it twice.

But, the gang leader thought to himself, no one knows about the smaller one hidden beneath the berth in the cabin of his boat. The one just sittin' there waitin' for us, holdin' the pay for over four thousand grunt workers who ain't gonna get squat tomorrow, 'cause we're gonna get there first.

"I'm just sayin', Paulie," whispered Frank one last time, "that I'd have felt safer if we'd brought more guys."

"Will you put a lid on it," answered Paulie. Turning back toward the men behind him, his gaze centering on Frank, he growled, "I'm sure the damn Bat has bigger fish to fry tonight than us."

"Oh, come now, Paulie," a harsh voice said from somewhere in the darkness. "I've got all the time in the world for enterprising little guppies such as yourself."

"It's the Bat," screamed one of the gunmen. Waving his automatic about wildly, his hand trembling, he gibbered, "The Black Bat, the damn Black Bat—he's here!"

"Am I," the sinister voice questioned, "or am I just a bad case of the nerves?"

Frank had dropped his satchel of burglar tools and explosives at the first hint of the menacing voice, clawing for the revolver tucked inside his waistband. Paulie, for all his supposed grit, had done the same. His hand pulling his weapon, he aimed it at the random darkness, screaming;

"C-Come out, ya coward, ya. W-We, we… w-we're not afraid of you."

"All right," answered the dark voice calmly. "As long as you aren't afraid."

And then, before any of the thugs knew what was happening, a form none of them would swear the next day was truly human was among them. It fell on them from above, a man-like darkness with bat wings that one moment was not there, the next was, crippling the thugs one after another with iron blows. As the gang swung wildly, trying desperately to injure the sinister shape, trying to strike or stab, or to take aim, the Black Bat moved between them effortlessly, more playing with the five well-armed men than anything else. He smiled at their pathetically slow attempts to fire upon him, their aim always off, their trigger fingers always seconds too late. There attempts to strike him were even more laughable. He dodged their fists with such ridiculous ease an observer might have thought they were watching a well choreographed dance.

"Put your weapons down now," the Black Bat commanded, growing bored with the quintet's pitiful resistance, "and I *might* let you live."

"I quit!"

The voice was Frank's. Instantly upon hearing the offer made by the avenger in their midst, the youngest of the crew hurled his weapon away from himself, thrusting his hands immediately into the air. As the splash of Frank's revolver hitting the water sounded, another of the gang followed suit as well, dropping to his knees as an added sign of surrender.

"Screw this," yelled one of the other gunsels, however. "You're not takin' me!"

The man studied the deep gloom before him, his eyes darting from shape to shape. Finally, when he was certain he had spotted their foe he fired his shotgun, both barrels carefully aimed directly at the Black Bat's midsection. The hero, obviously aware of the man's every move, flipped out of the way with a practiced ease. The retort of the weapon echoed up and down the docks, louder than all the previous gun fire the gang had unleashed put together. The man grinned for an instant, seeing the wobbling body there in the smoke desperately grabbing at its abdomen, frantic to hold its shattered insides together. And then, the thug's eyes went wide as he realized the man he had shot was not the Black Bat, but his own brother.

"Louie!" he screamed, rushing forward to catch his slain sibling, "it ain't possible—it had to be the Bat."

"No," came a voice behind the man's head, a touch of a .45 sliding up his neck. "This is the Bat."

The automatic barked and Louie fell the rest of the way to the ground as his brother's head exploded in a crimson splash. The sight spurred Paulie to make a desperate attempt. He emptied his revolver in the Black Bat's general direction, firing wildly as he tried to flee the scene. With a motion resembling boredom, the black-garbed crime fighter snapped off a single shot. Off in the distance, the gang leader's head splattered across the docks.

As the sound of police cars disturbed the tired poor of the Red Hook ghetto, the Black Bat pulled two pairs of handcuffs from the multi-pocketed compartment belt he wore, quickly securing the remaining thugs, the two wise enough to surrender, to a more than adequately sturdy fence. By the time the pair of squad cars arrived the scene of all the gunfire, the Black Bat had reached his coupe and was miles away from the river.

✠　✠　✠

WELL-RESPECTED ATTORNEY TONY QUINN SAT WITH HIS HEAD COCKED at an odd angle, listening to the noise coming from the band on stage. The bizarre tilt of his head did not seem out of place to anyone who knew him even casually, however, for all of New York City had heard of the fiery young attorney, and all of them knew he was blind. Those who were more familiar with the young Mr. Quinn, however, knew the slightly off positioning of his head was as much a part of a disguise as his dark glasses.

"You know something, sweetheart," he said, addressing the remarkably comely blonde sitting across from him. "I'm as bored as bored can be."

"Wishing you were out prowling the waterfront," she answered, "like last night?"

Tony risked shifting one eye in the direction of his fiancée, Carol Baldwin, for the briefest of seconds. The woman was an amazing beauty. Although a mere five foot four, the platinum blonde was the center of attention for every stray eye in the room. She shimmered with sophistication, and yet there were subtle things in the way she sat, the way she moved, which told those in the know that she was no cold fish. The fact that she was engaged to a blind man made more than one jealous low-life crack bitter jokes over how unfair God was to allow such injustices.

Such jibes only amused Carol, however, for she was, of course, one of those very few who knew that Tony Quinn was not blind at all. She also knew his connection to the city's black-garbed protector, namely that supposedly blind attorney Tony Quinn was the Black Bat, that his once all-too-real blindness had been secretly cured by an a one-in-a-million operation she had arranged, and that now her fiancé divided his time between protecting the innocent in court as the highly respected Tony Quinn, or on the streets as the fearsome Black Bat.

"What would you say," Quinn replied, a strain of mischief in his voice only she could recognize, "if I told you that recently I've been wishing for something else?"

It had been Carol's own father's eyes, donated by her when he had died, that had restored Quinn's sight. Indeed, if regaining his vision had been all the exhaustive, experimental operation had accomplished, Tony Quinn would never have become the Black Bat. But he had gained more. Not only could he see as well as any when the lights were on, after the operation he could see equally well when they were extinguished. Moreover, all of his other senses had been heightened to superhuman levels as well. It was when these advantages had been thrust upon him that he had struck upon the idea of becoming the Black Bat. And, ever since he had concocted that notion, he had become the hero of all the millions living in New York City who had no where else to turn when evil crawled forth from under its limitless supply of rocks.

"And what have you been wishing for, Tony Quinn?"

"You, sweetheart," he said softly. "I mean, I know most men are supposed to love the idea of long engagements, but, well…" Quinn pulled awkwardly at his collar for a moment, then finished saying, "do you think maybe ours has been long enough?"

And then, the young lawyer did something unprecedented. He reached across the table and took Carol's hands, not with the false feeling about he would normal employ to safeguard his dual identity, but the way any man would. He took her hands in his, and he turned his face toward hers.

"You may remember there was a rumor running around at one time that I might be in love with you."

"Now that you mention it," the blond beauty replied coolly, "I do seem to remember something to that effect."

"It's no rumor, darling." Carol's face went suddenly still, all movement draining from it. As the band continued filling every corner of the Stork Club with the turbulent rhythm of their latest hit, the two lovers lost track of all around them. Despite the thundering drums and dozens of horns, let alone the constant clatter of the sound of scores of heels thumping smoothly against the highly polished dance floor, at that moment they only had ears and eyes for each other.

Carol's face was open to all, with not the slightest morsel of restraint or coyness in effect to hide the rising hope flooding her entire being. Afraid to speak, not wanting to do anything that might shatter her momentary rapture, she held herself in check, saying nothing, biting her lower lip against the instant when the dream she was having would shatter.

Squeezing her hand, Quinn told his long-waiting companion, "Those guys from last night, they're a perfect example of what I'm talking about."

"What do you mean, darling?"

"When I first started this little nighttime diversion of mine," he answered, "I got knocked around quite a bit. Sure, I have certain advantages, but I brought home a lot of bruises, welts and broken bones—yes?"

"Oh, yes," Carol agreed. "I was there; I remember."

"Well, it's been a long time since I've had much trouble. Or since there's been anything that really needed the Black Bat's attention. I went out last night because Leonardo Paglo is a good man who employs a lot of men—men who need their pay at the end of the week. When I got that tip from the grapevine the Venture was going to be hit, well… sure, I had to go… but…"

"But 'what,' Tony?"

"It was just so easy." Quinn let loose a small sigh, one made up partly of frustration, partly of acceptance. "Do you know, while they were shooting at me, trying to stab me, there in the dark, half the time I wasn't even using my eyes anyway. Five men at close quarters..." the band hit a high note so loud and jubilant Quinn was forced to go silent for a moment. Then, when the noise level returned to merely raucous, he continued, saying;

"One of them, he tried to get me with his shotgun. I, I guess I've been doing this so long, I just knew what he was up to. It was so simple for me to maneuver one of the others into his line of fire..." As his voice trailed off, Carol managed to quietly breathe a single word in his direction.

"So...?"

"So," he told her calmly, "in that moment, two things hit me with sparkling clarity. The first one was what I've been saying, and it's been building for me for a long time now, the whole fact that this all seems too simple, too easy, as if there really is no need for the Black Bat anymore."

"And the second thing...?"

"When the thug with the shotgun cut his own brother in two, I had a thought, and I've had them before... what if he had been able to hit me? What was the purpose in it? I wasn't there saving the world, or the city, or even a single human life. I was just there rounding up hoodlums. And, if you want to get technical about it, and that is a lawyer's job, you know, they hadn't even done anything yet. Yes, we know they were going to, but three men died over nothing more than money. Pieces of paper—just an idea. I killed them to keep them from someone else's little green pieces of paper, and I might have died trying to keep them from those little pieces of paper."

All around the two, the Stork Club was blaring with noise and festivity. Women screamed as men twirled them, threw them in the air, jumped and leaped and moved with them to the pounding music. Through the growing storm of joyous noise, Carol blinked her eyes, her hands trembling within Quinn's. Straining to hold back the tears she felt growing within her, she asked simply;

"And so..."

"And so, I thought, what if that stupid punk had actually shot me, and I never got to do this again?"

someone to take care of us. You remember your twenties, don't you—back in the 1800s, right?"

"The counselor," Warner responded with a mock growl, "is definitely out of order."

"Strike it from the record," answered Quinn with a laugh. Letting the joking tone melt from his voice, the attorney said, "it's true, though. I think I've just come to that point where it's time to take another step further. You know, you find yourself just doing the same old thing all the time, and you just sort of realize, maybe it's time to grow up a little."

The two men talked for some time after, the conversation going across other relationships they remembered fondly, and some they had barely escaped.

Finally, however, the Commissioner brought the conversation around to the matter over which he had called their meeting in the first place. Warning Quinn that he was about to put on his official hat, he said;

"I've got a very strange duck locked-up downstairs. The DA's office doesn't know what to make of him—we don't either, my goodness… I mean, Lord, I… I don't know where to begin. I mean, he's part of something… hummmm… not sure I should go there—"

"Warner," asked the attorney quietly, "what is it? Why did you ask me here?"

The commissioner's face sank into hard lines surrounding a fixed stare. The transformation was so complete, and so rapid, Quinn almost betrayed his surprise. Through a supreme effort of will, however, he continued to look off into space as if he were as blind as he pretended. Warner was so absorbed in trying to find a way to present what he wanted to say, however, it was possible he might not have noticed any slip on the young lawyer's part anyway. Still, Quinn was glad his iron control had continued to serve him. After a long handful of seconds passed, he asked;

"Commissioner… is everything all right?"

"Tony, I have a favor to ask."

"Ask it, old friend."

"This fellow downstairs, no identification, his fingerprints give us nothing—he's a first-timer and, well, everyone seems to think we should just ship him off to Bellevue and be done with it." Warner sighed, his eyes downcast toward his desk. His fingers gripping one pile of papers before him in particular, the commissioner wandered away from the subject, saying;

"It's not bad enough the staggering amount of missing persons reports we're getting. Now in the middle of it we end up stuck with this oddball..."

"Crazy...?"

"I'm not certain," answered Warner. Quinn struggled to maintain his composure, continuing his practiced pretense of be blind while all along his better-than-human eyes were watching his friend's face contort and grimace. He knew the commissioner would never have allowed so much raw emotion to show if he thought anyone could see him. Something about this prisoner was bothering him like no other. Tony Quinn could not argue that his curiosity had definitely been aroused. Finally, having no other recourse, the older man took a long, deep breath, then finally finished, saying;

"He certainly says crazy things, and it's obvious he believes them, but he seems to believe them with such conviction... listen, Tony, my idea was... I guess it's because of your condition, but I've always felt, watching you when conversation is important, you have a way of listening that is so intent, I was thinking that if you were to volunteer as his public defender, a little pro bono as it were..."

"You were thinking that if anyone could tell you what to do with this egg, it would be me—correct?" When Warner nodded, Quinn stared, waiting for an answer. After a moment, feeling the fool, the commissioner laughed;

"Yes, my boy, yes. Old idiot that I am, I'm standing here nodding at you. Forgive me, would you?"

"Oh, that's what I heard rattling."

Warner gave the younger man a harsh look, then rolled his eyes at his own foolishness—glaring at a blind man—and rose from behind his desk to escort his guest down to the cells in the bottom of the building.

✠   ✠   ✠

"HELLO, MY NAME IS MR. TONY QUINN. I'VE BEEN APPOINTED BY the courts to be your attorney."

Quinn held out his hand to the man he had been told was directly across from him. One of the two officers assigned to protect him informed him that his client was wearing handcuffs and could not take his hand. Nodding politely, the young lawyer asked if chains and guards were really necessary. The officers informed him that due to the violence incurred during the suspect's capture, and his bizarre behavior, it had been insisted upon by the commissioner. Since Quinn knew Warner was on the other side of the wall listening to the proceedings, he knew no one was playing him false.

Still, he had to wonder. The man before him was amazingly thin, as if he had not seen a proper meal in months. With the country not yet even beginning to recover from the terrible Depression which crippled it so for the preceding decade, coming across men with vacant eyes and a starved look was no out-of-the-ordinary occurrence. Having them listed as dangerously violent, however, struck Quinn as just a trifle odd. The chained man did not appear to him strong enough to give a grade school child much trouble. Still, Warner had claimed the man was an unusual case. Putting aside his prejudices, Quinn threw himself into his role as blind attorney and pulled his outstretched hand back. Then, apologizing to his client, he began again.

"So, you've given your name as Murr, is that correct?"

"That's what it calls me—Murrrrrrrrrrrr. Had another name. Don't remember. Not important. Am Murr now."

Quinn regarded the man, taking him in through his dark glasses. He had to make his assessment quickly, of course, since he could not allow others to realize he was studying the man with his eyes. What he noted did not please him. The man chained before him was gaunt and pale, as if one starved in darkness for months. He was a quavering stick of a human being, but there was something disturbing in the aspect of his eyes.

"'It' gave you this name? Who, or more exactly, what is 'it,' Mm. Murr?"

"It? It is all."

Quinn watched the man's eyes as he answered. They shone back at him with the light one saw in those of an ill-used dog, that electric flash of love learned through terror.

"Which 'all' would that be, Mr. Murr? Forgive what may be impertinence on my part, but what do you mean by 'all' in this context?"

"All," said the starved man loudly. "All is all. They are all. Come to Earth in the great far gone. Conquer, they did. Yaksh, Tond, more. All did fall. Fall before their wind and fury. Tremble in the shadow of their basalt cities—their terrible, windowless towers—"

Quinn listened while the man rambled, stealing glimpses of the prisoner's guards from the corners of his eyes when he could. Both the officers were watchful enough, enough that is, to make certain an emaciated man in chains could not escape their domination. The lawyer could easily see they were not really listening to Murr, however. Whether it was because they had heard his mad ramblings before, or because they just did not care, he could not determine. The knowledge was enough to suit his purposes.

"Lords of all, they were. Before man walked erect, before the birth of the dinosaurs, their dark towers ruled over all. Held sway over all. Frightened the length of the solar system, they did. Terrified most of the galaxy, they did."

"That's all well and good, Mr. Murr," interrupted Quinn, "But you're speaking of the past. Where is this 'it' now, sir? And why did it give you the name 'Murr?'"

The interview went on in much the same fashion for another thirtysome minutes. Quinn continued to probe, trying to determine who Murr really was, the identity of his mysterious 'it,' the origins of its name for him, et cetera. All he accomplished was the coaxing forward of the same set of insane facts over and over. Or, at least, that is the way it appeared to Murr's guards and the commissioner. Quinn noticed something else, however.

As Murr spoke, he seemed to mumble a second set of information. Aloud, in his fervent voice, the one so reminiscent of a tent revival meeting, he continued to extol the virtues, fighting prowess and all round wonderfulness of his mysterious 'it.' Beneath his breath, however, he muttered a different message, letting a few words quietly slip out sub-vocally in between each sentence.

Only someone with the extra keen hearing of Tony Quinn's alter ego could possibly catch what had to be a subconscious attempt to relate a different message. Indeed, so low was the secondary message transmitted, so terrified was the voice attempting to send the message, Quinn had to question the man several additional times just to give him enough time to get his desperate communication out a single time in its entirety.

After the interview was finally completed, much to the grumbling relief of the two guards, Murr was returned to his cell while Warner and Quinn met once more in the commissioner's office. The moment the door had been closed behind them, before either of them had reached their seats, Warner had started in on questioning the younger man, wanting to know not only his opinion of the prisoner, but also why he had questioned him for so long.

Quinn made the excuse of hoping to pierce Murr's veil of madness, wishing to determine whether or not the man was faking his insanity, or, if actual, to reach some solid facts which could be used to identify him. He made his case as a matter of pitying the prisoner, knowing full well that most people were willing to extend such charity to anyone a blind man pitied because of their, at least, subconscious pity for the blind. As for his opinion of what to do with Murr, Quinn agreed that the man was quite mad, insisting;

"Without question he should be confined for study. But in a prison facility. I think this sense of his that there is this all powerful 'it' out there somewhere, most likely just waiting to get him back, is a plea for help."

"But, do you think someone is really after him?"

"I think it likely."

Warner smiled, and Quinn knew he felt the same. The two talked for a while further, then the commissioner noted the time, making a fuss over having devoured so much of his friend's morning. Quinn suggested he could make up for it by taking him to lunch, to which Warner readily agreed. As he grabbed up his leather attaché case and his cane, however, the younger man pretended to suddenly remember an appointment he simply could not break. Thanking the commissioner for his generous offer, Quinn shook his hand, then made his way carefully for the door, insisting he had to free Warner from his obligation. The commissioner thanked him again for his time and promised to make up the luncheon debt another day. Quinn swore to hold him to it, then made for the stairwell, desperate to shed the guise of a blind attorney for something a bit more stimulating.

"And so, you're saying this guy was actually speaking in two voices at once?"

The man with the amazed tone in his voice was Butch O'Leary, a giant of a man with courage to match. He was a huge, ungainly tower of a human being, one forged with gigantic shoulders and tremendous hands, fingers cast in steel that looked as if they might only be comfortable when curled into fists. Like many men hewn to the same great proportions, O'Leary was not the brightest man in the world, but he was a good and loyal friend of Tony Quinn's, and one of only a trio of people who knew the attorney's dual identity.

"I know it's hard to understand," answered Quinn. "Even I could barely pick it up. But the more I listened to what he said over again in my mind, the more I think there might be something to it all."

"Fine enough, sir," answered the third man in the room. His given name was Norton Kirby, a seemingly pleasant, middle-aged, balding man of medium stature. Those there present in Quinn's bedroom knew him as Silk, however, once one of the smoothest con-artists in the country. Having left that life all far behind, however, the dapper, quick thinking ex-criminal now posed as Quinn's valet and chauffeur. "But what might all this have to do with us? Or should I say, with the Bat?"

"You think this may be something for the Black Bat to look into," asked Carol. Sitting on the edge of her fiance's bed, she gave him a comic frown as she mock-growled, "so much for those wedding plans."

Kirby and O'Leary both smiled at such a notion, but Quinn put up his hand, smiling himself as he told his friends the idea was not actually the joke it might seem. As both men's faces settled into a mild shock, the lawyer explained;

"Carol's not kidding, boys. We're seriously thinking it's time. After all, if I look at it realistically, there just isn't the need for the Black Bat there was a year ago."

"But, boss," interrupted O'Leary, "you'd really give up being the Black Bat?"

"Chalk it up to lousy planning," Quinn joked. "We simply did too good a job cleaning up the city."

"That is kinda true, ya know," agreed the larger man." I ain't nearly as worried about my maiden Aunt Margaret walking home alone at night as I use'ta be."

"Granted," admitted Kirby with a slight hesitation, "but are you seriously talking giving up being the Black Bat? For good?"

"I think the police can handle things from here on in," answered Quinn. "Neither Carol or I wanted to marry and start a family in a world that wasn't safe enough for children, but we've put quite a dent in evil's backbone here in New York—"

"Indeed," responded Kirby, "but what about Europe? What about Germany? Do you think these Nazis are going to leave evil bent over and crippled? They're looking more and more each day like something to stiffen Satan's spine."

"True enough," agreed Quinn. "But Europe is always tearing itself apart. Always has. And they're a long way from here. I don't think we have to worry so much about them."

"So then, I don't get it," said O'Leary. "This Murr guy. Is this something the Bat is going to look at, or was you just thinking out loud, or what?"

"Well, to be honest," the young attorney admitted with a boyish grin, "I was thinking we might make this my, or actually, the Black Bat's bachelor party." As the others in the room stared at him, Quinn explained;

"Murr talked of this terrible god thing with such zeal and conviction, you would swear he was on to something. It's obvious he's just a madman, but this is the kind of thing a year ago we would have chased down with a vengeance. Look at the voodoo pranksters we've broken up, the supposed haunted houses, that witch woman racket, the phony fortune tellers who were fleecing people trying to contact their dead relatives, all the rest of it. Let's face it, we know there's nothing to this supernatural nonsense—right?"

Both men hemmed and hawed a bit, but finally they admitted that they too felt there was nothing to such beliefs except the vicarious fun people had in scaring themselves a bit. That much agreed upon, Quinn said;

"Well, this Murr, anyone who could hear the terror in that second voice of his, I think like me they'd want to put their concern to rest. So, what I'm proposing is, we three visit the site where he says his 'it' can be reached, and we do a bit of snooping. Maybe take a little brandy and some cigars, you know, for when it all proves to be a bunch of hooey."

When the others looked at his askance, Quinn threw up his hands and admitted he was joking about making a party out of the evening, but that he was still serious about looking into Murr's story. Curbing his playful side, he added;

"All I'm really saying is that if there does prove to be something there, some kidnapping ring or something from which he escaped, all right, we'll have one last adventure. But really, flying snakes from another world that wages inter-galactic war... Mr. Murr has obviously bent his mind on too much Buck Rogers."

"I liked the serial," said O'Leary with fondness. "I didn't miss none of the parts. Me and Silk saw all twelve—it just ended last month."

"Yes," agreed Kirby with a slight embarrassment. Justifying himself, he added, "that Constance Moore is quite something to look at. But more to this fantastic adventure you've outlined. When were you thinking we would execute this little scenario?"

"Tonight," answered Quinn, his eyes twinkling with excitement. "I think the sooner we prove there's nothing too all this, the sooner I can hang up the cowl of the Black Bat without regrets, and Mr. Tony Quinn, successful young attorney can finally sent out the announcements a certain Miss Baldwin's mother has been waiting to see for far too long."

☩   ☩   ☩

THAT NIGHT FOUND KIRBY, O'LEARY AND QUINN SITTING IN THE nondescript roadster the attorney kept for those evenings which demanded the presence of the Black Bat. As always whenever the three of them went out together, Kirby had taken the front passenger seat, allowing O'Leary the wheel, while their friend had remained hidden in the back seat. After all, it would not do for the supposedly sightless Quinn to be seen driving a motor vehicle. And, since he was sporting all of his secondary persona's garb save his mask, it behooved him to stay as out of sight as possible.

But, now that the trio had not only reached their destination, but had watched the area carefully for almost an hour, the time had come for them to take one last look around before they exited from the car. Despite the fact they expected Murr's story to be a complete fantasy, nonetheless they had come prepared. Each man was heavily armed. Both of Quinn's friends had masks, simple pullover affairs to help keep their identities private. The men, especially Kirby, were far too closely associated with the younger attorney for them to even hope that something they became connected to would not draw suspicion down upon Quinn as well.

"So, are we looking ready?"

"Think we might be, chief," answered O'Leary. "The streets look pretty deserted. I mean, nothing's moved since we got here. Besides, I don't think no one's gonna see us getting out, especially from this space." The large man had been able to find parking not only under a pair of trees, but along a stretch of sidewalk where the streetlight was out of order. Indeed, quite a number of the lights were out in that neighborhood, a fact not lost on the leader of the trio. As they all checked their weapons one last time, Quinn said;

"Murr's mumbling voice put the entrance to this hidden world inside that deserted building across the street." Sliding his mask on, his voice grew darker as the Black Bat added, "1443... that one with what's left of a taxi drop awning."

"We see it," confirmed Kirby. "No one's been in or out of that doorway, or any other on the street, really, since we got here. Of course, why would they? Look around, the whole block's shuttered up and abandoned."

"I wonder why," said O'Leary. "They're always tearing something down in this city. What're they going to do here?"

"Could be they're thinking of expanding the local power station. It's just over a block."

"And yet here we still sit in a deserted neighborhood. Maybe this is all for nothing," offered O'Leary.

"It could be, indeed," agreed the Bat. "And wouldn't that prove my point about my usefulness? But, on the off chance this feeling that's been nagging at me ever since I met Mr. Murr turns out to be something, let's check this one out as thoroughly as anything else we've looked into over the last year."

"Might as well go out with a perfect record—eh, Mr. Quinn?"

"I'll take one if I can get one," answered the dark and menacing figure in the back seat.

Reaching for their door releases, both men marveled over the complete and absolute change that came over their friend in that moment. When Tony Quinn became the Black Bat, he did more than simply put on a menacing suit and strap on a set of .45s. It was more even than the different tone he gave his voice, the way he walked taller than Quinn and looked people squarely, harshly in the eye. There were fundamental differences between the two of them—Tony Quinn, the crusading lawyer who championed the little guy, who fought for justice wherever it was needed, throwing tremendous resources in defending the slightest case.

The Black Bat, while obviously a hero to the downtrodden and a protector of the weak, somehow seemed made of far tougher stuff. He was a wrecking ball that constantly threw itself against the tallest towers evil could erect. He was a relentless hunter, one who fastened his sights on the biggest targets, men with entire armies at their disposal, and who brought them down one after another with ruthless efficiency. He seemed in the final shakeout to be made of iron, hard and primal—a wild, destructive power beyond mere muscle and blood.

The Black Bat was, to them, practically a force of nature. How Tony Quinn thought he would ever be able to put aside such a vital, overwhelming persona for that of family man and husband, neither man could understand. Of course, neither of them had ever married. Perhaps, they thought, it takes something more, something special to be able to do what their friend was contemplating.

Each had to admit that Carol made him happy. They had, in many ways, the perfect relationship—passionate and yet comfortable. She loved both the men he was, unquestioningly and unconditionally. As for Tony, his whole life revolved around his fiancée. The only reason they had put off their marriage as long as they had was his insistence that he make the world a better place for themselves and their children.

"Tony," said Kirby, his hand held up as if to pause their assault, "if I could just say a word." When the Black Bat nodded, the one-time confidence man, now butler and fast friend continued, saying, "I just wanted to… well, I wanted to let you know that I would have supported you as the Black Bat and followed you into Hell and back for the rest of my days if that were to be my lot. I know Butch here feels the same."

"Damn right I do," the larger man added quietly.

"But all the same, if tonight's the night you ring down the curtain on the Black Bat, I tell you now, both of us will stand beside you in that decision, too. You've kept us both from making a great number of mistakes. I guess what I'm trying to say is, we were both happy to back your play when it meant putting our lives on the line. If you say it's time for you to get married after tonight, we'll back that play, too."

The Black Bat wavered for a moment. So moved was the man beneath the mask, he found he had to pull it up over his head for a moment so he could respond.

"Silk," he answered finally, "And you, too, Butch—I hope you both know I couldn't have made it this far without the two of you. I would hope you'd know that. And, maybe my time fighting crime is done. Maybe it's not. Before we make any final decisions, let's go see what lies behind the doors of building #1443 and find out if Fate has run out of uses for the Black Bat."

So saying, Tony Quinn pulled his cowl back on and once more transformed himself into The Black Bat. Their far simpler masks in place, Kirby and O'Leary followed him out of the roadster and into the moving shadows spread thickly across lower Manhattan's Houston Street. Their mood, although lighter than usual, was still thoughtful, attentive and suspicious. Although to their conscious minds such seemed practically a waste of time, the habit of it had become ingrained in their behavior.

And, such was a lucky thing, for anything less would have doomed the trio to a quick and horrible death, and all of humanity to a short and brutal future of being first slaves, then food.

✠　✠　✠

THE DOOR THE TRIO MEANT TO PASS THROUGH WAS EASILY REACHED, AS was the interior of the building beyond. Using the flashlights they had brought, Kirby and O'Leary made a quick examination of the first floor rooms, while the Black Bat searched the shadowy darkness needing nothing more than his amazing eyes. When none of the three found anything of even remote interest, they removed themselves to the basement.

After a quick but thorough inspection, they found the lower level to be simply dirty, as was the way with most abandoned buildings. They established that the layers of dust were fairly uniform, showing nothing much in the way of traffic outside of the footprints and droppings of rats. Search as they might, however, they found nothing more of interest, certainly not anything in the way of an entrance into a subterranean underworld of some sort. Confirming there was nothing to be found, the Black Bat lead his fellows back upstairs, then cautioned them to wait, whispering;

"I have an idea. Keep a low profile. I'll be back in a minute." So saying, he exited back out into the street. Taking note of the buildings to either side of 1443, he realized the entrance to the one to the left was as unprotected as the one he had just used. The one to the right, however, was boarded over, some of the boards then held in place with chains. Reentering 1443, he called to his friends in a low voice.

"Let's take a look for a way into the next building over," pointing as he added, "that direction."

In but moments Kirby found a entranceway, one that had been cut through from the one building to the other through the back of a closet. The trio gave one another looks. This might mean nothing, of course, but it seemed more to give some credence to Murr's bizarre tale. All of them immediately cranking their attention levels up to a higher state of alertness, they stepped through to the next building one after another.

1447 turned out to be not so uncomplicated as its neighbor. The trio made their way only through the first few rooms before discovering a great hole torn through the floor. There was no doubting as least a part of Murr's story now, for there before them was a great and jagged entrance to whatever world might lie beneath the surface of the Earth. Leaning over the edge, playing their lights cautiously in the darkness, the men saw a similar hole torn through the floor of the basement as well.

Instantly the Black Bat made hand motions to his friends instructing them to make their way to the basement. As they went searching for the stairs, he deployed the cable from his compartment belt he had used so many times in his never-ending battle against evil. Securing it to a timber, he flipped his body out into the open air and then swung to the basement below in one smooth motion. Once settled on the solid flooring, a quick snap of his wrist freed his cable, allowing him to recoil it for storage back in his belt even as he looked about himself in the darkness.

The eyes of the Black Bat, able to see in total darkness, were amazed at what they found there in the neighboring basement.

A tunnel had been burrowed upward from beneath the building, one so deep it showed no bottom to even the hero's fantastic powers of sight. And, there was no doubt from the way it had been dug that it had indeed been tunnelled upward from some unknown point below. As the Black Bat's companions gathered next to him, they threw their flashlight beams down into the cavernous hole, but still no end to the terrible pit could be discerned.

And, terrible it was, especially for the Black Bat. An odd, repellant odor, just the barest hint of a bad flavor, like the blood taste one got if they put their tongue to a penny, hung over the hole like a cattle skull suspended as a warning over some remote pond. With his intensely heightened senses, the smell was more than a trifle sickening, it was repulsive, a sickly stagnant foulness that promised to grow stronger with every foot for those who might descend into the darkened circle.

And yet, as they surveyed the black hole, there was no doubt that others had gone before them. The dust in this second basement showed that countless feet had gone forward down into the depths. Hundreds, maybe thousands, there was no way for any in the threesome to tell. Leaning further over the edge, the Black Bat decided to play his one last trump card. He could not see anything except an endless burrow, and his sense of smell had proven not only useless, but almost a detriment.

Closing his eyes, however, cutting himself off from his friends, the basement, from everything he could, the Black Bat calmed his nerves, relaxed himself as much as he could, and then simply *listened*. He held his pose, hearing nothing out of the ordinary for some time. And then, he began to hear something. Actually, in a way he could not tell if he was hearing something, or feeling it, but slowly, a terrible, ominous whistling sound, like a vast but faraway wind came to him. It grazed his ears, his cheeks, this soft eeriness, this velvet knife blade of a sound, leaving him with an odd, clammy feeling.

"What is it, chief?"

The Bat turned to O'Leary. When his friend turned toward him as well, the larger man could not stop himself from doing a double-take. O'Leary blanched as he looked into the eyes of the Black Bat. Never had he seen such an expression etched there. It was not fear, but it was a type of wonderment terribly close to it, a look that might be worn by one who thought they should be afraid, but could not figure out why. More than simply concerned, the big man reached out and touched his friend's arm, asking;

"Are you all right?"

The Black Bat jumped slightly at the touch, no more than a nervous twitch, actually, but it spoke volumes about his condition to both his companions. Never one to play the fool and hide behind false bravado, the hero admitted;

"I don't know, Butch. Can you hear the sound coming up out of the pit?" When both men responded in the negative, the Black Bat tried to explain what he was hearing. As he spoke, he realized he was beginning to sound irrational. Stopping himself, he said;

"Guess I'm starting to chatter like Murr."

"Which says to me," interrupted Kirby, "that maybe there's something to Mr. Murr's ramblings after all. Maybe far too much."

"But, the things he had to say, they were so fantastic... so unbelievable..."

"Yes," admitted the older man, "but now here we are, and the unbelievable is catching up to reality second by second." Silk went quiet for a moment, then said softly;

"Tony, I know you think sometimes I can't let go of the past. But remember, you were just a boy when the Great War, the war to end all wars, as the fools called it, finally came to a close. Its terrors were supposed to be the end of it all. Men slaughtered by the tens of thousands, whole countries losing entire generations... it was a horror too great for most people to believe. Most still can't get the facts of it straight." As the Black Bat and O'Leary turned to face him, Kirby continued to whisper, saying;

"And now, all across Europe, after all they suffered, they're doing it all over again. With bigger bombs, and better tanks, and larger cannons... and the planes, so much faster, so much more deadly, rivers of blood, oceans of it, pouring over the world. Who's to say that stink you smell isn't just that horror reaching straight through the world for us?"

The trio stood silent for a moment until the Black Bat snapped his fingers.

"Something just came to me," he told the others. "I forgot for a moment, it was only in passing, but earlier today when I was talking with Commissioner Warner, he made mention that missing persons reports were up dramatically. All the signs we saw here of footprints in the dust, did anyone see any that were going out?"

All of the trio thought for a moment, then turned to search. After several minutes, they realized that wherever they could actually make out a direction, all movement seemed to head only downward, down into the darkness, into the endless depths, down to the terrible smell, and the horrible chilling wind that whispered its cackling invitation to pain and death. Steeling himself, the Black Bat came to a decision. Turning to his friends, he told them;

"I want you two to get out of here." Instantly both men protested, but their friend was firm. "Listen to me—believe it or not, I'm still the one in charge."

"But we can't leave you here," protested O'Leary.

"Why not?" The Black Bat drew himself to his full height, beginning the unconscious transformation from Tony Quinn, the man with friends and a future, to the uncompromising hero who accepted no restrictions nor refused any challenge. "How many times have we assayed a situation, and then you've gone off to follow my orders while I've moved ahead into the thick of things?"

"But this, this..." the big man's teeth chattered slightly, forcing him to seize control of himself so he might finish. "This is different."

"I'd ask 'how,' but we don't have time for it. Besides, I'll tell you how it's different so you won't have to bother. It's worse. None of us knows how it's worse, we just know it's true. Deep down inside, ever since we found this pit, you can feel it grabbing your guts and twisting—can't you?"

Both of the Black Bat's companions dropped their heads, looking toward the ground. Both wanted to protest further, but they could not. The Bat had taken control from them, forced them to admit the obvious.

"There's something terribly wrong somewhere down there, we can all of us feel it in our blood. I'm going down. Someone has to. Just like someone else has to alert the authorities. Silk—"

"Yes, sir..."

"I want you to make two calls. First, you need to get in touch with the police. Tell them about the missing persons angle. Fake something up. Don't tell them who you are, of course. Throw them an angle that will send them here by the carload. You can still con a cop—yes?" Choosing not to dignify the question with an answer, the ex-confidence man merely asked;

"And the second call?"

"Get the military on the horn. Same thing. Fifth column, terror saboteurs, tell them Hitler's trying to cut into the bagel business— I don't care what you tell them, just get as many men with as many guns as you can into this street before the next few hours run out."

"And me, boss?" The Black Bat turned to O'Leary. Looking up into the large man's gentle eyes, he said;

"Butch, you get to Carol. Stay with her, keep her safe. Protect her for me from whatever the hell it is that's coming." As the Black Bat moved for the edge of the pit once more, O'Leary called out to him;

"That all, boss?"

"There is one more thing you can do, Butch," he said. Finding the spot where most of those who had gone before must have headed downward, he placed one foot on the lip of the rubble there in the basement, then added;

"Tell her how much I really do love her."

And then he was gone into the darkness.

✠   ✠   ✠

THE BLACK BAT MOVED DOWN THE ENDLESS TUNNEL SLOWLY. IT WAS not difficulty which impeded his process. Indeed, after only a few hundred feet he found a ragged but serviceable set of stairs cut into the side of the cylindric tunnel in a spiraling fashion. No, what had slowed his descent was caution. The stench he had noticed above only grew stronger as one went further downward. Also, the terrible whispers he heard on the wind seeping upward only grew more hellish, more damnable, with each further step.

"What in the name of all that's holy could be going on down at the bottom of this thing," he wondered.

The Black Bat was puzzled, for this was certainly not his first excursion underground. Far from it—he had been in tunnels and caverns of all manner, not only in New York and the surrounding area, but in many spots around the world. Generally moving inward into the Earth cut odors completely. Sounds, of course, did echo upward with far more volume than they traveled in the other direction. But, he wondered with increasing agitation, what in heaven could be making such sounds?

Having traveled nearly an hour, the Black Bat took a moment to assess his situation. First, he found a solid place to stand, then stretched all the muscles he had been using during his downward march in the opposite direction. He also worked on the tightening he had felt setting in around his neck and shoulders. Something told him he was getting close to his destination. He had no solid clue to go on, just a feeling deep within himself, one that had served him well many times over the past year.

Moving forward once more, further down into the darkness, the Black Bat pulled one of his .45s. It was an unconscious gesture, the back of his mind making certain he was prepared for what was coming. Unfortunately, there was no way any man—not even the Black Bat—could prepare themselves completely for what awaited him. As he continued downward, the Bat began to hear a familiar sound hidden behind the now stronger wind. It was the slight noise made by breathing men—men attempting to hide their presence from another.

Staring forward, the Black Bat saw through the darkness that a reception committee awaited his arrival. He made out the forms of a dozen people lining the walls of a large open area. From the way they were holding themselves back against the walls, he had no doubt they were there waiting for him.

But, he wondered, how could they have known I was coming? And, just what kind of gang of thugs is that?

So as to not alert those waiting for him to his knowledge of their presence, the Black Bat continued to move forward, simply slowing his pace to give himself time to think. Less and less was making sense to him as he surveyed those hoping to ambush him. Yes, they were armed, but with rocks or hammers, some with chisels. And, they did not look the part of enforcers. Most were scrawny, resembling more refugees from the Hoovervilles of Central Park than any kind of enforcers.

In fact, the Black Bat told himself, you know exactly who these poor bastards remind you of—Murr.

That threw a bit of caution into the avenger. As Tony Quinn, he had been warned that Murr had a strength far beyond what one would expect. Could the same be true of his fellows? Worse yet, from the way the attention of those below was fixed on him, it seemed obvious those awaiting him could see in the dark as he could! Never one to hesitate, however, the Black Bat merely took a deep breath, thinking;

Well, only one way to find out—

And then, opening his arms to their full extent, the Black Bat leapt the last twenty feet down to the floor of the pit below. The pose frightened many when he used it due to the extension of the batwings built into his jacket. The wings had a dual purpose. They could not allow him to fly, but they did create drag, slowing his descent slightly. It was usually a great trick.

Those in the pit, however, were not frightened in the least by the bat-shape, or the fact that it fell slower than a body should through the air. They merely raced forward, their single-minded purpose being the destruction of their target. The first to approach made a wild swing, apparently assuming his adversary could not see in the dark. The Bat sidestepped the man's clumsy attack, grabbing his wrist as he went by. Then, twisting his body, the Bat forced the man to turn violently, allowing him to hurl his attacker into several of his fellows.

As the rest rushed forward, the Black Bat did his best to not injure his assailants. They did not strike him as murderers up to no good, but more as Murr had, a victim of some unseen force. He had faced such enemies before, evil men who stole the will of others, using the helpless and the weak as pawns in their nefarious games. If possible, the masked avenger would not allow himself to become as casual a killer as those he battled.

On the other hand, he did not despair if he heard bone shatter when his fist connected with a jaw, or when bringing his .45 down on this or that skull. The innocent always suffered in times of war, and that was beginning to look like what he had entered. Who or whatever Murr's "it" was, it had troops to spare. And, ragged though they might be, they were strong, and could find him in the dark. Realizing he was wasting time tangling with underlings, the Black Bat decided to do something more drastic about his situation.

As two more of those sent to greet him charged forward, his hand darted to his compartment belt. Each had a viciously sharp tool which they swung for the Black Bat's head in unison. On the one hand, the silent, perfectly choreographed fighting style of his enemies had been quite unexpected, different as it was from the usual uncoordinated rush he was used to. However, after only a few moments the Bat had adapted his fighting style to take such precision into consideration. Grabbing the downward striking hands of both men at the same time, he twisted and slammed the pair one into the other. Then, as he allowed the men to fall, he swallowed a deep breath and released the capsules in his hand.

Instantly, huge deep green plumes of tainted smoke filled the air. The Black Bat's attackers raced forward, no more fazed as to his whereabouts by the growing billow than they had been the darkness. But, when they did so, they fell into the Bat's trap, for the green trace running through the smoke bombs was a powerful knockout agent, one that dropped all his attackers.

Beneath his mask, especially treated to help protected him from the vapors, the Black Bat allowed himself a small grin, thinking;

Maybe I should have just started with the gas.

The next moment, however, his eyes jerked wide as an unknown voice sounded in the back of his mind, sneering;

yes—perhaps you should have at that—

✠   ✠   ✠

For an instant, the Black Bat turned from side to side, uncertain as to from where the voice might be coming. Then, fantastic as the idea seemed, he realized that over the noise of the coughing and gagging assailants all about him, that he was not hearing the voice, not with his super-sensitive ears. He had to be hearing the voice within his mind!

Unbelievable as the notion was, still, if it was the only possible answer outside of himself having taken leave of his senses, he decided to test it. Clearing his head, he thought;

Who the hell is this, and how am I hearing you?

sad, pathetic little one… strong enough to resist me, too weak to do any more—come forward, speck—I would see you myself before you die

The Black Bat stumbled slightly, thrown off by all that had just happened. A hundred thoughts slammed through his mind, all falling one atop another. Foremost among them was his memory of himself and his friends sneering at the possibility of the supernatural.

Having followed the feel of the bizarrely-singing wind down from the surface, the Black Bat continued to follow the strange breeze. How it could be generated, he had no idea, but it was the only clue he had to the location of the owner of the disembodied voice he had been hearing within his head. Trailing the wind around a series of passageways, the Bat found himself drawing closer to an area awash with lights.

What the hell could this be?

what else could it be, little one, the voice within his mind asked him. *it is my home*

And with those words ringing inside his head, the Black Bat came around the last corner into the impossible. Before him, extending upward hundreds of yards, practically all the way back to the surface, and downward what looked like thousands more, stood seven massive, windowless towers carved out of the bedrock of Manhattan Island. A small part of the Bat's mind was relieved no more of his previous assailants were about, for so stunning was the sight he actually found himself frozen in momentary immobility.

How, was the only word his mind could form. How was it possible? To carve such an extensive cavern, unnoticed, undetected? To erect such cyclopean buildings, towers rivaling the world's mightest skyscrapers—it was a project unheard of, unbelievable—impossible. In any rational sense what he was seeing simply could not be, and yet, and yet... there it was, shining in a light which seemingly had no source.

it appears you admire my home

The Black Bat spun around in a complete circle, searching for the author of the words whistling within his brain. In every direction, however, he saw naught but the incredible excavation, or the rubble left behind by who or whatever carved out the callosal sub-city. Feeling himself slipping toward the cliff edge of madness, unable to handle the wealth of information flooding his mind, the Black Bat screamed upward into the maddeningly insane cavern;

"Where are you? Show yourself!"

no need to excite yourself, little one... you had but to ask

And then, the Bat found his understanding of the world crashing inward upon him as suddenly a massive, barely understandable form flashed into being before him. Suspended in the air, floating serenely between the city and the massive outcrop upon which the masked avenger stood, the thing which could not be drifted mockingly.

is this what you expected?

The Bat fought the sensation to simply collapse. Large the thing was, like a whale, or deep ocean kraken. The horror had no wings, and yet remained airborne comfortably, as if inflated with gases, though its shape did not suggest such was actually the case. Long it was as well, and thin, a polypous, utterly alien being covered from one end to the other with dangling flanges, some singular in nature, others dividing into appendages—not as arms transform into hands and fingers, but more in the manner of tree branches subdividing down erratically until ending in multiple leaves or fronds. Struggling to find a way to deal with that before him, the Black Bat shoved aside the need to understand what he was looking at, concentrating on simply believing that he was indeed seeing it so that he might begin to cope with it. His mind diving in dozens of directions at once, he latched onto one cold line of logic which reminded him that the rest of the people he had seen this thing deal with, it had treated without regard or respect.

So far it's been talking to us. Even if it's just amused, it's better than nothing. Talk back—answer it's question. Wake the hell up, Quinn!

And, that thought shouting down all others, the Black Bat struggled to regain control of his senses, calling upward;

"I'll be honest, I didn't know what to expect."

and you amaze me, little one... no other mind reached has maintained itself... all have fallen gibbering... you please me

"That's great news." Part of the Black Bat could barely believe the words leaving his mouth. Corners of his mind were screaming at him to flee back to the surface, others to throw himself on his knees, to make obeisance before it was too late. Scorning such advice, he shouted;

"What's with the summer palace here? In fact, if you don't mind, why don't you tell me who, what, why you are—what's going on here... the whole ball of wax."

The air pitched all about the Black Bat, the wind which came from nowhere suddenly hurling itself in all directions. Without the floating creature telling him, somehow the Bat understood that control of the air was one of it abilities.

That's how it flies, he thought. The wind in the tunnel, where there shouldn't be any, that thing creates it. It can control the wind!

Instantly the Black Bat's mind seized on the idea, proving to himself that his brain was still his own, that staggered as it was, it was not completely over-awed by what he was seeing. A sinister chuckle sounded in the back of his mind, however, preceding the flying polyp's answer to him.

intriguing you are, little one, in that you resist... still are you not one to command or dictate... all you need know is that your time is over... soon the towers will break through to the surface and the rule of man shall end

And then, the Black Bat looked upward. Far above, suspended over the tops of the horrid creature's bizarre city, he saw hundreds of human beings mindlessly working—some chipping away at the ceiling, others taking what they carved off and using it to build the towers even higher.

up they shall go, onward and onward until finally the new is crowned by the old... then shall humanity be washed away... then shall the elder race return to prepare for the future

As the horrid creature's words slithered into his brain, suddenly the Black Bat's mind was filled with an overwhelming array of images. In seconds a flood of the terrible thing's memories spilled through his brain giving him the entire history of the monstrosities on Earth. Even if he had been prepared for the waves of alien thoughts, he knew full well he would not have been able to make sense of much of it. Caught unawares, only the most major points made any sense to him whatsoever. In the moment it took for the horror to flash the history of its race through the Black Bat's mind, he saw the things' arrival here hundreds of millions of years before the age of the dinosaurs. He witnessed their endless struggles with other alien races, saw the face of the planet devastated countless times.

your time, the time of man... but a falling of the leaves... now, your winter is here... your time is done

And in his heart, the Black Bat knew what the great floating leviathan meant. It had sent out its telepathic messages and drawn thousands of human beings to do its bidding. The poor and the destitute, its message had captured their starved minds and brought them to its lair in the dark caverns beneath the city. The creature, it seemed, had created the original tunnel to the surface, and could have easily built the towers standing before the Bat by itself. In truth, most likely the work would have gone faster if the floating horror had done all itself. But, the monstrous thing had found it amusing to enslave the humans. Their minds bent to its will, the creature had somehow given them the abilities the Bat had already encountered, night vision, incredible strength, more—all so they might build the windowless city it wished completed.

construction of the towers will signal the time of the gathering...

The Black Bat did not need to hear the words of the horrible thing. Its plan was clear—there were hundreds more like it waiting in caverns all around the world—dormant, resting—drifting in near-eternal slumber awaiting the rebuilding of their sky-breaching towers. Once the work there under Manhattan was finished, the thing's design was to simply erupt outward, claiming such structures as the Empire State Building and others around it as the crown for its great construction. It then planned to sink the rest of the island and flood the underworld, the signal that would summon forth its monstrous kind.

"You, you c-can't..." the Black Bat said in a horrified stammer. "Millions... millions will die!"

they will die anyway... after all, little one, all things must eat

And, so saying, the flying polyp send out one of its irregular limbs toward the ceiling of the cavern. The various ending phalanges roped around several dozen of the workers above. Without so much as a thought, the horror pulled them from their work and stuffed them inside its great and terrible maw.

And, at that moment, the Black Bat's mind overcame the monstrous incomprehensibleness of the floating thing before him. No longer did it matter that the thing above him defied all logic. No longer did his mind need to understand how such an impossibility could possibly be. None of that was important. In fact, nothing at all was important to the Black Bat other than destroying the horror there in the cavern. Pulling his .45s, the masked avenger sneered;

"So, all things must eat, eh? Then eat lead, you son of a bitch!"

Stepping backwards with each shot, the Black Bat fired round after round, emptying both automatics into the great creature's hide. Ejecting his clips, he reloaded with unbelievable speed and then repeated the process. The Bat knew, of course, that mere bullets would not injure the flying polyp, but that had not been his intent. Timing his attack so that his last shot would come at the exact moment his back reached the entrance to the great cavern, he turned and then fled into the darkness beyond.

flight will not help you, impudent one

With a casualness that should have been impossible for something so large, the terrible creature drifted down to the entrance to the tunnel to the surface world and began forcing itself within the narrow chamber. Ahead of it, the Black Bat had already reached the daunting upward climb and was racing to put as much distance between himself and the creature as possible.

Even as he did so, the Bat knew he was abandoning the thousands of human beings the creature had already called unto itself, but he saw no other alternative. Indeed, considering the tinkering done to them by the horror, most likely they were already doomed to spend their remaining years as mumbling madmen like Murr. Whatever the case, he could not think on such things then. The only thing he dare concentrate on at that moment was flight.

Got to get as far as I can before that thing catches up to me.

this is that distance, little one

The Black Bat swallowed hard, knowing he had only managed to get a few hundred feet up the tunnel. He did not break his pace for a moment, however, reaching into his compartment belt even as the terrible creature's hideous voice sounded within his mind. Knowing the thing pursuing him was too large for the tunnel, that it would be scrapping the sides as it ascended after him, the Bat began dropping his entire arsenal down behind him without bothering to aim. Smoke bombs, tear gas grenades, explosive pellets—one after another he threw them below, running as fast as he could up the treacherous stairs at the same time.

Beneath him, the flying polyp endured the minor irritations for a moment, then finally grew indignant. Within its cold, alien mind, it had been fascinated by the fact a mere human being might have the will to resist its mental commands. In truth, it had not tried overly to break the upstart's will. Much like a cat with a mouse, it had in its own way enjoyed toying with its unexpected prey. But now, its otherworldly brain had begun to reason—

Suppose this scurrying speck represents some new breed of human? What if there were many like him who could resist the call? If he were to alert the others, they might become quite bothersome.

As yet another grenade exploded against its outer membrane, the flying polyp decided pursuit was too risky. If the human escaped, or worse, if it could contact others of its race with its own mental powers... the thought was practically inconceivable to the horror. But, so thinking, it called out—

this will end—now

And, actually irritated by a mere human to the point of concern, the tremendous polyp halted its upward motion, choosing instead to use its great wind powers to drag the Black Bat down to it—exactly what the masked avenger had been praying for.

Several hundred feet above the horror, the Bat could feel the wind beginning to grow. From the beginning, he had known his only chance for escape was to get the polyp to follow him, and then to annoy it into filling the tunnel with wind. He knew if the creature simply continued to pursue him, it would overtake him easily. But, the Black Bat had counted on the alien's overwhelming arrogance to cause it to attempt to flush him out of the tunnel by using its ability to manipulate the currents of the air. And, the simplest strategy to do that would be to first blast upward to shake him loose, and then to catch him as he fell helpless to the bottom.

As the wind began to build, chilling the already cool temperature of the tunnel, the Black Bat continued to gain as much altitude as he could. He could already hear the strange piping sounds of the creature moving in the air, but the current was still not strong enough to affect his footing. Purposely filling his mind with thoughts of fear, the Bat struggled forward, yard by yard, foot by foot, at some narrow junctures making his way by inches. Digging his gloved hands into the walls, he tore his leather-reinforced gauntlets to shreds, but he managed to hang on. Thinking only of failure, feeding the creature below the comforting terror it wished to find within his mind, he crawled when he had to, never stopping from gaining as much ground as he could.

so, little one, do you still wish to feed me?

The flying polyp, believing that which it read within the Black Bat's mind, actually allowed him to gain hundreds of yards, amused to see him scamper so diligently. Finally, however, when the Bat was less than a few hundred yards from the top of the tunnel, the horror knew there was no sense in being careless. Reaching inward, it called all the air within the shaft to itself, and then forced it upward as violently as it could.

The Black Bat was immediately torn from the stairway, flung upward at a tremendous rate. Having known that moment would come, however, he recovered quickly, drawing his body into as tight a ball as possible. Then, when he felt the raging air beginning to lessen in intensity, he extended his arms, and unfurled his batwings to their full length!

Noooooooooooooo!

Instantly, as the Black Bat dropped the pretense within his mind, the flying polyp read his true thoughts, seeing his intent. Without hesitation the terrible creature began forcing itself upward once more.

you shall not escape me!

"Don't count your chickens til they're hatched, you sausage."

The Black Bat had risked all, daring to hope his wings would give him the power to guide both his ascent and eventual descent. And, sure enough, once the lift from the polyp's wind had ceased, the Bat had been able to direct his fall, returning himself safely to the stairway—only yards from the exit back into the basement of the building from which he had originally descended. It had been a perfect plan—

Except for one small detail.

"The Black Bat!"

As the Bat came charging into the now well-lit sub-structure, he found a score of heavily armed police officers and some military personnel surrounding the opening. As guns were raised, all pointed in his direction, the Black Bat shouted;

"Below! For God's sake—*look below!*"

Fortunately, one rookie did. Instantly the man screamed, emptying his service revolver wildly over the edge. As others reacted to his startling behavior, they too followed suit, first peeking over the edge, then sending whatever firepower they had down toward the approaching insanity.

"Bullets can't hurt it!"

The Black Bat bellowed his warning more than once, but he could not be heard over the terrible din caused by both the weapon's fire and the nearing horror's screaming winds. Knowing there was nothing more he could do there, the masked avenger raced up out of the basement to the abandoned building above.

"Good Heavens," cried the first to see him. "It's the Black Bat!"

"Commissioner Warner," cried the Bat. Throwing his arms in the air, not wanting to risk his friend being hurt, he feigned surrender for a moment, then threw himself forward faster than any of those in the room could anticipate. Catching Warner squarely in the chest, he slammed the older man against the room's largest window and, even though it was boarded over, he managed to smash their way to the outside with the impact.

He regretted the fact his friend had to take the brunt of the blow, but it was the only way to get him outside in time. Inside, the sound of multiple gunshots and the screams of the dying came in a never-ending torrent. Rolling off the commissioner, coming up on his feet directly in front of an amazed lieutenant, he shouted;

"Get the Commissioner out of here. Draw your men back. All Hell is about to burst out of that place and it can't be stopped!"

The officer was about to attempt to arrest the Black Bat, a part of his mind not only knowing such was his duty, but that such would also make any New York City policeman's career. Then, as his mind focused and he realized those inside were still shooting and screaming over something that was not the Black Bat, he hurried to help Warner to his feet, even as the masked avenger raced down the abandoned street.

As he ran, the Bat saw several cannons being placed in position, backed by a number of approaching tanks. Exhausted from his monumental ordeal, still the hero allowed himself a brief grin. He had no idea what kind of cons Kirby had used to get both the police and the army there in such force, but he had expected no less from the man. Heading for the military vehicles, he was about to search out the highest ranking officer and explain what was coming, but events made such tactics useless.

"Jesus, Mary and Joseph—"

The cry was just one of hundreds as the front of 1447 was shoved roughly outward from within. As policemen and soldiers stared, the great mass of the flying polyp began to drag itself outward from the ruined building, a score of human arms and legs hanging from its horrible maw. Needing no orders, their terrified minds reacting without thinking, every man in the narrow street turned their weapons toward the approaching monstrosity and opened fire!

A score of hand-held machine guns threw gobs of lead into the approaching creature. Two .50 caliber Ma Deuce guns had been positioned in the street as well, and both of them began emptying their beltloads of armor-piercing shells into the flying polyp. Along with the lead from a hundred different hand guns, shotguns and rifles being fired by police and soldiers, heavier artillery began to make itself felt. Both the small bore cannons there in the street also roared, slamming great explosive rounds into the monster's hide. The tanks fired as well, the three which had clear shots at the horrid creature staggering it with each new volley.

The Black Bat continued to run, not out of fear, but it an attempt to draw the horror into the line of greatest fire. He had no idea what effect conventional firepower would have on the possibly immortal monster, but he knew there was no better time for humanity to discover if this particular enemy had a weakness for lead poisoning.

The Bat ran, calling on every ounce of reserves he had, pushing his body to its absolute limit. Sweat was pouring off his head, down his neck, into his eyes, cramps were beginning to form in the corners of his muscles. His lungs were accepting less air with each gasp he made, using that which he took in quicker. Still he ran, making his way through the impressive military column one torturous step at a time.

And still, the terrible polyp followed. Even as huge chucks of it were blasted free from its massive frame, still the monster floated onward, its mind bent to only one task—destroying the insignificant human that had defied it. As it made to do so, however, it did not ignore those firing upon it. Columns of wind were thrown forward from the creature that crashed against men and their machines like iron mountains dropped from on high. Men were crushed instantly, their bodies reduced to wide puddles of mixed fluids and piles of meat squashed as thin as a magazine.

Some it did not bother to crush. Those it simply jerked upward to its terrible form and slid them inside itself, consuming them clothing, weapons and all. For others, it had a worse fate. Many it found it could reach telepathically. Those, it simply turned on those it could not sway, ordering them to kill their fellows for it.

We're losing, thought the Black Bat in horror. We're losing.

For an instant, the masked avenger stopped in helpless terror. He had thrown all the energy he had, used up all his weapons, to draw the creature to the surface where he was certain Kirby would have assembled some kind of task force for him to use against it. His plan had gone perfectly. The only problem was proving to be that it simply was not enough. Even as he stared, the terrifying hellthing had slaughtered almost every officer and soldier in sight. Its violent wind attacks had silenced both cannons and tanks.

come now, little one... enough is enough... time to die

"No!" screamed the Bat, turning on his heel. "You won't get me—I'll hide where you'll *never* find me!"

So saying, the Black Bat darted into a side street, racing for the only other option of which he could think. Allowing his mind to hold only images of hiding, he dragged himself forward, his legs stiff and protesting, lungs feeling as if they were filled with flame. As he swung his arms, he winced from the pain stabbing through them both. Still, he continued onward, knowing he had only minutes before the monster would be upon him.

The streets behind the Black Bat were now eerily quiet, the flying polyp having slaughtered all those who had stood in its way. In truth, the horror was greatly reduced from its many battles, but it was still airborne, its mind consumed with the idea of eradicating the Bat once and for all. Coming to a massive chainlink fence, the masked avenger pulled both his .45s and shattered the lock with a shot from each.

Then, he disappeared inside the first major building before him. The flying polyp, as close to feeling a true emotional response as the alien creature was capable, battered its way inside the structure, smashing walls, throwing its great bulk this way and that, determined to find the Black Bat or bring the building down upon him. The creature felt something akin to frustration, for although it could hear the Bat's thoughts, his continuing chant of needing a place to hide, it could not locate him that way. And then, a sudden violent humming in the distance alerted the terrible thing to its prey's whereabouts.

Damaged by its unexpected battle with the humans' machines, still it had more than enough energy to take care of one simple, defenseless human. Tearing its way through the door behind which it knew the Black Bat awaited, its winds hissing ominously, it thought to him—

and now, at last, it ends... farewell, little one

And, as the polyp flew through the entrance to the main generating room of the central power station for all of Manhattan Island, tangling itself in the wires the Black Bat had strewn in its path, the desperately tired avenger whispered;

"Yeah, farewell. See you in Hell."

And then he threw the connecting switch, and the world exploded, the air filling with fire, and the monstrous stench of a roasting god.

✠   ✠   ✠

"GOOD TO HAVE YOU BACK WITH US, TONY."

"Goo-Good to be back, I-I guess."

Tony Quinn awoke in a hospital bed the next day. Although he found he had the presence of mind to feign blindness, just in case there was someone present outside his immediate field of vision, the precaution was wasted. None were with him save Kirby, O'Leary and his fiancée, Carol.

Finding his mouth terribly dry, he got across with hand motions and a few words his concern over Tony Quinn being hospitalized. Kirby assured him every hospital in the city was packed to overflowing. The flying polyp's mental orders to the soldiers to attack each other had spilled over for miles in every direction.

"People were busting each other's heads from the Bronx to Jersey. No one's thinking anything of you being here. Don't worry yourself over that, lad."

Getting their friend a hot cup of tea, the trio first eased his sore throat, then answered his many questions. Yes, the creature had been destroyed. The police and the military, it seemed so far, were agreeing to cover up the truth of what happened in lower Manhattan. Their telling of the events the night before hinted at an anti-government strike foiled by a brave join effort. The identity of the thwarted assassins would be kept a secret for the time being, the story went, while investigations continued.

The quartet chuckled slightly over the fact political business was going on so smoothly as usual. The three not in bed did their best to make their friend comfortable, to answer all his questions, and to not ask him the thing they all wanted to know the most. Finally, however, a wicked grin on his face, Quinn said in a low, conspiratory tone;

"I'm thinking you're all wondering what decision I've made about the Black Bat."

"Now that you mention it," answered Kirby for the group in a tone so blasé he might merely be agreeing that it did indeed look like rain, "I think that did cross our minds earlier."

"Tony," said Carol, "you've been hurt. You know you don't have to say anything now."

"No," he disagreed. "I do." Reaching out slowly, his arm sore from a dozen bruises, his side badly burned from the fire at the electrical plant, he wrapped his fingers tenderly around those of the woman he loved, then said softly;

"I'm sorry, dear, but after this, I think the Black Bat is going to have to stick around for a while longer."

And then, it was Quinn's turn to be surprised. The young attorney fell back shocked as his friends and fiancée all suddenly crowded forward, joyously shaking his hand, slapping him on the shoulders, or trying to hug him. As Kirby and O'Leary congratulated each other on knowing their friend would never hang up his cowl, Carol shoved the two aside and threw her arms around Quinn, telling him;

"Oh, Tony, I'm so happy. I'm so proud of you."

"You... you're, you're glad we're not getting married?" As the two men next to her dropped their celebrating down to a whisper, lest they attract unwanted attention from outside in the corridor, Carol said;

"What does that matter? A piece of paper—a bunch of words. Do we need those to stay together, to love each other?" As Quinn simply stared, she told him;

"Back when you lost the use of your own eyes, why do you think I donated my own father's eyes in the hopes of you regaining your sight? Did Tony Quinn, lawyer, need them? No, he didn't. But I knew there was a bigger man, a greater man waiting within you that needed them. When you took up the mantle of the Black Bat, that was when we took our vows. When you strapped on your pistols for the first time and went out hunting evil, that was the moment we were married." Brushing his rumpled hair back from his brow, the beautiful blonde told her man;

"Do you think some simple attorney could hold onto Carol Baldwin? Really? Did I ever seem that tame to you? What is it you want, Tony—a girl in cotton waiting for you with your pipe and slippers, or do you want me waiting for you the way I do now—the way I wait for the Black Bat to come home?"

O'Leary started to make a ribald comment, but Kirby judiciously elbowed him in the ribs to make him think the better of it. As he did, the big man still managed to point at Quinn, chuckling as he said;

"Look at him; he's blushing."

"I probably am," admitted the younger man with a grin. "But probably not why you think. I guess I needed what happened yesterday. I needed it to remind me that the forces of evil never disappear. That none of us can ever relax for a minute—that when we do, that's just when the never-ending rot returns to try and ruin all society has built."

"Now you're talking, boss," said O'Leary with excitement. "That's telling them."

"I remember something you said a year ago this very day," remarked Kirby. As all turned toward the one-time confidence man, he quoted as best he could;

"It went, 'we'll use whatever means we think best in our fight against crime.'" Remembering the moment clearly, the words coming back to him as completely as if he had only just said them, Tony Quinn took over, repeating;

"We'll fight them with their own weapons—with treachery, intimidation, theft. We'll worry them until they're as jittery as a one-legged man on a tight-rope. We'll work with the police or against them if need be. We'll make our own laws and we'll enact our own judgment."

"Oh, Tony," whispered Carol, her eyes moist with tears, her pulse racing. Pulling the man she loved closer, she told him, "I'd trade a thousand lifetimes with some work-a-day lawyer for only an hour with you if I had to. *You.* The *real* you—*the Black Bat.*"

"And we'll never quit," O'Leary added, "Right, boss?"

"Never."

THE END

C.J. Henderson (1951-2014) was the creator of both the Jack Hagee hardboiled private eye series and the Teddy London supernatural-detective series. Over the decades, C.J. wrote over fifty books and novels, hundreds of short stories and comics and literally thousands of non-fiction articles. His work has been translated into languages found in every corner of the world. To find out more about this fascinating fellow, to read free short stories or to perhaps comment on this book, visit his website at www.cjhenderson.com, or write to the publisher at www.boldventurepress.com.

Printed in Great Britain
by Amazon

37326154R00139